THE
KINGDOM
OF SWAY

THE KINGDOM OF SWAY

ELSEN BOSO

Publication Details
Interior and Cover Layout: Pickawoowoo Publishing Group
www.pickawoowoo.com

Book Cover Artist —NvtHarper

An extract from the Covenant of Light

It is written that in the beginning the Hiatus Forest was the only intelligent life form. Then there was only the Forest.

Over many centuries the Forest grew more and more powerful and from the nucleus came the Proto Forest. From there became the Woodland and then the Plains.

With each new creation the Hiatus Forest expanded until there wasn't any other force that could withstand the Forest's Will. First, the Wind and the Rain submitted; the Thunder followed by cowering before the might of the Forest and the Lightening withdrew - bowing in deference. Only the Light remained constant and strong.

In time the Forest became the Light and the Light became the Forest.

As one they ruled.

Chapter 1

LIKEA

Aria urged her horse ahead of the mounted guards and rode towards her waiting husband. As she drew level with him, she slowed her mount to a walk.

Prince Vidal grinned and reached out and took her hand. He raised her hand to his lips and gently kissed her fingers and knuckles. He sweetly whispered something, and Aria laughed. Aria pulled her hand free and encouraged her mount into a gallop. Prince Vidal gave a shout of delight and slapped the reins of his horse and raced after her. Vidal's horse was faster, and he soon overtook his bride. He reached out and wrapped his arm around Aria's waist and drew her onto his saddle.

Still laughing Aria submitted to his embrace. She slipped one of her arms over his shoulder and drew his head down and they shared a passionate kiss.

"I love you, my Bride," whispered Vidal sweetly, softly with a playful smile never leaving his face. He placed his hand under her chin and gently tilted her head, so he could look upon her face. He shook his head in wonder. "My Father and Mother will love you dearly."

"I confess I am a little afraid. I have but met them the once and that was some time passed." Aria said with little concern in her voice. Vidal chuckled. "Don't be. I'll be here by your side for as long as the Light allows. We Lions live long. The King will be doubly delighted once he knows you are breeding. My family has had little luck begetting an Heir and now the King will have two more."

"Why are you the only Heir to the Kingdom?" Asked Aria curiously.

"It is in our history. The Queen has brought forth many a cub, but none have lived longer than a few years. I am the only one to reach a good age. The strife dated back many years when my Father was but a youngster himself. There was a broken law and my family was punished." Vidal shrugged and lifted Aria back onto her mount before continuing his response. "One of my ancestors broke the Covenant and the punishment has been meted down our lines." He grinned, again lighting his mood and his amber eyes twinkled. "Worry not, my Lady. I live, and you and I will go forth with love and honour."

Regaining his composure on his horse Vidal glanced behind. His guard was still some way back but coming on steadily. Instinctively sensing something amiss, Vidal frowned. "Aria stay with me." He said quietly and suddenly.

"What is wrong?" Aria asked as Vidal took hold of her reins.

He smiled. "Maybe nothing, but me likes not this track. It is overgrown and there is little room to manoeuvre..." He smiled as she brushed the thick light brown hair away from his face. "I also think I need a ribbon."

Aria laughed. "Maybe a haircut."

Vidal laughed again. Taking hold of the reins from Aria's horse he turned themselves around and began to walk them back to the guard.

Helment, the Captain of the Guard, upon his own mount, watched his royal charges as they began walking back. "Faith, the Lady has tamed the Lion," he said in gentle amusement.

Likea stopped his restless search of the scrub and looked at the royal couple.

Vidal sat proud in the saddle. His long hair was blowing wild in the soft breeze. His yellow vest straining against the bulk of his powerful chest muscle. He was leaning slightly towards Aria, as though listening intently.

"The Lion has merely been subdued - not tamed. My lady has her own weapons, but My Prince is still the most fearsome of warriors." Responded Likea.

Helment nodded in agreement. "Tis the truth - I still bare scars from his youthful escapades." He shot a sly sidelong glance at his lieutenant, then smiled maliciously, as his eyes gleamed with merriment. "Lady Aria is with child. My Prince Vidal told me so last evening."

Likea looked at the captain whose smile was well hidden in the depths of his thick, shaggy grey beard. "That is good news. My Liege will be well satisfied to have Vidal's Heir."

Helment nodded. "Tis true. The old Lord has waited many seasons, but the news will please him. My Prince has charged me to assign a personal bodyguard to the Lady."

Likea grunted and allowed his gaze to wander moodily over the dense undergrowth. With a frown he replied, "Then the better for him the sooner we are away from this place." He shook his huge head and his long black hair rippled with the movement. "This is ambush country and I have an uneasy feeling. Tis a pity that my Lady's family lives on this side of the Proto Forest."

Captain Helment nodded as he too scanned the verges of the tracks. "Tis her filial duty to honour her Pride but I agree. I could hope that the Emir lived closer to the Kingdom." He shot a quick look at Likea and smiled wickedly. "You are My Lady's bodyguard."

Likea started in surprise and jerked at the reins of his mount. "Me! I am not qualified!"

Helment laughed softy. "I chose you and the Prince agreed – what other recommendation do you need."

Likea, again, frowned. "But, Captain, my Majority is Horse. It is not fitting that I be My Lady's bodyguard."

Helment shrugged. "The Prince is pleased with my choice. Would you tell him that his judgement is faulty?"

Likea bowed his head in obedience. "Tis indeed an honour." He mumbled. Helment gave him a hearty slap on the back. "You are worthy – you are my finest warrior. Save the Prince there is none braver or fiercer in battle. As for your totem I can think of a dozen times I have needed a Horse more than I have needed a Wolf. For one thing - your legs are longer and your speed is greater. Now – enough – keep the mind on edge. I do not like this country and my bristles are inclined to rise."

As he spoke he lifted his shaggy head higher and sniffed loudly at the air. "I do not like this place - come it is time we joined the Prince." Helment kicked his mount into a gallop and raced towards the royal couple. Likea paused only to draw his sword and glanced back over his shoulder at the following guard." Prepare," he ordered. "The old Wolf has the scent." Then, he too, nudged his horse into a gallop. As he neared the Captain, he heard a whoosh as the air parted. An arrow sped past his shoulder and he saw Helment jerk involuntarily as the arrow sunk deep into his left arm just below the elbow.

The Captain howled loudly. With his uninjured arm he pulled the arrow free. He flung the arrow away and drew his sword. As he did so he kneed his mount in front of the Prince. Likea saw another arrow strike his thigh and yet another ricochet off his thick waistcoat. Helment's eyes glazed in fury and pain. He grimaced, exposing his fang like teeth and then howled again.

Likea threw him another glance as he sped past him. Helment was beginning to transform into his Wolf Majority. By now, the guard had formed a uneven ring around the Royals. Likea pushed his way past the milling horses to stand directly beside Aria. His sword slashed in a continuous arc movement as he brushed the flying arrows away from his Princess.

The milling horses powdered the hard dirt track into a fine yellow dust that rose and covered the both soldiers and horses. Through the billowing film, Likea saw an arrow strike the Prince high in his chest and for the briefest of moments, the battle noise died to a whisper. Likea peered into the melee around the Prince, and he witnessed Helment get struck with another arrow; this time the arrow brushed his neck and Likea saw the blood flow. Helment howled, and Likea saw him slip from the saddle and into the danger of the stamping, snorting horses. Helment disappeared from sight.

Soldiers were falling all around him. Those mortally wounded were trampled and the others who were quick enough or not so badly injured slunk into the undergrowth and continued to fight on foot. Those soldiers were at their most vulnerable as their metamorphosis gripped their bodies and the human weapons slipped from fingers as their hands turned to paws.

As the battle intensified, so did the noise of the fight transform. Human sounds gave way to the pure animal sounds of growling Dogs and the mighty roar of the Bears.

The dust parted for a moment and Likea saw Helment, the Wolf, bleeding and lame, take one of the haflings by the throat and bodily lift it from the ground and shake the dog vigorously. He saw too, Vidal, slumped over the neck of his stallion. Blood was streaming down his neck dyeing his clothes red.

Likea hurriedly guided his mount to Aria and gripped the reins of her horse. "Lady we can't hold them – we must run!"

"No! No! Vidal is hurt, and I won't leave him." She cried with tears streaming down her pale face.

"Lady, his horse will bring him – we can't stay here! We have lost too many warriors and still the haflings come. I must get you to safety!" Suddenly, Likea groaned as a shaft pierced his chest. In pain, Likea continued to speak. "Lady, please, I beg of you - my Prince is badly wounded let my Brothers take him away. Give me leave - we cannot fight the curs that strike from cover and use ungodly weapons..."

Aria shook her head and wiped tears from her eyes. She flinched as an arrow plucked at the loose material of her sleeve. She moaned and called Vidal's name over and over. Making an abrupt decision while still gripping the reins of her horse, Likea reached out and snatched Vidal's reins. With the loudest voice Likea could muster he shouted; and the many riderless horses rose on their hind legs and pawed frantically with their front hooves. Under the cover of the protective wall of the horses, Likea ordered the remaining warriors to retreat. Now the haunting sounds of the wounded horses mingled with the cries of terror as the mounts were savaged by the hafling dog pack.

Likea forced the horses forward, passing their rearguard and onto the open track. He kept a rapid pace until the horses were sweating, their eyes wild and foam spat from their gaping mouths. Finally, he eased them into a walk. Aria reached out to touch Vidal; His body lolled uncontrollably. Aria sobbed and called his name. Likea watched compassionately for a moment when he began to dismount and upon awareness of others behind him, Likea turned to see his three remaining loyal warriors.

"My Brothers are almost spent so we cannot run, and we are too few to fight. Our Prince is mortal - if he must die then let him die in his Kingdom and not here amongst evil. My Lady must be saved and that is our duty." He turned to the tallest of the three soldiers. "Torbay, I have need of a Raven. I need you to fly as you have never flown before. I must send you to the Kingdom."

Torbay bowed his head. "I am yours to command Likea." he said.

"I can only give you the Second Life my friend." Likea spoke sadly.

Torbay gave a compassionate smile. "What more do I need?" he answered rhetorically as he dismounted and knelt in the sand to begin his transformation. The soldier fell forward and Likea swept him into his arms and cradled him as one would a beloved. The body curled and withered but Likea did not release his hold. His gaze never leaving Torbay's face. Within moments, Likea could hold the whole of the body within his gloved hands. Gently, he opened his hands an out flew a huge black raven. The bird circled once and then flew straight up into the blue of the sky.

Likea slowly rose to his feet and watched the raven until it disappeared. He turned to the remaining soldiers and suddenly became aware of the arrow that still pierced his chest. He gripped the shaft with both hands and pulled - the arrow came away and a trickle of blood stained his tunic. He looked at the arrow and flung it into the thicket with disgust.

"Leeba I have a use for your four legs. You will ride with the Lady and I. She must be protected at all cost. Citor - you will take the Prince home. Tie Prince Vidal to his saddle so he won't fall. Your strength and stamina will see you through. You should keep to this track. When you near the Proto Forest you will be safe, and Torbay will find you. Take Torbay's mount and ride in relay until you have freed the Prince from this form or this life."

Aria whimpered softly but she grasped at Likea's sleeve. "You can't do that - he lives still. See you – Likea - see you; he lives still," she cried and her tears continued to fall.

"Lady if he doesn't ride then he will die here, and his life form will stay here. Here is where evil spreads. He must return to the Kingdom for he is a Chosen One. You will condemn him forever if he stays."

"But he lives. He still lives! Likea, please, I beg of you listen to me!"

"Nay Lady. His wounds are too great. Our Prince is no longer. Even the Royal Physician will not be able to stop the decay. Understand me Lady Aria - he has had no time to begin his metamorphosis - he is still human." He slowly shook his head sadly, and with his eyes never leaving hers Likea continued in a softer, gentler tone. "Either way, he is dead to you. Vidal is no more."

Tears streamed from Aria's eyes and she swayed in the saddle. Likea steadied her so that she wouldn't fall. "My duty is to protect you for you are the living." He whispered to her before turning back to Citor.

"Go!" He commanded. "You must get to the Forest before he dies."

"Likea - they are closing - I smell them clearly," Lecba called urgently and then he turned his nose disgust for he could also smell the scent of fresh blood.

Likea swung back into the saddle. "A moment in time is all I can give to say your farewell my Lady." Aria stared at him, despair in her eyes but still she reached for her lover and drew his head to her breast. Torn between her heart and duty, she kissed him gently, feeling the warmth of his breath on her lips. "Oh, my love," she whispered. "My sweet love."

She brushed his long hair away from his face and wound. "Goodbye my love, forever."

Citor bowed to Aria. "I will care for him, My Lady." He said as he took the reins firmly in his hand. "I will return for you Likea. Brave Heart." He said as he touched his heels to his horse. Holding both his and Vidal's reins Citor set off at the gallop with Torbay's horse following.

Likea turned to Leeba. "We will be better served by travelling across country. By your reckoning Fox, how far are we from the Forest?" He asked.

"I know not of the dangers but at least two days. There is no way of knowing neither how far the rot has spread nor what lies in our way, but I think at least two day."

Likea nodded as he gigged his mount forward. "Just as long as we keep ahead of them. My Liege Lord will send reinforcements, but we must be alive to have use of them..." He glanced behind at Aria. "Leeba, old friend, I fear you must be our diversion. Take My Lady's shawl and my glove and lead the hyenas on a merry chase. Give us the two days then save yourself."

"I am yours to command." Leeba responded taking both shawl and glove. "I know this area a little and remember a river about one hour from here - we should part there."

"Agreed." Likea stopped and waited for Aria to catch up. He reached over and took the reins of her mount. "You must hold on for now for we will travel fast. Do you understand?" Aria nodded sadly, she couldn't muster the strength to vocally speak even if she wanted to. He stared at her for a moment then nudged his horse into a gallop.

Behind them they could hear the heavy sounds of running feet and the shrill, excited cries of the fast closing pack.

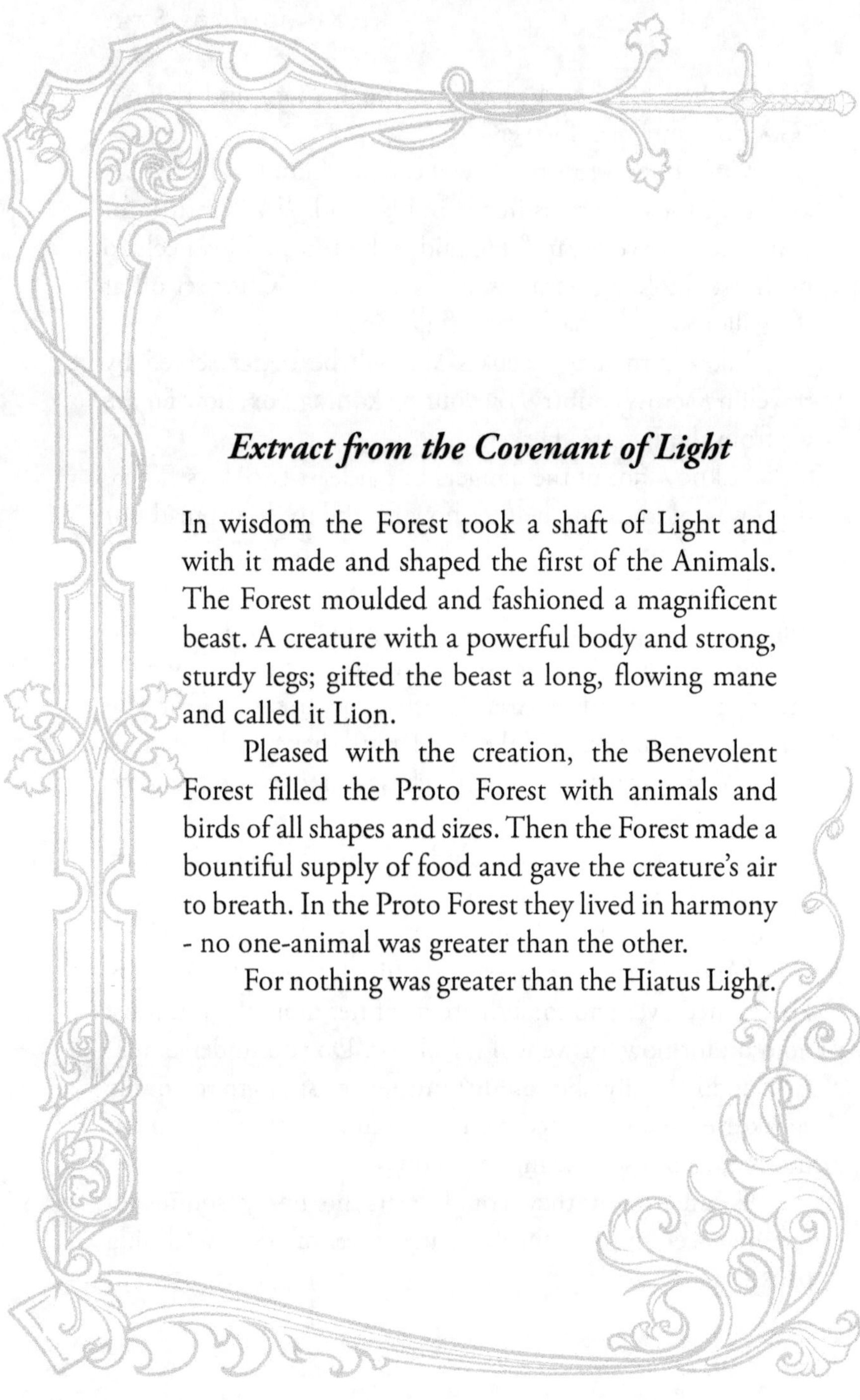

Extract from the Covenant of Light

In wisdom the Forest took a shaft of Light and with it made and shaped the first of the Animals. The Forest moulded and fashioned a magnificent beast. A creature with a powerful body and strong, sturdy legs; gifted the beast a long, flowing mane and called it Lion.

Pleased with the creation, the Benevolent Forest filled the Proto Forest with animals and birds of all shapes and sizes. Then the Forest made a bountiful supply of food and gave the creature's air to breath. In the Proto Forest they lived in harmony - no one-animal was greater than the other.

For nothing was greater than the Hiatus Light.

Chapter 2

LIKEA & ARIA

At the wide river Likea, Aria and Leeba with their mounts entered the water. Although the horses were almost spent they managed to swim to the middle of the river. As the river sloped and began to deepen, Leeba guided his horse closer to the bank while Likea and Aria remained in the deep water. At every overhanging branch Leeba touched the shawl and glove to the leaves and branches so that the haflings would take the bait and follow a false direction. They travelled in this manner for some distance and now the horses began to struggle as the current of the water gradually flowed faster.

With no warning, Aria's horse stumbled. Out of surprise, she lost her grip on the reigns and began to fall. Witnessing what had happened and with Likea's quick reflexes, his strong arm shot out, gripping her waist tightly and he lifted her with ease out of water and up before him on his saddle. Her horse resurfaced and Likea ordered the steed to join Leeba in the shallower water.

"Leeba take my Lady's mount with you – the dual set of prints might convince the haflings that she rides with you. My horse will carry us far enough. Go now and Brave Heart, little red Fox". He shouted.

Leeba waved and guided his own horse towards the river bank. Another salute and he and both horses disappeared into the thick undergrowth. Meanwhile Likea slid out of the saddle and into the quickening current of the water. He swam beside his horse and Aria, occasionally grasping the stirrup, taking a minute rest. In this manner, they covered a vast distance until Likea spied a rocky outcrop jutting into the river. Pausing for a moment, he ordered his horse to swim towards the shore and guided the horse out of the water and onto a small sandy beach.

Breathing heavily, he ordered both Aria and the horse to stay where they were. Likea quickly climbed the breakaway and with shading his eyes, he searched for signs of pursuit. Satisfied the haflings weren't close he returned and lifted Aria off the patient horse and carried her to a fallen tree and gently sat her down. He then returned to his horse where they gently and affectionately touched heads. Likea whispered his thanks for the courage and the stamina given that day.

He opened his saddle bag and withdrew a gourd of wine which he carried back to the Princess. He guided her shaking hands while she drank the peppery, sweet wine. When she pushed the gourd away he sat down beside her, and he took a drink. As his breathing eased he took her hands. Her fingers were cold to the touch and he gently massaged them to give them some warmth. His face was filled with compassion as he stared at her tear stained cheeks and dark ringed eyes.

"Lady you must listen to me and pay me some mind for we haven't much time." He murmured.

She turned slightly to look at him and Likea felt his chest tighten with sympathy for the utter misery he saw in her eyes. "Please Lady Aria, listen." He paused briefly and when she nodded slightly he continued. "We must get away from the river bank. My steed is worn out, so we must walk." Again, he hesitated. "If we get separated always walk west.

Always follow the Light - always. You must go deep into the Forest. The deeper you go the safer you will be. My Liege will find you - you must believe that - My Liege will find you."

Aria shivered and pulled her trembling hands free. "Not the Forest. No, not the Forest! It is a terrible place! It is evil!" She cried and furiously shook her head.

Likea put his hands to her head to cease her shaking. He, however, shook his head vehemently. "Do not fear the Forest. For all that it looks dark and cold the Forest will keep you safe. You are from the Plains and know not the Forest as we do. Deep in the woods there is no evil. The animals are ours and they will know that you carry the Heir. They will do you no harm. The haflings will not follow you into the centre and there you will be safe."

He stood and helped Aria to her feet. She leant heavily on his broad arm, staggered a little as she stepped forward and gripped Likea's hand as he steadied her.

"Now we must go - I'll help you walk until we can rest or until my horse can carry you again." This time, Aria nodded wearily in agreement but as she stepped forward, she noticed a thin trickle of blood staining his tunic. She raised her hand, touching the wound. "You are hurt!" she said.

Likea chuckled. "Faith Lady – the haflings might use ungodly weapons but they are too puny but to prick at my chest." He gave a soft laugh, and Aria gave him a tiny smile.

"Your Majority must be Horse." She said, "For no other has the build of thee." Likea nodded. "I am Horse." He answered with pride. Taking her elbow, he guided her past the thick growth of the river bank and into grasslands beyond. "My Lord chose well to make thee my bodyguard." Likea bowed his head. "My Prince and my Captain gave you to my protection, but it is also my honour to serve you." He said. Aria gave him a sidelong glance. She was tall, but he towered over her. His tunic of thick woven material made him seem huge, but she noted his enormous arms and bulging muscles and realized that his clothing really did not exaggerate his true size.

"How much time are we ahead of them." Aria asked as she pushed past a leafy branch. Likea sighed. "Leeba has all the cunning of his race but I think he can give us no more than one day." He paused. "And that is if they take the bait. The dogs are not without intelligence and they will suspect sooner or later that we have split up. Hopefully it will be later."

"But how long will it be before My Liege finds us?"

Likea didn't answer; instead he concentrated on removing a series short, prickly scrubs from the path he was making. He beckoned her forward and as she pushed past him she glanced up at him. His face was set into grim lines and he was frowning heavily. "Likea?" She prompted him... "Well?"

"Lady I do not know. He will send the Eagles and the Falcons first but from the air they cannot help us except to be our eyes. The haflings will see them and they will then know where we are and set their traps accordingly." "How long?" she asked again. Likea paused but Aria eyed him steadily. He grimaced and shook his head. "Depending on how many battles he must fight to reach us, but I think at least six of the Light times."

Aria looked shocked for a moment but quickly recovered and even managed a small smile. "Then tis well that I have the best of my Mate's warriors to protect me." She said lightly." Nay, Lady this warrior would like the company of one Helment. I think we will have need of his wisdom and cunning."

Throughout the rest of the light time Likea lead his small party westward. The way was rough - the terrain stony and the brush thick and full of thorns. Several times their way was barred by deep ravines or thickets so dense that the way was impassable. Likea kept slowing his pace so that Aria could keep up but gradually she weakened and began to fall behind. He paused briefly and lifted her into the saddle and offered her another drink from the gourd.

"We will rest soon, Lady. Brave Heart." He said as he took the rein and led the horse into the maze of vegetation. They had been steadily climbing for the last hour until; finally, they reached the summit of a large, rocky breakaway. Likea handed Aria the reins and told her to stay while he searched the blind side of the hill. Shortly he returned and brought his party to the far side. Once there he lifted Aria down and taking her hand led her to a shallow cave. The cave had been hollowed out by both wind and rain and although the walls were still rough and sharp in places the floor was covered in a deep layer of soft sand and was warm to touch.

"We will rest here for the dark time." Likea stated as he removed his saddle bag.

"But it is still Light time - there must be a good portion of light left," Aria responded. "Nay. This is the fringe of the Badlands. Darkness will come soon and be complete. There will be no night light and I must find food for my brother and us. We all need rest. Now - Lady listen to me - I beg of you. While I am gone keep a watchful look about you. Be alert. At the slightest sign that you think there maybe haflings - mount my horse. He will bring you to me."

Aria gave a slight shudder and her lips trembled, but she nodded bravely. "I understand." She said. Likea smiled and bowed in deference. "You have the Lions heart Lady... My Prince chose well, his bride."

The mention of Vidal brought the tears back to her eyes. The fragile courage she found within herself, crumbled and she began to cry. Likea stepped forward and she motioned him away with a quick thrust of her hands. He nodded just once, picked up the now empty gourd and turned away. He quickly strode down the slope to where the vegetation began. Once down the rock face he searched amongst the rocks and bushes for food. Luck favoured him, and he found a wild fig tree. He plucked one of the small pear-shaped fruit and bit into the dark brown fruit and tasted it. It was slightly tart and not very juicy, but he finished eating it and then proceeded to pick the fruit with both hands until his pockets were full and wouldn't hold anymore.

He glanced up at the rock face and could see his horse standing quietly. Satisfied that there wasn't any immediate danger he searched further and found some dry, yellow stalks of pearl grass. The seed hadn't fallen yet so the heads were full of the coarse grain. Taking his knife, he cut a large sheath of the grass and tied it together with his wide flaxen belt. A brackish stream was nearby. He scooped away the rotting weeds and filled the gourd. He wrinkled his nose in distaste at the sour smell but fitted the cork to the gourd and pushed it inside tunic. He looked around quickly and seeing nothing amiss bent and gathered the sheaf of grass, He tucked it under his arm and began the slow journey to the summit of the breakaway.

At the top of the hill; he spoke softly to his horse. The beast whinnied and began to pick its way down the slope. Likea waited until he could see it grazing on the pearl grass before he returned to Aria. He found her staring intently at the direction from whence they came.

"Darkness is coming. I can see it engulfing the land." She whispered in awe. Likea dropped the sheaf and stood beside her.

"Keep a careful guard now. As the shadow eats the Light you will see the smoke from their fires. This will tell us how close they are. Watch now. I must hurry to prepare our fire to cook our supper."

"Light a fire? But they will see our smoke." Aria stated, her voice fearful.

"Nay." Likea said. "Not while we still have the light." He removed his sturdy, woven coat and spread it over a large stone. He then beat the grass against it until the seeds shook free. He scooped the seeds together and with a smaller stone he ground the seeds into a coarse powder. He took a small sachet from his saddle bag and from it he sprinkled some of the bluish coloured powder onto the crushed grain. Tipping a little water from the gourd Likea had at last fashioned a stiff, flat cake out of the mixture.

He quickly prepared a fire out of some of the grass stalk then struck two stones together until he caused a big enough spark to ignite the straw. The fire flared briefly then burnt steadily. Likea balanced the cake on both his sword and knife and held them over the fire until a fine brown crust formed.

By now the shadow was closing fast. Aria gave a muted cry and Likea looked up. "See the fire – see them! There are so many." Likea removed the hardened cake from the flame as he stood he stamped out the small fire.

"Do not fear Lady. The fires are not even close. Leeba has done his work well."

"But so many?" she asked. Likea shook his head solemnly. "Tis a sorry time. The rot has not been contained and has spread further than the wisest predicated." He glanced at Aria. "They won't travel far in the darkness. We will be safe this night." He said "Come. Sit you. The shadow is almost here and soon there will be no light to see by and we must eat."

Just then the horse returned. Likea spoke to it and the horse retreated to the far side of the hill. Kneeling to cut the seed cake into slices and with the figs spread them onto his coat. "Tis the best I could do at so short a notice."

Aria made no attempt to eat. "First we should look at your wound." She said. When Likea made to protest she held up her hand. "I am Lion and can see in the dark to eat - I know where my mouth is but I cannot see to fix your wound. Now! Before we eat." She ordered.

Likea scowled but obediently stripped away his web spun shirt and exposed the arrow wound. Aria touched it lightly with her fingers. "It is messy and deep." She muttered pulling his shirt from his hands. "It has been bleeding since mid Light. Even horses don't have a limitless supply of blood." By ripping a sleeve from his shirt and screwing the material into a twist Aria gently inserted it into the wound. "At least the river washed it clean. Tomorrow we should look for the Taba root to seal the hole. Your shirt is tight, and it should hold the twist in place."

Likea redressed then picked up the food and carried it to the caves entrance. He sat down and when Aria joined him, he offered her the food. She accepted a slice of the seed cake and with her hand motioned him to eat. He slightly inclined his head and he too took a piece of the cake and a fig which he offered to Aria.

She smiled and squashed the fig over the slice. She took a nibble and raised an eyebrow. Likea looked abashed. "Tis all I could find."

"Eat - my bodyguard must remain strong." She commented and handed him a thick slice of the cake. Nothing loath Likea picked up a fig. He ate well but Aria continued to nibble at the slice. Suddenly she jumped and stifled a scream as the night shadow passed over them. Without warning the light died and utter darkness took its place.

Likea shifted his body a little and she sensed rather than seen the movement.

"Are you alright, Lady?"

"Yes. My eyes are becoming accustomed. Does night always come thus - without twilight?"

"In the Kingdom, no. Here I don't know. I have never been this close to the Badlands before. I have heard stories which are told around the dinner table. "Last dry-time, Petrov, the Eagle scout was out this way. The night caught him, and he was forced to land. He flew again in the early Light. It was he who told me the little I know. The disease had not spread so far then because it happened some distance from the Forest." He sensed her uneasiness and tried to reassure her. "Eagles are notorious liars though and I suspect he exaggerated."

"I do not think he lied. I can feel the evil of this place."

"Worry not Lady. We survived this day and will survive again tomorrow. Rest now for the sand is soft and still warm. I'll keep watch over you."

"No Likea - I'll take this watch." Likea opened his mouth to rebuke however Aria stopped him from talking. "No! Do not argue. My eyes are sharper than yours and I'm not so tired. You must be tired for you swam far in our journey down the river."

"Lady I beg of you. I cannot sleep while you are awake. Let me take the watch." He protested.

"Likea I… I have not had a chance to grieve. Give me the solitude I need to make my peace and to give vigil to my beloved Mate." She pleated.

Likea swallowed loudly and bowed his head. "I had not forgotten. I knew not how or what to say." He stood up to move back into the cave. "Wake me when you tire." He lay back in the warm sand and for a time watched the still shadow where she sat. He heard a sob and then the beginning of the Passing Lament. He woke several times and he lay awake for a few minutes and listened to the sounds of the night. He heard Aria then slept some more. The next time he woke he lay listening and somewhere in the distance an animal screamed in pain. He squeezed his eyes closed as if it shut out the horror. Close by he could hear his horse breathing and giving the occasional whiffle through his nose. Aria still whispered her prayers to the Covenant for Vidal's passing. Occasionally, she would give a small sob as her voice caught in emotion. Not wishing to disturb her Likea waited patiently until at last she finished. He stirred noisily to alert her and softly spoke her name.

"I must have been sleeping too long for I am stiff and the bed hard." He said.

In the darkness he could hear her sniff but when she spoke she sounded calm though her voice was husky with suppressed emotion. "You needed the sleep more than I." She responded.

"Yes - but I will watch now. Try to sleep, we march at first Light and the day will be long. Go into the cave where it is warmer." He suggested.

Since the night was so dark he sensed not saw her shaking her head in refusal.

"No, I will not sleep this night. I have offered penance for Vidal."

Likea slipped his coat around her shoulders and she hugged the warm material closer.

"Lady - the Lord Vidal is no more. If Citor reaches the Forest, then the death might have been interrupted but he will not be the Vidal that you knew. The Hiatus Forest extracts a huge payment for the lives we are given. He will be a servant to the Forest and in all likelihood, he will not remember who he was or where he came from. He might remember some, but he will not be the one you loved."

"If Citor didn't reach the Forest - what then?"

"Unless the physicians reached him — then he will be dead." he answered bluntly.

Aria suppressed a rising sob. "Will he become a hafling?"

"No. Citor will see to that. My Prince did not have time to begin his metamorphosis. He will pass as a human. Citor will then return his body to the Kingdom."

"I'll never see him again." She snivelled.

Likea didn't answer her and could not find any words to comfort her. They sat in silence for a long time until Likea thought she had fallen asleep and when she finally spoke it was also a whisper – as if she was talking to herself. "My family are all from the Plains. None of us has ever been this way before. My Liege had sent Vidal on a goodwill mission. That is how we met, you know."

"Yes, Lady," Likea murmured.

"That was before the haflings had become an army. I have never seen anyone so handsome and strong. Our warriors were puny in comparison. They were so envious of him. I loved him the first time I saw him." She gave a soft laugh. "He had ridden far that day – his coat was dusty and his mane uncombed. He greeted my Father as was his duty and the Emir invited him and his entourage to sit with us for a meal. He begged to be excused for a short time but when he finally rejoined the banquet he had bathed and changed his clothes. We could not work out where he found the water for the Plains are dry at that time of season." She laughed again." Apparently, he had commandeered most of his warrior's horses and rode back to his caravan. He carried water back with him and bathed outside our camp. Our warriors cursed him for he had put them to shame. That night he asked my Father for me."

She stopped - lost in thoughts of a happier time. Likea could not bring himself to speak, he simply sat and waited for her to continue. She sighed.

"He said he had only ridden to impress me. Foolish, brave Lion - I didn't care and now he is gone. We were together for such a short time." She began to cry again and Likea reached into his saddle bag and took out another, smaller gourd. He passed it to her nudging her elbow, so she would know where it was. "Drink a little – it will warm you." He said.

Aria sipped at the strong flavoured wine and it seemed to comfort her. When, at last she spoke again her voice was strong. "He left the next Light time for he needed his Father's permission. My Liege and Vidal's Mother came back with him. We were joined and so began our union. My Liege stayed a little longer, but he had word of the haflings. They returned to the Kingdom, but Vidal and I remained as you know for you were there. I had forgotten you came with Helment to escort us to the Kingdom." She took another sip of wine. "Tell me what happening here - Vidal never would."

An extract from the Covenant of Light

Before the Covenant the Animals had the freedom
of the Forest and they roamed where it pleased
them.

But it was inevitable that the creatures would
come to the boundary of the Proto Forest. It is said
that the Animals looked out of their sanctuary and
into the wide, open plains - which they gazed in
awe at the Woodland and the Sky above them. It
is said that one by one they ventured out of the
Forest. Tentatively at first, then bolder and more
assured. The Birds took flight and they soared and
sang in exhilaration at the feeling. The Rabbit, the
Deer and the Fox ran and played in the long grass
and then the other creatures followed them.

Chapter 3

THE HAFLINGS

Likea tried to marshal his thoughts before he answered. "The subjects of the Kingdom of Sway are not given to question the Covenant of the Hiatus. They are happy to believe and not to doubt or ask for other answers. What is – Is. That is the way of the Covenant. The hafling problem is not well known and the Covenant is not fully understood. Even the soldiers do not understand, but we believe, and so we fight."

"Please explain what you do know because if we are separated then I will need to know as much as possible."

Likea grimaced and frowned a little. "It is difficult." He paused for a moment. "The Monarchy always thought they could control them, and so as not to cause panic, the haflings were seldom mentioned. Not that My Liege deliberately tried to suppress the talk, but it was never encouraged so most of what I know is only rumour."

"Go on." Aria encouraged him.

"We always had a few haflings, but the numbers were small, and they assimilated into our society without any trouble. They were poor, ill formed creatures but they were part of us and so we cared for them. At that time there wasn't any trouble, but the King before My Liege allowed one of his relations to sit on a medical panel. His totem was Tiger and he married the King's youngest daughter. I'm not sure how it began but the version I heard was that he began to experiment with the haflings."

"But what exactly is a hafling?"

"He is neither human nor beast. Something in their metamorphosis went wrong. They have no control over their change. Sometimes they are animal and sometimes human. That is a genuine hafling. When Ambrose started to experiment that is how they were. It was disconcerting when their unexpected transformation took place as they were speaking to you. Anyway, Ambrose wanted to eliminate one of the forms and make them stable."

"But we can all change into our Majorities until we receive the Second Life."

"Yes, but we change voluntary and the haflings couldn't. You see when they die they become nothing. They couldn't achieve the Second Life and they couldn't become human. They would depart in whatever form they existed in. Ambrose violated the Covenant when he convinced some of them that he could alter their structure. He assured them that he could help them achieve a Second Life and to fulfil their Majority. In that way they could enter the Forest.

Likea stopped talking for a moment and listened to the night. When he could hear nothing, he continued.

"The experiments went wrong. During one of the transitions some of the haflings were freed from the laboratory and into the compound. Nobody knows if it was because they had been fasting or because of the altered structure but they attacked some of the workers. They tore many of the achieved animals apart."

"No! Oh no!" Whispered Aria, horrified.

Likea nodded. "Cannibalism. The King ordered all the haflings banished. He had no choice because they couldn't tell which had been altered. The warriors rounded them up and they were escorted to the east of the Kingdom. The King could not destroy them because of the Covenant so banishment was the only answer. An agreement was reached in regard to their territory and it was duly bound. We cannot violate their borders by the law of the Hiatus. Ambrose had failed - he had halted the rapid transitions, but they were still neither human nor beast. He had also changed their temperament and because they had killed and tasted flesh they had no chance at all to enter the Light. In the main they were unrepentant. The Council thought that natural attrition would eliminate them, but the haflings learnt to breed and over time they became a reasonable force, but, they had no leader. So, as we practice and teach the Light of the Hiatus Covenant, they teach and practice a policy of death. Those that didn't submit to their will were destroyed. Soon much of the east was under their control. The King and Council had little idea what was taking place outside the Kingdom but gradually word filtered through to the King that the haflings were almost to the edge of the Proto Forest. Of course, they were really concerned because the Forest is sacred to us. The King send his oldest son, My Liege, to assemble an army and rode to the border. There emerged the haflings leader - one by the name of Tonka. His totem should have been Lion, but he was neither."

Likea paused and sipped at the wine. When he continued, Aria noted the pain in his voice. "His cross - breeding had made him an alien of both forms. Cannibalism had extended his teeth into fearsome weapons, almost long as my fingers. His mane covered most of his neck and shoulders and hair grew from most parts of his body. His eyes, black and cold. His nose retained a vague human shape and for the main he apparently walked upright. It is said that a most terrible sight had ever been witnessed. Most of his warriors were canine and they too had altered appearances. They carried their food with them - caged rabbit and squirrel. Those warriors who witnessed the sight seldom speak of it."

Likea stopped again and spat to clean his mouth before he continued. "Tonka said he didn't want war and he reminded My Liege of the Charter they had been given. Under those terms he was forced to retire. He didn't retire far but spread his army all along the edge of the Forest. Tonka withdrew. In the meantime, the King had sent Jayca the Advisor in amongst the haflings. He reported back that the haflings were afraid to enter the Forest and that is why the advance had stopped. Your Father's army and that of the Kingdom were too large for Tonka to fight in the open. No more was heard of them for some seasons until Lord Vidal came this way to seek your Father's treaty. Lord Vidal's column was set upon, but they beat the haflings back. On his return to the Kingdom, he reported the desecration that you seen this day. This land was once beautiful and safe to travel - now it is known as the Badlands. Lord Vidal also reported some of the haflings had entered the Forest. This action was in direct violation and opposition to the Covenant. My Liege assembled his army and we rode to confront them. Word came from our scouts that Tonka had outflanked us and was riding on toward Sway. My Liege split his forces. Prince Vidal and Helment came this way and My Liege and I returned to the Kingdom. We fought many battles, but we could not capture Tonka. We heard later that he had returned to their birthing place. We could not follow and now it appears he has rebuilt his army."

He gave a low sound, like a chuckle. "One good thing though - those that entered the Forest were destroyed. The Light obliterated those who transgressed the law and no other hafling will try to enter the Forest again." Likea said with some satisfaction. He paused for a moment "I trust in the Light that Torbay flew safely for he is our only hope." He added soberly.

"What will happen to me if I am captured?" Asked Aria. "I cannot metamorphosis for the safely of my baby."

Likea closed his eyes as if in prayer before he answered. "He will force you to kill, once that happens, you will be named Hafling. There will be no escape." He answered her brutally. Then in a softer tone he added. "He knows not that you are breeding so he will try to break your faith with soft words and persuasion. He would like to have you to mate so the process he uses might not be so swift. You will be safe until your belly swells. Once he knows that you carry the Heir his methods will be cruel and barbaric. Death will be the easiest course unless you transform. As a Lioness you will have some chance to escape, and perhaps, reach the sanctuary of the Forest."

"To transform is to destroy all I have left of Vidal," Aria whispered now understanding her predicament.

Likea continued speaking, "He will destroy the baby regardless of any argument. Make no mistake Lady Aria – Tonka and his dogs are mutants. They care nothing for the Light or anything that we believe in. Their Gods are excess and this day. They care nothing for the re-birth for they are outside of the Covenant and for them there is no way back."

Aria didn't reply and Likea didn't elaborate on his remarks. He remained silent to allow her to digest his works on her possible fate. Aria didn't speak and shortly he offered her a wild fig which she took with a murmur of thanks.

"What happened to Ambrose?" she asked.

Likea made himself more comfortable before he answered.

"He and his family were sent into the Proto Forest - they were ordered never to return. The old King had no heart to put them to the sword."

"Why not? They transgressed the fourth journal of the Hiatus."

"His daughter had married Ambrose. He could not cleanse him and allow his daughter grace. Instead he had the royal physician make a transition to Ambrose. He ordered him to be turned yellow and black. The yellow was to tell the Kingdom of his treachery and the black denoted that no subject give him aid. Some say it broke the old King's heart to brand his daughter. But he did it. He had her branded silken white - that was for the royal blood but bastardised. The gossips in the palace still say that she was the beautiful human in the Kingdom.

"Was the family ever heard from again?"

"Nay. There are rumours that they left the Proto Forest and went deeper into the Hiatus. There was also a rumour that the line continued but there is some doubt about that. If we enter the Forest as human and are there for time, then that is how we remain, but humans are forbidden to enter the Forest and will do so at risk. If we chose to attain the Second Life, then as our Majorities we seldom return to Sway - and it wouldn't be of much use since we cannot speak. Ambrose and his family were refused the Second Life, so they entered as human and that made it impossible for them to breed." He shook his head. "Nay – that family were expelled forever."

Suddenly Aria clutched his arm. "What is that phenomenon - see there to the east?" she exclaimed pointing to the horizon.

Likea stood up and brushed down his tunic. "That is the opening of Light. It will be fully light soon – we must hasten."

"Dawn! - But so sudden?"

"The sins of the haflings have caused the whole of the Badlands to be unbalanced - you saw the night fall. Nothing here is normal. Come away Lady, we must hurry."

He helped her to the horse and then led the way down the hill. He stopped at the fig tree and picked more of the fruit. He gave them to her to carry and bade her to eat as they travelled.

Their pace was slow; they sometimes followed a track although most were badly wide enough to take a horse. The thorns picked at their clothes and scratched at their skin. Once, in the distance, they could hear barking but that sound soon faded leaving a deathly silence broken only by the soft tread of the horse and a persistent buzzing from some insects that stung and swarmed around their face and crawled into their eyes.

"There isn't any birds - no sounds at all," whispered Aria.

Likea grunted. "The birds have wings. Only a few were ever captured by the haflings. When the flowers and the grass started to wither and die they fled; wise birds."

He stopped and listened intently. Satisfied that the pursuit was still far away he again took the lead by cutting a swath with his sword, wide enough for an easier passage. Twice he stopped and hacked through the thick cord of a spider's web that had become entangled around the horse's legs. Aria shuddered and looked frantically around for the host. Likea made no comment but he gave her a cheerful grin.

They pushed on steadily until their way was barred by a gaping chasm. Sulphur smelling smoke belched from the pit and into the air. Aria gasped as the smoke bit at her throat and tears streamed down her cheeks as her eyes watered. Likea's firm hand steadied his restless mount and he quickly led his charges away from the smoke. He took them upwind a short distance then stopped to regain his laboured breathing. "We will have to go around. Go further upwind from that abomination." He gasped.

"Likea I'm fearful - this place is evil." Aria shivered. "I hate this."

"Brave Heart, Lady. Look hard in the distance - see – that is the Forest." He pointed to the painted line on the horizon.

"It seems so far away and how can we be safe there? It is forbidden to enter the Forest," she whimpered.

"We will keep to the edge of the trees - that is allowed."

"But you told me that if I was pursued to seek the centre of the Forest,' she protested tearfully.

"To save both you and your cub the centre is the only haven you have. If you are alone then the haflings will follow in number. Some will, some might, reach you and drag you out before the Light can respond. The Forest is not evil. How can it be? It is our Light." He said patiently. He continued. "Lady, listen to me. When we spend or tire of this life we go into the Forest, from whence we first came. It becomes our new home. By entering it as a human you, yourself, will remain in that form, but your cub, because it is unborn will remain pure providing that you do not bring it to life while within the Forest. I will willingly condemn you into the hereafter as human for the sake of your cub and the Kingdom's Heir." He brushed a hand over his eyes and wiped away tears that he did not realise had formed. "I can do nothing else, Lady. Forgive me."

Touched, Aria reached out and touched him lightly on the forehead. "I understand," she gave him a slight smile. "After all, it may never come to that. Brave Heart Likea - my warrior - My Lord chose well." Likea bowed his head in deference.

Once more they pushed on through the dense bush. With the gentle sway of the horse's stride Aria fell asleep. Likea spoke softly to his steed and the horse regulated its steps to accommodate the sway of her sleeping body. She awoke to the hollow sound of the horse walking over rock. From her higher advantage she could see the coming shadow of the night.

Aware of her awakening, Likea halted and he lifted her from the mount and when she swayed he held her by the elbow until her stiff legs were stable enough to hold her weight.

"We will rest here this night." He pointed. "See there - the Forest."

Aria peered through the deepening gloom. "It seems so close."

"Two hours on the morrow, by my reckoning. I haven't heard any sounds of the chase, but we will not risk a fire. I found some berries and figs along the way, so we will have something to eat."

Likea let Aria take the first watch. Although he was tired he slept fitfully and was awake when she called him. It was bitterly cold, and the wind howled and moaned through the trees. Likea gave Aria his coat and settled her down beside the horse so that she might get some benefit from the animal's body warmth. The night passed without incident but even with first light the wind still moaned. The coming of light did, however, reduce the cold.

As the sun rose, the gentle breeze became a wind so strong that it carried fine grains of sand and dust, but it also contained a strong smell of burning wood. Likea stared towards the east intently until the flying sand made his eyes hurt. He couldn't detect movement but still he felt uneasy. Coupled with the sound of his horse's stamping and its restless movements he returned to the campsite. He stroked and smoothed his horse with soft crooning sounds before he woke Aria.

Aria slowly sat up and looked about her for a moment she looked serene until she remembered the events of the last few days. Slowly misery etched lines on her face and a dark bleakness shrouded her eyes.

"We have to leave immediately. Something is disturbing my horse."

Aria quickly rose to her feet. "I'm ready." She stated.

Likea smiled. "I cannot believe your courage." He said.

Aria looked surprised. "My courage? I am only trying to survive for the sake of Vidal's Heir. For myself I care nothing."

Likea shook his head sorrowfully. "That is part of the grieving process. I have known strong beasts to wilt under less adversity than you have faced."

The horse began pawing at the ground again and its eyes flickered wildly. Likea grimaced. "We must hurry," he said almost to himself. He quickly lifted Aria into the saddle and this time he gave her the reins. Leading the way, he took his little party once again into the scrub and scrawny woodland.

"The wind is behind us which is helpful and hopefully the smell of the smoke will mask our presence to any hafling that may be ahead of us." Aria didn't answer, and he glanced over his shoulder. She was trying to protect herself from the stinging sand that bit at her unprotected arms and cheeks. Likea stopped and quickly removed his coat which he placed over her head and shoulders. She murmured her thanks as Likea turned away.

They travelled for some distance before they spoke again. Aria settled herself more comfortably and spoke.

"Likea what happened to the guard we left behind?' she asked softly.

He didn't answer immediately, and she started to repeat the question when she noticed that he was intoning a prayer. She waited until he completed his homage and the repeated her question.

"Most of the guard were killed. Hopefully those who weren't completed their transition and made their escape.

They earned the Second Life and if their injuries weren't too serious they had a chance. Those badly injured are in dire jeopardy - I pray they were put to the sword but I haven't heard of any pity among the haflings so I have great fear for them"

"What of Captain Helment? I know he had been struck several times."

Likea grinned. "The old Wolf became a new Wolf. He was still tearing out the throats of the jackals even as we rode way."

"I'm glad. He was a kindly old warrior."

Likea laughed at her description of Helment. "He was the most fearsome of warriors that I have ever known." A sad frown reflected on his face. "I will miss him." He said simply, and Aria nodded in agreement.

The travelled as swiftly and as quietly as possible but the way was so rough that they often had to change course. Likea searched endlessly, his eyes restless, his head turning every which way. He noted a huge storm building and he hastened his stride.

Without warning a tremendous rumble of thunder rolled overhead and the noise shook the ground. He quickly grabbed at the reins and grasped them tightly with his other hand he gentled his unsettled horse. The clap of thunder was only the prelude to the violent storm that followed. The darkened sky was constantly ripped apart by brilliant and deadly flashes of lightning. The wind howled and whistled amongst the stunted trees and competed in volume with the thunder that snapped and rolled across the sky. Long, thick tendrils were ripped from the climbing vines and tangled around their feet. The horse stumbled but Likea held him firm. The wind screamed in velocity as it tore whole trees from the stony ground and ripped the wiry grass out by the roots.

Likea struggled to get Aria from the saddle and hold onto his horse at the same time. He dragged them both to the nearest, largest tree where he pressed Aria tightly up against the trunk. Still holding his horse, he stood in front of Aria to protect her from the flying debris. A Large branch snapped from the trunk and plummeted down, striking Likea on the shoulder. He grunted in pain, but the violence of the storm was so loud that Aria didn't hear his involuntary exclamation. He felt the reins slip from his fingers and his horse move away. He raised his uninjured arm over Aria's head, giving what protection he could.

As quickly as the storm started the thunder and the wind stopped and then came the rain. A wall of water appeared before them. Likea stepped away from the tree truck and called his horse. The animal hadn't fled and was standing dejectedly, close by. At Likea's call it trotted over to them.

"Come Lady, mount. It isn't far, and the horse can carry both of us. The sooner we reach the Forest the better." He tried to assist her to mount but his arm wouldn't bear the weight and he faltered.

Aria turned around and noticed his arm hanging limply at his side. The blood from the wound, diluted by the rain, stained his shirt and dripped into the sand.

"You're hurt! She cried.

"Tis nothing and we cannot dawdle here. Mount you — I'll help as best I can."

When she started to protest, he took her by the elbow and brought his horse closer to them. Commanding the horse to be still, Likea gently pushed Aria who looked closely at his face and seeing the pain etched with the stubborn set of his jaw she submitted and swung herself into the saddle. Likea mounted with some difficulty but he managed to seat himself behind her. Obedient to the pressure of his boot the horse walked forward. The rain was so heavy that Likea could barely see the faint trail and allowed the horse to pick its own path. Abruptly the dense thicket parted, and they found their passage barred by a fast-flowing river. The Forest loomed comfortingly close - just beyond the water.

"How can we cross - you won't be able to swim?" asked Aria in concern.

"I can't but you can. My horse will carry you."

"No! I won't leave you here."

"We have no choice and we will waste valuable time to look for a ford. I haven't any idea how many haflings are living on this side of the river. We have been lucky so far, but they must find us soon."

"No - either we both cross here or we find a ford. I won't leave you here alone." Said Aria stubbornly.

The horse whinnied and swung its head around and nuzzled Likea's boot. Likea leant forward and caressed his mount's neck. He nodded once and sighed in defeat.

"We will cross here, he said, 'my mount is strong enough to carry us both across."

Aria smiled in relief. "Good." She said relieved.

By now the rain had tapered to a drizzle but the wind was again gathering strength. Aria shivered with cold from the wind and the wet clothing. She pulled Likea's coat closer, but it was soaked and offered little respite.

"I must get you to safety. You will be with the fever if you don't get warm." Said Likea.

Suddenly the horse reared and Likea almost slipped from the saddle. He fought to control the frightened beast and to regain his seat. The slippery mud made the task harder but with brute strength he managed to regain control. As he did so, an arrow struck Aria in the fleshy part of the upper arm and glanced off. She screamed, and the horse raced forward, down the muddy bank towards the river. Mud flew in all directions as the beast tried to keep its balance in the mud but at the river's edge it plunged into the water without hesitation.

Arrows were falling all around them, one brushed past Likea's head while another pierced his wounded shoulder. Aria felt him shudder and slide away from her, over the rear of the horse and into the water. She glanced back and tried to stop the horse, but the beast ignored the pressure of the rein and raced on. Likea was standing in the shallower part of the river, his sword drawn and already fighting the savage, screaming packs of hafling hyenas that were pouring out from the hedgerow. Several of the haflings were still loosing arrows at her, but the range was great and most fell short. Aria jerked the reins and to make horse stop. Over her shoulder, she turned to looked back at the fighting.

Likea, sword still swinging, had begun his metamorphosis. His body rapidly taking on the shape of his Majority. One group of haflings kept pushing him backwards into the deeper part of the water. Suddenly, Likea slipped, and disappeared under the water. He surfaced briefly a little further downstream, his transformation reverting to his human form. He looked around and focused on Aria.

"Go. Ride for the Forest. You can't help me now." He shouted at her and then again sank beneath the raging water. Aria choked back a sob as she waited for him to resurface. An arrow thumped against Likea's thick coat. She looked away from the river to look back at the second hafling pack. They were wading towards her. She threw one more glance downstream and then touched the horse's flanks with her heels.

The whizzing sound of a flighted arrow sounded past her ear. An arrow struck her leg. She screamed in pain as the arrow penetrated deep into her thigh. Momentarily her sight failed but the horse never faltered. It swam rapidly through the water; it mounted the far bank and galloped headlong across the open ground leading to the safety of the trees of the Forest. It carried her into the Forest at a gallop and Aria made no attempt to check its speed.

Finally, exhausted the beast slowed to a walk. Aria, blinded by pain, exhaustion and grief fell from the saddle, landing heavily on the ground, striking her head against a stone. Her last conscious thoughts were of Vidal and the sweet smell of pines. The horse stood still for a while – watching her - then it slowly walked away.

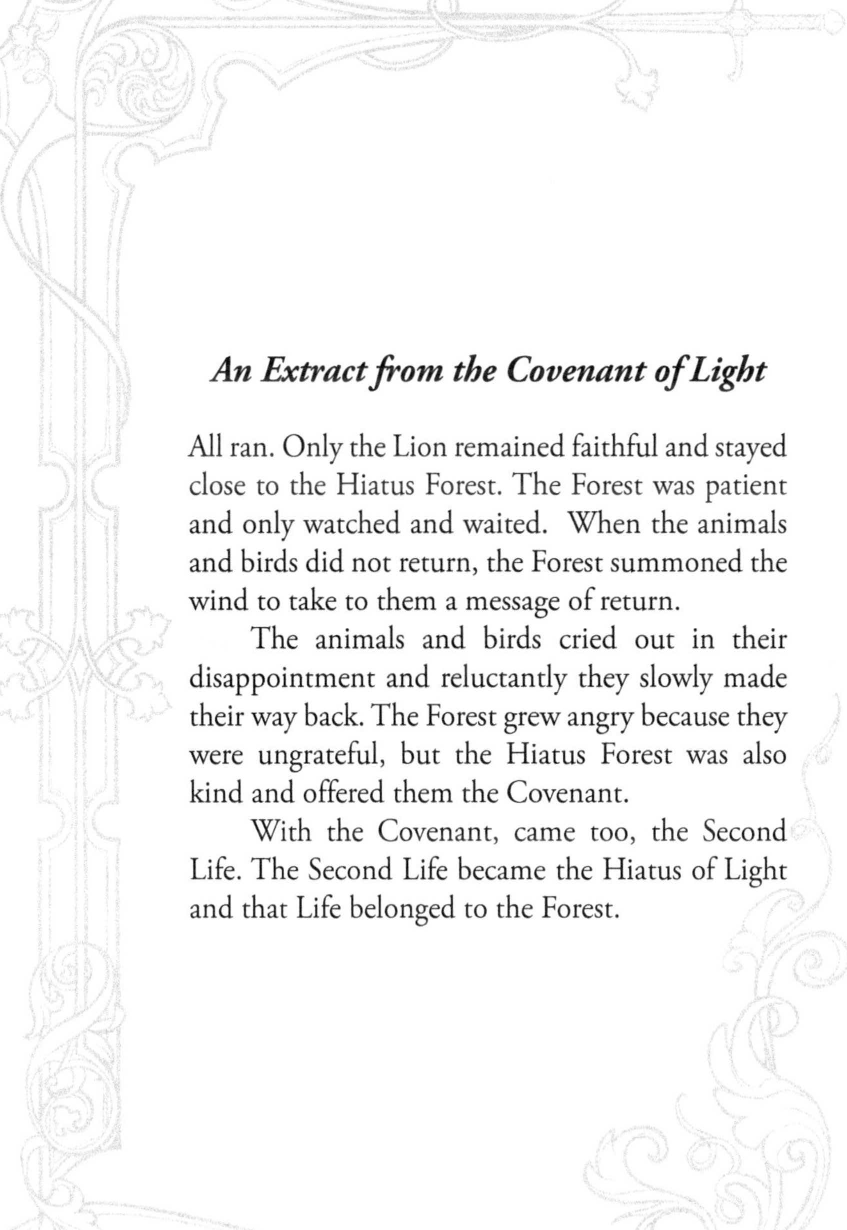

An Extract from the Covenant of Light

All ran. Only the Lion remained faithful and stayed close to the Hiatus Forest. The Forest was patient and only watched and waited. When the animals and birds did not return, the Forest summoned the wind to take to them a message of return.

The animals and birds cried out in their disappointment and reluctantly they slowly made their way back. The Forest grew angry because they were ungrateful, but the Hiatus Forest was also kind and offered them the Covenant.

With the Covenant, came too, the Second Life. The Second Life became the Hiatus of Light and that Life belonged to the Forest.

Chapter 4

HUTT

Citor rode as he had never ridden before. Twice he was set upon but rode through both ambushes without allowing the horses to break stride. At the pace he set, the arrows and stones flew harmlessly by. Once passed the second trap he stopped and changed mounts. Vidal lay in the saddle without moving, causing Citor to check that some life still remained within. The life signs were faint but still there.

All through the darkness of that night, Citor rode. He relied on the horses to gauge the road for the most part he could see very little. By mid-morning of the following day, he sighted the Proto Forest in the distance. Grinning in fierce triumph, he allowed himself to relax a bit. Not long after and without warning, his horse faltered causing Citor to jump from the saddle. He recovered quickly, bounding to his feet then rushing back to the labouring horse. He pulled hard on the reins and forced the horse to stand. He then quickly stripped the heavy saddle from his mount and flung it into the ditch that ran alongside the track. Pausing only long enough to briefly touch the horse with his forehead and make good the Covenant bonding before swinging himself into the saddle of his relay mount. He touched the mount with his boot and set about fulfilling his mission.

He was closing rapidly on the sanctuary of the Forest when Vidal's horse stumbled. He reined in quickly and turned. The horse was covered in a foaming sweat and it snorted as it gasped for air. Citor dismounted and hastily released the cords that bound Vidal to the saddle. He lifted Vidal down and carried him to his own horse and tied his Prince to the saddle. Vidal's horse snickered and Citor release it from its burden and set it free. He returned to his own mount, but his horse wasn't in any condition to carry two. To his left, in the distance, he could hear a pack of the haflings coming. They howled as they caught the scent. Wasting no time Citor grabbed the reins and pulled the horse forward.

"Come noble horse. We are on a mission to release our Prince from this life. Our journeys end is in sight and then we can both go the Light." He coaxed the horse forward and to his relief the horse trotted forward and Citor ran beside it. He laughed out loud as both unburdened horses raced with him, passing him leaving him behind. The raucous cackle of the haflings was closer now but so to was the welcoming Forest. Citor's chest was heaving from the exertion but he daren't slacken his pace until they were but a few lengths from the first of the trees.

He paused to regain his breath and then to concentrate on awakening his Majority. The haflings had stopped some way. They were now regrouping and chattering excitedly amongst themselves. Two of the more adventurous ventured forwards but Citor gave them no more than a contemptuous glance. Slowly his human shape altered until a huge brown bear stood. The Bear lifted Vidal from the saddle and carried him into the Forest. He lay him down on a deep bed of fallen leaves. With reverence, the Bear carefully scraped the aromatic leaves over Vidal's prone body until it was completely covered leaving only the face clear. He intoned the warriors lament over his Prince and fallen comrade as he covered his Lord's face with leaves.

The Bear returned to the Forest's edge and slowly Citor returned to guard the body and wait for the Raven's return. The haflings had withdrawn and now the songs of the Forest filled the air. Citor smiled. He drew his sword and sat with his back against a large tree and as he laid the sword across his knees, he closed his eyes. The Forest had accepted the offering and now he could rest.

Citor held his lonely vigil for three more Light times before the Raven found him. With him, Torbay had brought Jayca the Advisor. They both landed at Citor's outstretched legs and Citor smiled a greeting. While he waited for Jayca to resume his human form, Citor picked up Torbay in his huge hands. He stroked the black feathers in a loving bonding. Jayca returned to his First Life form, out of breath and slightly flushed.

"It gets harder to change the older I get," he complained.

Citor grinned and released Torbay. "Perhaps it is too much fine living in the Kingdom." He teased.

Jayca scowled. "Perhaps only a Bear would think such thoughts. We Hawks always prefer to have our wits about us." But he grinned in good humour and patted Citor on the head. He sobered suddenly. 'Will you bring him out now, Citor?"

Citor nodded and slowly commenced his transformation. He lumbered into the Forest and found the mound as he had left it. The Bear cleared away the leaves, lifted the body, then carried his burden to the Forest's edge. He laid his charge in the long, sweet smelling grass and knelt over it. Jayca joined him and he too knelt. While Citor regained his First Life, Jayca intoned the Covenant Prayer of Thanksgiving. He offered the prayer to the Light of the Forest. Citor slowly resumed his human form and he too gave thanks.

"See Jayca, My Lord has departed. The wonder of the Forest took him, comforted him and made him whole again," wept Citor with joy.

Jayca didn't answer. He seemed to be speechless as he methodically ran his hands over the body. "Praise! The Boy lives! He was so near death and the Light absorbed him," said Citor excitedly. Jayca completed his examinations and sat back on his heels staring intently at the young boy before him. He stood up and brushed the sand and grass from his legs. He looked as though he would cry.

"Indeed, I offer praise for the Light that has restored this Boy, although my heart is heavy for the demise of our beloved Prince Vidal," He murmured sadly.

"Faith Hawk – look before you and believe thee eyes," Citor scoffed.

Jayca sadly shook his head and laid a hand on Citor's broad shoulder "The boy you see before you is not Vidal. A man entered the Forest and a boy returned. The Proto Forest is truly wondrous and creates the miracles of our lives, but it also extracts a high payment. My friend, Vidal has passed into the Light as our Prince. The Forest in its wisdom did know of our sorrow and gave us this boy in his place to ease our grief. But he is not Vidal." He said kindly.

Citor turned to Jayca and his face mirrored his disbelief and shock.

"Some part, some small part is surely Vidal," he pleaded.

Jayca nodded. "This boy is in some part Vidal and yet, this boy is not." He held up his hand to stop Citor from protesting. "Listen to me Bear. The Prince was almost to the end of his First Life. His body was bloodied, and his spirit was silenced when you carried him to the Forest. Is that not correct?"

He waited for Citor's assent before he continued. "Because his Majority lay still, the Forest could only give him back the First Life, so the Forest took the body and remade this Boy and gave him to us. Be not sad, Bear. Our Prince is safe, but he is where we cannot reach him."

Citor sunk slowly to the ground and began to mesh the soft grass between his fingers. He looked from the boy to Jayca. "I understand. Tis all written in the Covenant. Likea must have understood that when he entrusted the Prince to my keeping. The Horse knew."

"Don't be sad, my friend. Likea is wise and that he chose you to see this task through he showed excellent judgement. We are all subject to the Forest. It is our life and it both gives and takes." Said Jayca kindly.

Jayca started to pace restlessly muttering softly, "My Liege is coming at all speed, but I would delay his arrival just to save his grief for a while longer." Citor asked him to repeat himself. Jayca returned to where the boy lay and sat beside him. "Never mind that now. What of the Lady and the guards? What happened?" He asked.

"The battle was most fierce. They fired their ungodly weapons from the cover of the trees and brush. Lord Vidal was struck in the throat almost at once. Likea, the Lady, Leeba, Torbay and myself were all that escaped. Others were badly wounded although many were returning to their Majority. Likea ordered those that could run to do so, and those that couldn't run…" He shrugged. "Haflings have no pity. I don't know. We got away. When we rested for a moment Likea asked and Torbay gave himself to him. Likea dispatched him with all honour and Torbay was willing. It was the only way we had to bring you here to the Prince. It was then we separated. The Lady, Likea and Leeba went one way and I the other. The pack followed me, I could hear them behind me, but I had Torbay's horse and I so outran them. I passed through two of their traps to reach the Forest. If you listen carefully, you can still hear them. I fear their way is driven by hatred."

"What of Helment?"

Citor sadly shook his head. "No. The old wolf was struck several times, but he had completed his metamorphosis."

"Praise and thanks for that. The Wolf was a fine warrior. What of the Lady?"

"When I left them, she was unhurt. Likea was - he had an arrow sticking out of his chest, but he seemed hearty." Citor suddenly jumped to his feet and roared his grief to the world. It was a dreadful sound and the birds fell silent and the gentle breeze seemed to pause; even the chattering from beyond the hedgerow stopped. Jayca went to him and bonded to him by touch.

"Go into the Forest." Jayca said gently." Let the Light care for you."

Citor shook his head." No. Not yet. I will give thanks here beside the boy who was my Prince and now is not. It is fitting."

Evening came and coloured the sky in delicate shades of lemon and pink. The two soldiers sat side by side next to the boy they had been sent to protect. Sometime earlier, they had watched the darkness fall swiftly over the Badlands. Both had shivered at the sight. The howling and wild cackling coming from the Badlands had ceased as the blackness swiftly fell. Now, the soldiers listened to the gentle sounds of the night - the chirping of the night crickets and the occasional surprised hoot of an owl.

The muffled sounds of running feet coming from the direction of the Badlands towards them bought both soldiers to their feet. Citor drew his sword as the sounds drew nearer. Out of the darkness, and into the soft night light, Jayca espied a horse and a small red fox. Both were coming at speed. Citor relaxed and set his sword aside. Up above on a branch of a tree, Torbay made a chuckling sound.

"'Tis one of the horses from the guard. It must have eluded the Haflings." He laughed in delight.

"But who is its friend - the little red fox?" asked Jayca.

Citor watched the horse disappear into the Forest but the fox paused as it drew level with the soldiers. It stopped and sniffed the air before it trotted over to the body of the boy. It walked all around the still form - every few paces it would sniff deeply. It paused for a moment and it seemed to the warriors, that it bowed. Then, with one quick look at Citor the fox turned and trotted after the horse.

"Wait! That must have been Leeba…!" Exclaimed Citor, as he stared after the departing fox. "They must have been attacked again," he added and turned to Jayca. "For Leeba to undergo a complete and permanent metamorphosis the road must have been fraught with danger."

"Yes" Jayca agreed and then he frowned. "Come the Light I will fly. If Leeba managed to reach here then maybe the Lady and Likea are close by too."

"Likea would not leave her unless," he paused. "Unless he is dead." He added.

Citor shook his head. "This has been an ill-fated journey. First the Prince, then Helment and now the Lady and Likea. The King will be beside himself with grief."

"Brave Heart Citor. As yet, we have seen no evidence." He cocked his head to one side and listened. "The boy stirs," he said.

They knelt beside the boy who was struggling to sit up.

"Be still, Little One. Be still. We are friends," Said Jayca, reassuring him. The boy looked puzzled as he glanced from one to the other but he didn't shirk away from Citor's supporting hand.

"I am called Jayca, the Hawk and Advisor. This is Citor, a Bear and warrior of some note. By what name are you called, Boy."

"I am Hutt, a woodsman's fourth son..." The boy frowned. "I was injured. Why am I here?"

Jayca didn't answer him except to ask a question of his own. "Do you remember the Covenant, Hutt?" Hutt nodded. "Yes, but I do not understand it."

Jayca smiled. "Good." He said. The Twelfth Law states; should a human stripling, of years below that of Enlightenment, enter the Hiatus Forest and should that Youth be mortally wounded, then the Covenant of Light will take that Youth and hold him, protect him and nurture him until a life can be given to him. So, states the Covenant." Intoned Jayca.

Hutt still looked puzzled and Jayca reached out to touch his cheeks and smooth his hair.

"That means your first parent took your still body into the Forest. There you were lain and covered with the goodness of the Forest. Your parent gave you to the Hiatus to protect you until another human life was offered. The Forest has given you the life of our friend and companion. His life could not be saved so the Hiatus gave his breath to you. And so, you live."

"So, who am I now?"

"You are Hutt – a woodsman son. How old are you?"

"I was in my tenth period of seasons when I was struck," he said.

Jayca and Citor exchanged glances and nodded with satisfaction. "Tis the Twelfth Law - Hutt was beneath the age of Enlightenment."

"Which part of the Forest is your way Hutt?"

"I am of the way of the setting light and warmth."

"Do you know that area Citor?" asked Jayca.

"No. I never travelled that road. Maybe that way is also a Badland."

"I am of that way and I know of no Badland. We are not part of the Proto Forest but dwell apart from it by some good distance. Our way is green and plentiful," said Hutt indignantly.

Jayca touched the boy on a shoulder and gently shook him. "Hutt, you have lain comatose for many seasons. The way you knew is no longer. Mutant haflings have destroyed much of the outer part of the Kingdom. Maybe your home and parents too unless they were nimble and sought refuge near the Forest..."

"You lie!" Hutt cried.

"Lo Boy, my Majority is Hawk and I tell you no lie. The green land is brown. The plentiful of your way may be wild and wilted. The Light is weak, and the night is dark. It is unknown, but your way might have passed by with the coming of the mutant haflings."

"Then my homeland is gone," whispered Hutt.

Citor could see that the boy was upset and he slipped his arm around his shoulders in comfort.

Jayca continued. "Your way is unknown to me, but I say this only to warn you. This attack by our enemies is by far the strongest yet and we know not how far they have contaminated. Your family is here with Citor and me. When the King arrives, your family will be with him. The Kingdom of Sway is yours – the citizens of the Forest are yours. The food of the Realm is yours. Your new family is huge."

Citor gently pushed Hutt back down onto the grass. "Rest now," he said. The brightness of the morrow is still far away, and you will need your strength for you will have much to learn."

The warriors sat beside him until he slept. Before them they saw a boy, slight of build but with a promise to be tall when fully grown. His facial features undetermined although his jaw looked firm and strong. His hair a reddish coloured untidy mop. Both soldiers studied the boy, and both turned aside. Both with tears moistening their eyes. He was not Vidal.

They heard them coming long before they could see them. They came around the edge of the Forest and the King rode with his army. Those that could fly took to the wing and arrived first. Then came, lion, tiger and cheetah, all manner of cat and with them ran hyena and dogs. The Light was high above the trees and still animals of all shapes and sizes came. Those with less speed but more strength came mounted on horses. Hutt stirred and upon waking his eyes grew wider and wider and his mouth dropped open at the sight. Animals and birds, he had never seen before came on and on. More and more birds landed. Once down on the ground they began their transformation and once completed they took to organising a camp. Except the eagles, the falcons and the other birds of prey. They rested briefly before again taking flight. The haflings who had reached the Forest and had been hiding in the undergrowth fled screaming - only to be attacked from above by the eagles and hawks. Hafling birds took to the air and engaged with the Kings warriors. Some fell to the ground only to be trampled by the horses and attacked by the mounted warriors. No mercy was given.

Hutt found the shelter of Citor's broad shoulders and followed the battle through the bent elbow of his refuge's arm. His eyes remained wide with wonder. Then his mountain moved and Citor fell to his knees; Hutt looked directly into the eyes of his King. Jayca had the presence of mind to pull the boy down and so they both paid homage due to the King.

Jayca was first to rise and he walked to the King's side. Citor followed and Hutt was left kneeling. He looked around desperately seeking a way out.

The Magnificent old man walked to the boy and held out his hands. Hutt instinctively grasped the hands and once lowered his head; The King cupped his hand under Hutt's chin and tilted his head up. Still Hutt kept his eyes lowered.

"Are you frightened of me?" asked the King, his voice surprisingly gentle.

Hutt nodded dumbly.

"Why boy I mean you no harm?"

"You are the King," whispered Hutt.

"Yes but no citizen of mine was ever afraid of me. Look at me boy."

"I am afraid." Replied Hutt, shutting his eyes tightly.

"I mean you no harm. Look at me." Said the King and this time it was a command.

Hutt slowly opened his eyes and he looked at his King. The King was on his knees before him.

"You are Magnificent," said Hutt, awed.

The King smiled. "Surely, you have seen Majority before." Laughed the King.

Hutt nodded. "Yes, but not like you."

The King smiled again. "Allow an old lion to rise. The knees do not bend with a youthful spring anymore and the bones now creak."

Hutt stared as the King rose. Never before had he seen such a creature. The King was old. His hair was long - almost to his waist, and pure white in colour. In his prime, he would have exalted, for now though age had shrunk his body and wrinkled his face. He was still imposing and noble. His eyes still held the fire that had kept him King for so long. Within that fire, Hutt could see that he grieved. Hutt felt an overwhelming desire to please him and make happy to remove some of the misery so evident. He pointed to Jayca.

"The Hawk says that I am yours. This pleases me, but I think he lies. I am only Hutt, the woodsman's fourth son."

The King brushed a hand over Hutt's hair. "I know your name and I know you are a woodsman's son. Jayca speaks true for he is my Advisor and he never lies. Now Hutt, I need to talk with him and Citor. See there - my eagles are returning." He pointed. "Go and talk with them for a little while and then you and I will speak again."

Hutt grinned. "Yes, I would like to speak with them for I saw them in battle. I will be back soon." He promised.

The King watched him run across to the clearing. His headlong flight caused the birds to jump away and scatter. The King smiled again but when he turned back to the waiting warriors the smile had died from his lips and eyes.

"Tell me." He commanded. "Has there been a sighting of Aria?"

Jayca shook his head. "No, My Liege, nothing."

The King gave a low, grumbling growl. "What has happened here?"

Jayca began to explain about the boy, Hutt, but the King interrupted him. "I know all about the boy." He said.

He saw Jayca's puzzlement. "An owl told, and the crickets spoke this night last and this morning the same tale from the cicadas. Am I not the King? How else could I greet the boy - he is my son but not my son. I have no reason to cause him further anguish." He growled.

Jayca bowed. "No, My Liege. The boy is confused but he will learn. Lord, not one of us would joyfully bring you the fate of Vidal."

"Then it is well that it came by the creatures of the Forest. They found reasons to rejoice." He paused for a moment then added. "In all honesty they eased the pain of Vidal passing from me. They spoke to me as the Light and as free creatures. They made the pain less." His voice hardened, and his eyes were like flint. "But make no mistake – the haflings will pay dearly for their treachery."

He turned and beckoned his commanders forward. They came quickly, Hutt with them. The King glanced down at the boy that stood beside him. And then looked at Citor. "Bear, you will take twenty of my finest warriors and forty of the sturdiest horses. You will take this boy, Hutt, to the Kingdom."

Citor bent low. "Your command, My Liege."

The King bent forward and touched Citor in a bonding. "I cannot thank you enough for the homage you paid to my son. Ask what you will of me and it will be yours."

Citor blushed at the King's tribute. "There is nothing I require. It is my honour to serve, as my father did before me."

Hutt tugged at the King's sleeve and the King looked down at his upturned face.

"I would stay here." Said Hutt.

The King frowned. "You would refuse me?"

Hutt looked hurt. "No but I would rather stay here."

"No. I lost you once. I will not do so again. By my command you will go with Citor."

Hutt looked mutinous but Citor stepped forward, picked Hutt up and tucked him under his arm. He carried him to a horse and tossed him up into the saddle.

"Low One, you do not argue with the King." He said. He restrained Hutt from slipping out of the saddle.

"But I wasn't. I just wanted to tell him that I could serve him better by staying here." Protested Hutt.

"Enough! Make your bow and lets be away from here." Citor growled.

Hutt bowed with a flourish, but spoilt the effect by grinning widely and waving. The King smiled and saluted. He looked at Jayca. "He doesn't look like Vidal, but he has all his charm."

He watched Citor choose the escort from the primate division and nodded his approval before turning to address his officers.

59

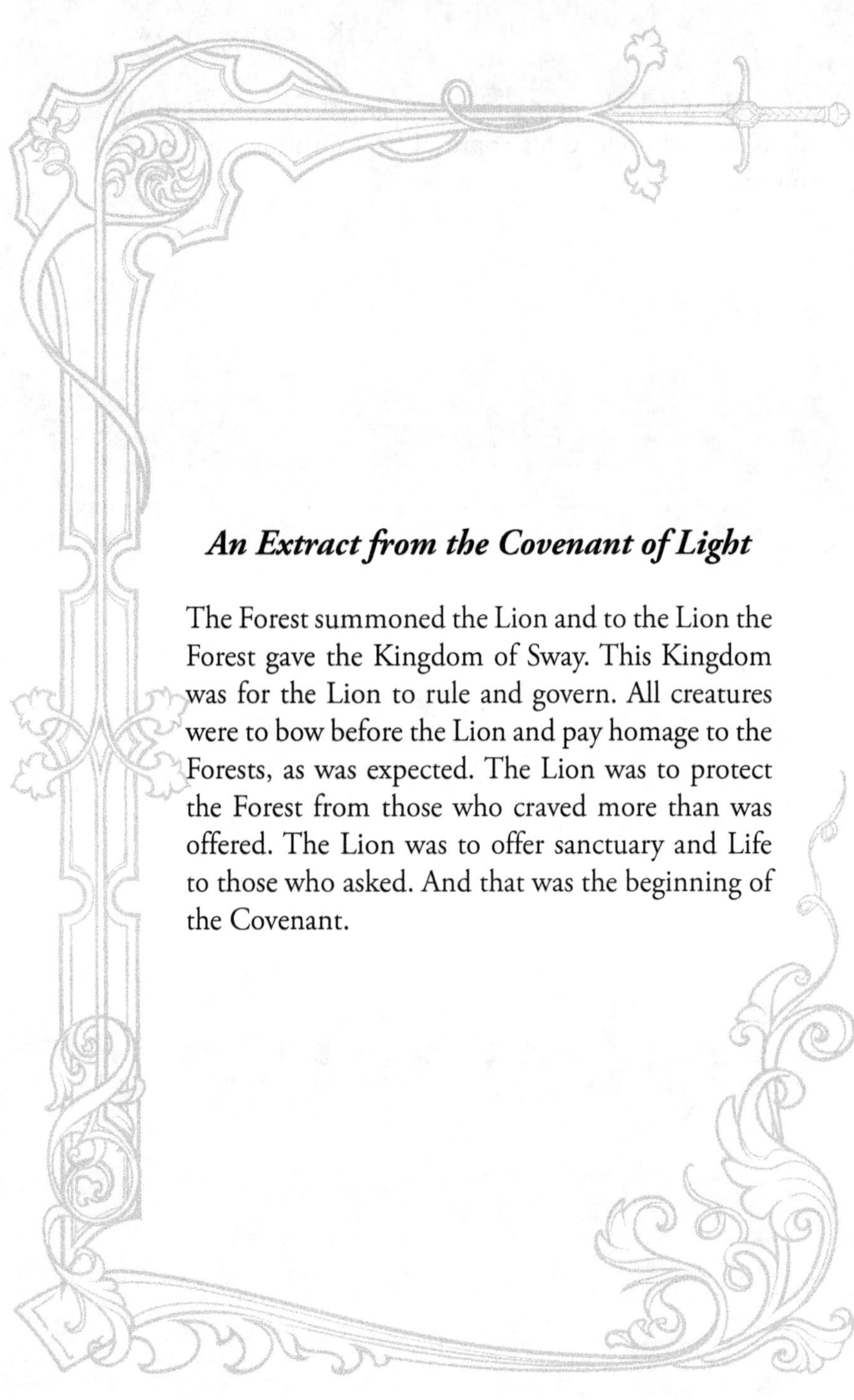

An Extract from the Covenant of Light

The Forest summoned the Lion and to the Lion the Forest gave the Kingdom of Sway. This Kingdom was for the Lion to rule and govern. All creatures were to bow before the Lion and pay homage to the Forests, as was expected. The Lion was to protect the Forest from those who craved more than was offered. The Lion was to offer sanctuary and Life to those who asked. And that was the beginning of the Covenant.

Chapter 5

THE BADLANDS

"I want three groups with two hundred warriors in each. One will return to the site of the ambush. They will track the Lady Aria and Likea. The second will ride the boundary of the Forest for their sign. I want them found!" The Kings eyes narrowed, and he spoke though clenched teeth. "Destroy the abominations as you find." He turned to a panther human warrior standing apart from the others. The King gestured him to come forward. "The third army will ride into the contaminated lands and as far as the haflings border, again, destroy all that isn't pure."

"Do we penetrate their land Sire?" asked one commander

The King clenched his fists and the scowl on his face deepened. "We cannot violate their borders else we defy the Covenant. For all I want the Lady and Likea returned, I cannot place the Hiatus Forest in jeopardy to save them. Essura, you will lead the panther army into the Badlands and I will command the army to search along the Forest. You will choose the commander to carry out the search from the ambush. Go now - before the word of our coming spreads too far."

The warriors saluted and ran to their waiting mounts. The King watched them go. "I would go with them." He said to Jayca. "What say you, Advisor?"

"You cannot go. You are the last of the Monarchy."

"Still I would avenge the loss of Vidal's Second Life."

"So would every soldier in your Kingdom. Let your decision stand, My Liege," pleaded Jayca. The King nodded. "It stands, but one day I will find Tonka before me and he will taste my sword," he vowed. "Come on. We are wasting time," he said impatiently and strode for his mount.

The King and his soldiers patrolled the Forest's edge for four days before he received any news. One of the sub-divided search parties, under the command of Duran, emerged from the Badlands and crossed the river to where the King waited at a make-shift camp.

Duran and his warriors were battered and weary; their losses had been considerable. The King ordered the search party to partake in food and drink while he ordered his servants to take care of their mounts. After they had eaten their fill, the King summoned Duran before him.

Duran knelt before the King; his head bowed.

"I have failed, Sire." He confessed.

The King masked his disappointed and waved Duran to continue.

"We cut no true sign of the Lady or Likea. Instead, we followed a band of haflings that were travelling in the direction that Likea should have taken. Only on one hillock did we cut sign that they might have been there. That would have been the first night after the ambush. After that we found nothing. The haflings must have set fire to the grass and undergrowth around that hill and destroyed any sign Likea might have left. I assumed Likea would continue west to seek the sanctuary of our beloved Forest. I divided my troops to give us a better chance of finding their tracks. Nothing - except heavy losses.

We were attacked three times in the one day. We pressed on but there must have been heavy rain in the area for even the haflings tracks had disappeared. The creeks and rivers we crossed were swift and swollen so even in the muddy banks we could cut no sign."

"Is the way very bad,?" asked Jayca.

Duran nodded miserably. "Tis unbelievable. The terrain is beyond description. Huge gaping craters spew a stinking odour; deep canyons that run for league upon league slash open the ground. The trees, the poor unfortunate trees are dying by the hundreds. Thick cords of creeper and vine cover the shrubs and choke the grass. The newer growth is not soft to touch but full of thorns. The first dark time we almost froze in the cold but by the light of the morrow the heat was intense, the water we carried dried in our sacks. By the second light time the weather was reverse."

He stopped and wiped his tearing eyes. "Forgive me Sire. The abominations that we witnessed are too terrible to comprehend." He passed his hand over his eyes again and sniffed loudly. "We found some crazed prisoners. They had been initiated, but the haflings didn't yet trust them." Duran looked directly at the King. "Some begged us, those that were still able - to end them. We put them all to the sword. It seemed the kindest thing to do."

The King rose from his nature-made chair and lifted Duran to his feet. His hand lingered on his shoulder to comfort him. "You could have done no more. Take your troop and return to the Kingdom. You have done more that should have been asked." The King said kindly.

"Sire - but the Lady and my brother Likea. We should stay."

The King shook his head. "No Duran. We will stay until Essura returns. We will continue to patrol just in case

Likea…" He stopped and shrugged. "Take your troop home warrior. We can do no more."

Duran bowed. "Then by your leave, Sire, allow me to take my men into the Sway woods. They would like to renew their oath."

"I could grant you no less a request. Rest your men for this dark time. On the morrow I will speak with them." Duran saluted and left the King alone with Jayca. The King glanced at him. "My family has paid a terrible price for the honour. Now it spreads to the innocent. There is no longer an heir to the Kingdom and that might mean war from within. Any successor that I name will not suit." He shook his head in despair and for a moment Jayca saw the hopelessness in his Kings eyes.

"All is not lost, Sire. There is still time for…"

The King slumped back into his chair. "Time for what? I can no longer breed. I am the last of my line. The Chosen line." He rubbed his hand wearily over his eyes. "Yet the Covenant continues, and my faith is not shaken. What does it mean, old friend? You know the Covenant almost as well as I. Tell me, where is the way out?"

"Sire, I do not know."

"Nor I, and yet there is something," He touched at hand to his chest. "Here - there is something." He shrugged. "I know not." He stood up and strode to his work bench. "Bring me a list of all the candidates that are eligible. I will study them, but I know in my heart that none are suitable."

"There is time for that task later. Rest for now for you are tired."

"I will rest when Essura returns. Hear me and help me for I cannot rest. Aria is my only hope."

Essura returned with the bulk of his army three days later. He rode directly to the King and paid homage. "We chased them back into the Charter. They stood across the river and taunted us for they knew we wouldn't violate the Covenant. Of Tonka we saw no sign, but his army is far stronger that we imagined. He has even managed to contaminate the insect world." He looked at Jayca. "Even the birds are soiled. They were beyond our reach, but we thinned the mutants – those that we caught. But the rot has spread far and wide. I lost a dozen soldiers to snake venom." He paused but the King urged him to continue.

Essura looked at Jayca.

"Did Duran find them?" he asked.

Jayca shook his head. And Essura scowled.

"We found some haflings prisoners. None of ours were amongst them. We killed them too. They were contaminated - sickening to watch in their mutant state."

"How did your soldiers react? Did they object?" Jayca asked.

Essura snorted. "They fought each other to be on the execution squad."

He looked at the King. "Some were not badly soiled - those we gave a chance to redeem themselves - we freed them and sent them on their way. Most of them seemed pleased at the prospect of the blade."

"What now Sire?" asked Jayca.

The King sighed. "We go home. Although Likea was one of my finest warriors it would be too much to expect him to have survived this long against an army. However, since my faith is strong… Essura! Keep three squads here to patrol this line. The rest of the army will return with me to the Kingdom."

"By your command." Responded Essura.

"Sire I would stay with Essura," said Jayca.

"Yes, but you will have to return soon for we must prepare for the inevitable. Essura, exercise skills while you bide here. Give your men some time to go into the Forest. Jayca will explain what I want done. Now I will rest."

They watched the King approach the brush shelter, pause, then turn instead to walk towards the river.

Jayca shook his head.

"Now all he has left is the boy Hutt. No heir and then no Kingdom. What is your prediction, oh Wise One?" Essura asked.

"The King must name a successor. If there isn't an heir, then he will abdicate in favour of one of the Plains' families. Because there isn't a blood line then whoever the King names will have to defend his right to rule. That means fighting which is against the Covenant. If the Lady Aria was still with us, then the King could name her as his successor and that would bring her father to offer his sword. No usurper would stand against two armies."

"Can't he offer his aid voluntary?"

Jayca shook his head. "No, it is forbidden by law to increase his army. To protect his family it is the only way he has."

"The Badlands border the Plain so how can we be sure that they haven't been contaminated?"

"We can't."

Essura nodded thoughtfully. "Then it is as well he takes the army with him. I will prepare some battle plans."

"Yes." Replied Jayca. "That is what he wants you to do."

Jayca and Essura stood silently as they watched the King lead his army back to the Kingdom. The rest the King had wanted and needed seemed to have eluded him for when they saw him the following dawn he looked tired and old. He had taken leave of them in his usual calm manner, but he had a haunted look and his warriors avoided his eyes.

Essura slapped his gloves against his thigh as the last column disappeared from sight. "I will not submit!" he shouted. "The King is worthy of His Kingdom and I will not submit!"

Jayca looked startled." He is not beaten, and he will never give it up." He said coldly.

Essura glared at him. "Fool!" he snarled, and he strode away, shouting for the officers. They came running, and Essura glared at them fiercely. "We found nothing - nothing! That means until we find their bodies they are still with us. Understand! They are still with us!" He roared at them. "Now - Likea is a very good soldier. The Forest will be his goal. Two squads will patrol the far river bank at all time. It will be dangerous and at night it will be difficult to see. The abominations do not care for the dark either and Likea will know that. He will move at night. I want him found. If we find him then we will find the Lady." He turned to Jayca. "Old Hawk, I have kept only three Eagles, three Falcons and one Owl. You are my only nighthawk. Will you fly with the owl?"

"Of course," answered Jayca, offended.

Essura gave a slight smile. "I meant no offence, Hawk. I have the greatest respect for your age and confidence in your sight."

"Then I fly."

Evidence of the haflings return came on the second day following the Kings departure. On that day, the birds fought a bloody battle in the sky over the river.

Two falcons and one of the eagles were on a routine sweep when they were attacked by three mutant eagles. The mutants swooped on the two falcons. Outnumbered, the falcons relied on a superior speed to avoid the sharpened talons. Then simultaneously, the two falcons attacked one eagle. Under the combined weight of two, the mutant fell towards the ground. The other two mutants began to follow them down when suddenly the Kingdom eagle struck one of the mutants. The mutant couldn't regain its equilibrium and it plummeted to the ground, almost at Essura feet. The falcons had succeeded in forcing their victim low enough for their comrade to take over. Long talons and powerful legs gripped the mutant bird around the wings. Essura later swore he heard the bones crack. The eagle released the mutant and because it couldn't fly, it fell to earth. The eagle circled once, and then flew to assist the falcons who were now harassing the last mutant eagle.

The sound of cheering woke Jayca. Rubbing sleep from his eyes he joined Essura. He stared at the dead hafling and shook his head in disgust. The mutant was dead but in its final death throes it had transformed into a hideous sight. The trunk and legs were human, but the upper part of the body was eagle.

Jayca turned away. "Disgusting."

Essura agreed and toed the still form with his boot. He called two of his soldiers to dispose of the body into the river.

"If they regained their courage to attack us then Tonka must have returned. I will have to withdraw the patrols from the daylight hours. Tonka's army is too strong to fight on his terms. We will continue to patrol this side of the river. You had better fly and recall our patrols," instructed Essura.

"What about the dark time air patrols?" Jayca asked.

Essura shook his head." The owl is defenceless, and I won't send you up alone."

"But to cancel completely?"

"Not completely – you will still fly - but on this side of the river. Don't argue. If they have contaminated some of the eagles, then you can be sure they have touched the hawks as well."

By the time he found and warned the patrols Jayca was feeling weary. The creeping shadow of darkness was approaching – most of the Badlands was covered when Jayca caught a glimpse of a large pack of dogs moving through the bush. He circled and watched as the darkness overtook them. Still, he watched them until they stopped and built a huge fire.

Puzzled by their behaviour, Jayca couldn't see any other sign of movement but the pack had given him the impression that they had been following a scent. Jayca yawned. He knew that he would soon have to go to ground soon before the metamorphosis began to weaken. He circled lazily watching intently the area between the dog pack and the river.

Still nothing moved. He continued to sweep, each pass taking a wider circle. He spotted Walcott, the Owl, closing on him but he continued the sweep. Walcott joined him, flying at his wingtip.

"Are you insane? Essura says you are to return at once! You have been transformed for too long and you are in danger of going over your limit," Cried a worried Walcott.

"Hush! Will you?! I have a few minutes left. Listen. Walcott. Pay attention. Look there - between the dog pack and the river."

"Only if you agree to leave; Jayca you are out of time," said Walcott urgently.

"I can still make the Forest's edge if not the army. Look. See there. Near those large rocks. The shape isn't right."

Walcott stared then gasped in surprise. "It's a form - a human form. I'll go closer." He swooped lower then almost immediately climbed back to Jayca.

"I think it is Likea!" Walcott exclaimed.

Jayca quickly judged the distance to his army." It's too far I can't make it. You must go Walcott to alert Essura and bring him here."

"But what about you? You can't stay here."

"I will fly in a direct line to the far river bank. I'll be safe there and have time to transform. On your way back, sight on me to give yourself direction. But hurry Walcott - the dogs had his scent."

Walcott sped away without further argument. Jayca turned away and flew for the safety of the river. He landed clumsily and immediately began to make the change. As his human form took shape he sat in the grass to regain his breath.

He hadn't been there long before he heard Walcott fly over him on his return flight. In the distance he could hear Essura coming bringing with him his small army. Jayca waited patiently for them to arrive but he didn't look for them, instead he kept his eyes fastened on the far bank.

Essura jumped from his horse before the beast had fully halted.

"Is it Likea?" he demanded.

"I think so... But whoever it is, the pack had his scent and were closing in. Only the darkness saved him but the haflings are learning. I have been watching them - they are lighting beacons every few paces, in his direction. They will reach him soon and what a prize he will be."

"We will be there first. Wait here until we return." Essura ordered. He turned to a soldier standing beside him. "Toppett you and one other, get a fire going as soon as we cross the river. Beebee run back to camp and bring Jayca's medicine sack."

"If he is hurt you will need me," protested Jayca.

"You can't treat him in the middle of a battle. You will be needed here." said Essura.

To forestall further argument, he swung himself into the saddle and ordered his troops forward. Walcott was in the lead to guide them across the river and onto the far bank. The haflings were close. Essura could hear them as they trampled fallen twigs and branches.

"Three of you will not stop to fight. You will ride directly to the figure. Walcott will guide you. You are to pick up the figure and carry him back to Jayca. Do not stop. This is your task." Essura ordered harshly. Three of the soldiers nodded and moved a little way to the left to let the main body of soldiers pass. The beacon fires were increasing and now it was almost light enough to see by. Essura double banked his guards and now they rode two abreast. The haflings were close, but the light they had made blinded them to the horsemen who were still shrouded in darkness.

The mutants were still fitting arrows to their bows when Essura's army crashed through the night and fell upon them. The battle was swift. Essura's troopers gave no quarter and they trampled the haflings underfoot. Finally, their ranks broke and the haflings retreated. The soldiers tasked with securing Likea rushed past the fighting by using the light from the fires and made a rapid descent down the hillock to the river. Essura ordered his troops to retreat into the darkness and make their way back to the river. He spotted the fire on the far side and gave a shout in triumph as they splashed into the water. Safely on the other side he shouted with glee to Jayca. "We never lost a warrior." He yelled.

"Excellent! With what I could see it looked fierce..."

Essura sneered." Against us? If we could strike them in the open, we would annihilate them. They are cowards - a foulness to be squashed under our boots."

Jayca agreed but his attention was drawn to the soldier who carried the human.

"Is it Likea?" he asked anxiously.

"Yes. Get him down gently, Oaf!" Essura shouted to the soldier. He turned back to Jayca. "I think he is badly hurt - see what you can do otherwise we will give him to the Light."

Jayca quickly examined the unconscious Likea. He grimaced as many wounds were uncovered. He forced open Likea's mouth and poured in a black liquid from one of his many gourds. Most of the liquid trickled out of the corners of Likea's mouth. Jayca readjusted his approach and again poured more of the foul-looking liquid until he judged enough had been swallowed. He then started to work on the oozing wounds and the scowl that Jayca wore etched deeper on his face. After some time, Likea's wounds were scrapped clean and wrapped in some fresh, green pallor leaves that fell from around them. Jayca produced another liquid administering only a little to Likea before he signalled Essura forward.

"Well? I've ordered a litter made in case we have to carry him." Said Essura.

"He's very weak - blood loss mainly. He has several arrow wounds and at some stage he has received a heavy blow to his shoulder."

Essura stared at Jayca. "You look sick. What's the matter?" he demanded.

"Some of the hafling insects have been at him." He muttered.

Essura threw him a horrified look. Jayca caught the look and nodded. "It's alright. I destroyed them. Dirty, filthy haflings." He held out a closed hand.

"What's this?" Essura asked.

Jayca dropped the object into Essura's hand. "It's what they are using on the arrows."

Essura frowned. "Yes, but what is it?"

"It is bone. They are making their arrow heads out of bone." Jayca turned aside and spewed.

Essura dropped the arrow head and stared at the object lying on the ground. He also felt like he might throw up. He swallowed loudly and patted Jayca on the back. Jayca straighten up wiping at his mouth with his hand.

Essura nodded to where Likea lay.

"Will he live?" he asked.

Jayca shrugged. "I don't know. I have done what I can, and he seems to be resting easier, and in less pain, but is probably because of my mixture. I'll stay with him this night."

"Do you want to move him back to camp?"

Jayca shrugged again. "It matters not. I can do no more."

Throughout the darkness of the night Jayca sat beside his patient. He kept feeding him small measures of his potions. As the light came back to the Forest, Likea was sleeping peacefully. At first light Essura came to them.

"Well?"

"It will take a long time, but I think he might survive. He has the strongest constitution I have ever known. A lesser horse would have succumbed days past."

Essura snorted. "A lesser anything would have died. Never have I seen such wounds on a living form and I have soldiered long." Essura said admiringly. He paused, seeming to hesitate. "Has he been contaminated?" he demanded brusquely.

"I doubt it. Likea would have chosen his path, but to be sure we will guard him until we are certain. I will rest now. I have given orders to be awakened if he returns to us."

"Yes. Get some sleep - it has been a good work all around. Before you rest, advise me. Do I send word to the King?"

Jayca thought for minute before he answered. "Allow one more day. If he recovers soon then there will be something to tell and if he doesn't then there is no harm done."

All that day Likea did not stir. The watchers continued to spoon Jayca's potions into his mouth and they kept washing and cleaning his wounds. The haflings had returned to the river bank and shouted abuse. Some threw stones and fired arrows, but the range was too far, and they fell harmlessly into the water. Essura held back his men but he watched the haflings closely. It was late, bordering on dusk before the haflings retired and Essura returned to the camp. Jayca was awake and he found him with Likea. Jayca greeted him but didn't look away from his task of spooning yet more of a mixture into Likea's mouth. Suddenly Likea coughed and his eyelids fluttered. Jayca immediately signalled and four warriors came forward and held Likea down. Likea coughed again and this time his eyes opened. He struggled against the weight of the soldiers as they held him firmly down.

"Jayca," he whispered hoarsely, "Jayca."

"Tis I Likea. Lay thee self still less the wounds reopen and bleed again."

Likia stopped struggling and gradually the soldiers released their grip.

"Are thee touched by the haflings? Are you contaminated?"

"Nay. They never came close enough. They were closing though. I remember but I had no strength left to fight and I couldn't run. The Light was close to me then."

"We found you first. Tell me - have you taken or ingested the flesh or blood of ours?"

Likea gritted his teeth and started to struggle up. The soldiers quickly held him down and he could only glare. "Nay. Fool!"

Jayca smiled in delight. "Likea's fire returns. Soon you will mend but for now you need rest."

Likea gripped the sleeve of Jayca's tunic. "The Lady is she safe?"

Jayca dropped his gaze. "We haven't found her."

"No!' Likea cried his voice weak. "No. She must be.' His voice tapered off and his eyes closed as the medicine took hold and sent him back to sleep. Jayca covered him with a blanket and then stood up. He sent the soldiers away then looked at Essura. "You heard?" he said.

"Yes, come the Light I will send a Falcon. There is no hurry now. None at all."

75

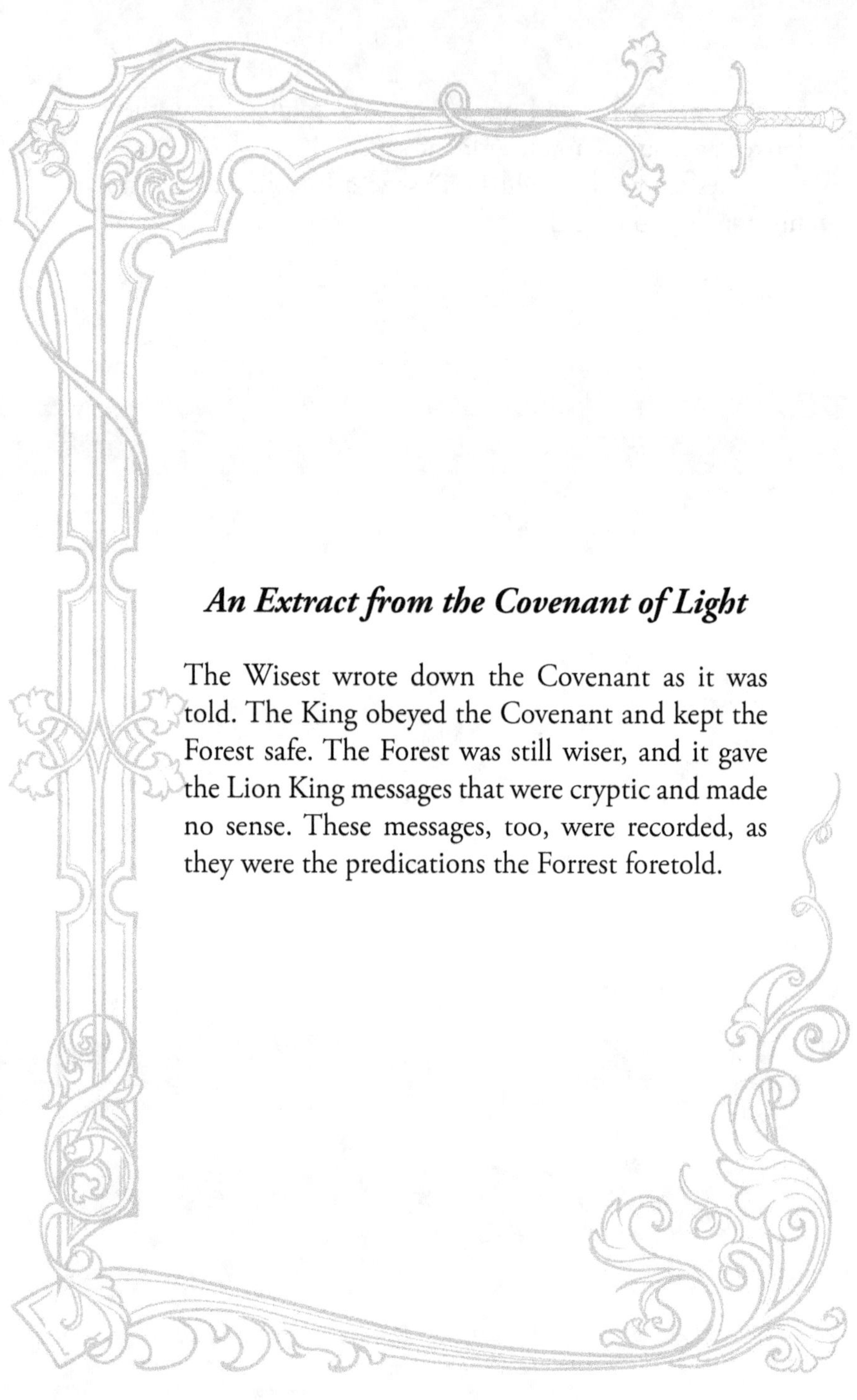

An Extract from the Covenant of Light

The Wisest wrote down the Covenant as it was told. The King obeyed the Covenant and kept the Forest safe. The Forest was still wiser, and it gave the Lion King messages that were cryptic and made no sense. These messages, too, were recorded, as they were the predications the Forrest foretold.

Chapter 6

LIKEA AND HUTT

For Likea's sake, Jayca kept him asleep for two more days. Every time Likea stirred Jayca would spoon more of his elixir into Likea's mouth. The enforced rest was doing some good because Likea's wounds were visibly healing quickly and as his strength began to return as he was waking at closer intervals. On the third morning Likea woke before the light came. He lay still so not to waken Jayca. He frowned and seemed puzzled as he tried to recall the last days. He stirred restlessly and started to sit up. Jayca woke and immediately reached for his bottles. Likea caught his hand and held it tightly.

"Nay do not drug me. I must speak." He whispered.

"'Tis better that you sleep. Thee, will be stronger faster. Come - release me and take my potion." Jayca coaxed.

"No! Listen to me. Why is the army here?"

"We were searching for you and the Lady Aria." Jayca explained patiently. "Now take the mixture."

"But the Lady. Why hasn't someone gone after the Lady?"

"We searched but she was nowhere to be found. Essura searched all this section of the Forest and into the Badlands. Likea you must rest."

Likea struggled to rise but Jayca pushed him back onto the make-shift mat.

"Likea. Likea – stop it. You must rest."

"She went into the Forest. Hear me dolt! She went into the Forest. She had my horse and went into the Forest," he whispered but his voice sounded urgent.

Jayca paused - the spoon poised in mid-air. "No lioness came out of the Forest. Citor was there with the Boy. Likea I tell you – no lioness came from the Forest."

Likea snorted angrily. "Fool! Dolt! She didn't metamorphose – she couldn't." He lay back, panting for breath.

Jayca wiped the perspiration from his brow with a damp cloth and then pushed the spoonful of medicine into Likea's open mouth.

"Then it is too late, and it doesn't matter. She didn't return and now she is human for the rest of her life. The Forest will be her guide to a settlement where she can live."

Likea beckoned Jayca closer. "You don't understand - the Lady is with child. She could not transform," he uttered weakly. He closed his eyes and his vision faded.

"With child!" repeated Jayca, shocked. He gripped Likea by the shoulders and shook him. "Likea! Likea! Wake up! Wake up Horse! You can't sleep now!" Shouted Jayca.

Likea didn't stir but Jayca's shouting brought Essura and the sentries running.

"What is it Hawk? Has thee brain snapped?" shouted Essura irritably. "Leave the Horse be - he needs to rest."

Jayca stopped shaking Likea; instead he grabbed Essura by the arm and dragged him away from the shelter and the guards. Surprised by Jayca's odd behaviour Essura submitted but once out of earshot he jerked his arm free with such power that Jayca stumbled and almost fell.

"Speak of your folly," Essura snapped.

"Likea just told me that the Lady went into the Forest," cried Jayca.

"So – he did save her. Why didn't she return? Tis too late now the Forest owns her," mused Essura.

Jayca gripped his arm again and shook it violently.

"You oaf of a Panther's breath! She is with child!" Jayca hissed.

"What?" thundered Essura. "You lie!"

"No! Likea told me but he fell asleep before he could continue."

"Are you sure? He is ill - delirious maybe? Perhaps he was dreaming."

"No, he was sane. The fever has passed."

"Then wake him. We must know more," Essura ordered.

"I can't wake. At least, not until the Light has travelled halfway. Essura we must be silent for the haflings would covet this news. No word must be spread here - tis too dangerous. For the capture of the Lady the haflings might be brave enough to penetrate as far as the Hiatus Forest."

Essura slapped his hands together angrily. He glared at Jayca.

"Halfwit! Why did you drug him?"

"How was I to know what he wanted to say?" said Jayca tearfully.

Essura glared at him for a moment longer then slapped him on the shoulder.

"Tis not your fault. My temper is as black as my hide," he reassured him but then he frowned. "My Liege must not know. The Royal party was away from the Kingdom for two seasons. It must have happened in my Lady's home place."

Jayca nodded. "Yes – otherwise Citor would have seen the Lady's swollen belly," he agreed soberly.

Essura took a deep breath "Advise me, Jayca the Advisor. What am I to do?" commanded Essura.

"My Liege must be told. He needs to prepare a form to enter the Forest. Likea must return to the Kingdom for the King will need to question him. He will have to go with much speed but without arousing suspicion. The haflings are separated from us by a single stretch of water."

"Yes yes. But how?" snapped Essura.

"Patience and let me think."

Jayca sat on a fallen tree truck tucking his legs up under him. Essura watched him impatiently and when Jayca signalled to him he almost ran to him. Jayca motioned him to sit.

"Send two falcons and one eagle. Send them at different intervals. Each will carry a part of one message that I will devise and inform you." He paused briefly then continued in a quiet voice. "Likea can't ride so he must be carried. We cannot send too many warriors for one injured horse no matter how brave that horse is. Choose seven of your best and let each take a second mount. Send them out by two and send one only with Likea. Send Likea first. He will travel the slowest and the others will catch him. It will appear to be normal patrols. The haflings shouldn't notice anything odd."

"Yes. I like it. Tis almost full light and the camp must be kept as usual. Return to your mat for you are never about this early. Come noon Likea must go but the birds must fly sooner. What is the message?"

"The first - it comes by three and the Lioness is the Forest. The second – It comes by two and the King must seek. The third - once only for a kingdom's sake. That should be enough. The King will understand. If we lose one bird, then there is enough of the message left for some sense to be made of the rest."

Essura stood and dusted down his tunic. He slapped his hands together and nodded solemnly "Good. Rest now Advisor. You will ride with Likea because the King will have need of you. We will wait another two light time and then we will also return."

The King finished praying and left the Prayer Tree to walk into the warm daylight. He blinked rapidly to clear his sight for it had been darker in the shade and the light outside was very bright. His gaze caught sight of Hutt on his own playing down by the stream; amusing himself with a type of catch-up game with some squirrels. He also seemed to be impervious to the frantic beckoning from his teacher.

The Queen joined her King and took his arm caringly. She smiled wistfully as she watched Hutt. The King glanced at his Queen affectionately.

"He reminds you of Vidal, doesn't he?" He asked.

The old Queen sighed. "Yes. He has all of his wilfulness and all his sweetness too."

The King nodded and they both fell silent, each remembering another time. The Queen rallied her thoughts first, and she looked up at her lifelong mate.

"Has there been any word of Aria?" she asked inquisitively.

"No. It's been too long now. If she had survived the chase, I'm sure she would have made contact."

"There is already talk of trouble amongst the other Prides. I heard it yesterday from my Ladies."

"Yes. Some of the Plains warriors feel they have the right to succession. The Emir is doing his best to keep control and to placate them. He is under a lot of pressure himself."

"Who do you choose?" Enquired the Queen.

The King hung his head. "None have the right. No matter who I choose there will be discontentment."

"If you do not choose will there be war."

"To have war is to become a hafling - we must not shed our blood. Only the Hiatus's chosen line can rule, and we forfeited that right through Ambrose. To choose from the Plains Prides is to almost have an unbeliever as protector and that is unthinkable. "

The Queen smiled at him and patted his arm.

"The Forest will provide – you must keep the faith. Brave Heart."

"I have doubted. Of all our offspring Vidal was the only one that survived long enough to take a mate and I hoped, I hoped. Now the haflings have taken him and given me a human child. I have doubted."

"My love, we both knew from your father that the price of Ambrose's folly would be high. I believe that the debt has been paid with the last of our offspring - Vidal. I could wish that Vidal be spared but it wasn't to be."

"Did you never question your faith? You knew the price demanded by the Covenant when my father spared Ambrose. You knew when we mated that all our offspring were fated."

She smiled a little. "I never questioned my faith. Oh, I had hoped that my children would escape their destiny, but I loved and enjoyed them while I had them."

She saw his distressed expression and smiled lovingly at him.

"Do not doubt my husband. The Covenant goes beyond your life. The Forest makes our lives and it will provide."

The King knelt before her, took her hands and granted a kiss.

"You are my strength. You always have been. But tell, why you believe when the wound of Vidal is still open?"

The old Queen helped him to his feet before she answered. She looked into his sorrowful eyes and smiled.

"The Forest has forgiven your family - you see it has given back Vidal in the form of Hutt."

The King looked across the field to where Hutt was playing. The tutors were running after him, trying to catch him but Hutt kept eluding them and then sought refuge in a nearby tree.

"That's Vidal's favourite escape route." The Queen laughed and clapped her hands.

The King chuckled. "He will get away too. Just watch - see there - through the limbs and down the far side."

"Shall we rescue the teachers?"

"We had better," agreed the King with a slight smile. He clapped his hands sharply and the teachers turned to look at him. "Leave him," he beckoned. "I'll speak with him later." The King waved them away and he watched them slowly walk towards the Learning Tree. His idle look was arrested suddenly as he saw the flight of a falcon.

"A message from Essura no doubt." He said.

"Shall I leave you?"

"No. We are too old to have secrets from each other. Come, walk with me."

The falcon landed and slowly regained human form before bowing humbly to the Royals.

"What is your message, Falcon?" The King asked almost impatiently.

"It comes times three and the Lioness is the Forest," replied the messenger.

The King frowned. "Thank you, Falcon, rest now." Replied the King. He took the Queen's hand and they walked away. He bent his head to whisper. "Aria is safe. She entered the Forest."

The Queen smiled. "I'm glad." She said and looked at her mate. "I'm sorry; does this mean that the Emir also has a right to claim the Kingdom?"

"None have the right. But he won't though, he gave me his word, although I am inclined to favour him above all other." Moments after his reply to the Queen, the King stopped suddenly and stared hard into the bright sky. "Look! An eagle! Essura is busy."

"There is another bird as well! It seems to be injured," exclaimed the Queen.

The Eagle was flying close to another Falcon. It looked as if it was trying to help the Falcon to stay aloft.

The King motioned to his guards and they rushed to assist. The guard with the most speed caught the Falcon before it crashed to the ground. The Eagle landed nearby and immediately began to transform his shape.

"What has happened?" The King demanded of the Eagle. "Why has Essura sent you?"

"We have messages of great importance. The Falcon was injured, and I had caught up to him. The haflings had loosened arrows and threw stones; he was struck. He was still able to fly and so we came together." The Eagle paused to regain some composure, but the King was impatient.

"What is your message?"

"Only once for Kingdom's sake." The Eagle replied.

"What does it mean?" asked the Queen seeking an explanation from her mate.

The King frowned deeply but he thanked the Eagle and sent him to rest. He walked over to where the injured Falcon lay.

"What does it mean? "Asked the Queen, repeating the question.

"Jayca must have sent the messages. They are cryptic, so they must be important. I wonder, yes, the message must be in three parts and the injured Falcon must have the second piece."

The crowd of on-lookers that gathered around the injured bird parted to make room for the Royals. Medics were slowly bringing the Falcon back to his human form. A large wound was now visible on his thigh. The Falcon saw the King and tried to stand to make a bow, but the King knelt before him and stopped the movement.

"Away all of you," said the Falcon importantly "This message is for the King."

The assembly of on-lookers rapidly broke up and the King leant forward to support the warrior.

"It comes by two and the King must seek." Said the messenger.

"Can you tell me more? What has happened?" asked the King.

Focusing his breathing through pain, the Falcon whispered, "We found Likea," and with that he fell back against the King unconscious.

The King waved the medics to return. "Take him for immediate treatment," he ordered, and the medics rushed to obey.

The King watched them carry the warrior to the shelters before he turned his attention to his Queen.

He smiled, and the worry lines seemed to leave his face.

"I see that it is good news," The Queen remarked. "But what?"

"Jayca is indeed wise. Likea must have recovered. Listen, My Dear. Forget the first part of the message that was only to tell me that Jayca split the message into three pieces. Now – the Lioness is the Forest: For Kingdom's sake: The King must seek. The message is simple - it means that for the sake of the Kingdom I must find Aria."

"I'm afraid I don't understand. Although she is an Heir in her own right, she is female and not of your lineage."

"Hark!" The King chortled. "If Aria is in Forest then that means she has taken human form - she can't rule. Jayca knows this but he sends me the third part - for Kingdom's sake. Why? And the second part - I must find her. That is not a request he summons me to obey. Jayca is devout, he would not order me, but he means me to make every effort. He would not do so – not for a human."

"I still don't understand." Grumbled the Queen.

"Aria must have chosen to keep – no take – the human life instead of the treasured Second Life."

"But why?" insisted the Queen edgily.

The King took the Queen into his arms and hugged her.

"To keep her baby safe." He whispered into her ear.

With realisation, she clutched at the King and her breath caught. "Sire. Beloved. Are you sure? Citor said nothing."

He probably didn't know but Likea might have known – he must have known. He made a super - human effort to protect her. If she is with child, then Likea would have been both Vidal's and Helment's choice to be her bodyguard."

He bent his head and kissed her.

"Your faith has been answered and mine renewed. The Forest has forgiven my family."

"How can we get Aria out of the Forest? She must give birth outside the Forest for an Heir. It is forbidden to deny the Second Life and we have no true humans to send in to get her."

"Likea must go. If he is her bodyguard then he has already accepted her life for his."

"He is injured. He cannot protect her. By Essura's report he cannot even walk and besides, he doesn't know the Forest." She protested.

"I know the Forest," said Hutt.

The King quickly spun around. Hutt was standing a few paces away behind him.

"How long have you been here, Boy?" the King roared at him.

The Queen gently placed her hand on the King's arm, and it seemed to calm him for a moment. With a deep sigh, he beckoned Hutt to come forward and placed his arm around the boy's shoulders.

"Hutt, I don't know how much you heard but whatever you did hear you must never repeat it. Do you understand me? It is very important."

"I understand, I am not a fool." Retorted Hutt

"But do you really understand?" The King persisted.

"Of course. Citor told me about the haflings."

Smiling, the King ruffled the boy's hair. "Good, now go and play."

"But you said you need a guide. I can do it." Said Hutt.

"My King! You can't send him he is but a child!" Exclaimed the Queen.

The King looked down at Hutt who smiled at him. He smiled back but when he turned to his Consort his eyes were troubled.

"What choice have I, My dear? I must name a successor, or we will have anarchy in the Kingdom."

The Queen shook her head. "He is just a boy.' She murmured.

Hutt grinned at her. "The Forest is my home. I lay within for season upon season and no harm came to me. Citor found me whole and asleep. The Forest cared for me and for me, there is no danger."

The Queen stared at her mate; penetrating deep into his eyes. "There is one other," she pleaded with him.

The King shook his head. "No. I will not call on anyone else. Likea will go," said the King with finality.

It took the guards several more days to bring Likea home. He was still weak, but his strength was returning. The medics examined him in detail and immediately ordered him to rest. Likea protested but was given little choice once he was threatened with a sleeping draught. The King did not call on him but sent for Jayca. Their conference lasted for some time and when Jayca emerged he immediately dispatched four Hawks to recall Essura back to the Kingdom. From there Jayca went to the woodsmiths and gave orders to begin gathering fallen timber and start shaping the wood into swords and pikes.

The King allowed Likea one more day to regain his strength before visiting him. Likea made to rise from the bed but was waved back down. Likea repeated the story of his and Aria's escape right up until the time he saw her ride into the Forest. The King listened without interruption. The King rose from his chair and began to pace. Likea watched him impassively.

The King turned abruptly, and Likea could see from His Majesty's facial expression that he had made a decision.

"Although you were made, and you duly accepted the bodyguard position and that, by law, you are compelled to fulfil that role I am reluctant to suggest;" He stopped. "Likea I ..." and his voice tapered off.

"My Liege, before you ask of me a favour I have to refuse. I have been tasked to protect the Lady Aria and to do that I must first find her. That chore has precedence over everything else. I cannot accept any other chore at this time. I am sorry to disoblige you, but I am the Lady's bodyguard."

The King stared at him and gave a long sign of relief. "Likea, you do realize that you will lose your Second Life if you enter the Forest and stay longer than four dark times. I can't ask that of you."

"You don't have that right to ask. The law has stated my position." He smiled at the King. "I am comfortable with that position."

The King reached out and gripped Likea's arm. "The medics tell me that it will be many more days before you are fit enough to travel. I will prepare some maps for you. The Boy, Hutt, says he is familiar with the area, so I will send him to the scribes to add any guidelines he might contribute."

"Then have them work fast for I am leaving at first light."

"That is too soon, they say you can hardly walk." argued the King.

"Sire, I know that time isn't on our side. I do not know how long it will take to find the Lady and she was beginning to swell. I will need all the light possible. All that the Lady is and all that she carries is something that must be kept from the mutants."

The King acknowledged the truth of Likea's words for he nodded sadly. "You will have the finest and best I can provide. They must leave you at the Forests edge." He paused. "You will be on your own."

Likea smiled. "I will need a new sword."

"The woodsmiths have been set to work as we speak." He inclined his head in a manner of a bow.

"Brave Heart, Likea." He said as he turned to leave the shelter.

Likea could hear him roaring for his aides and he smiled to himself. He settled back in his bed and closed his eyes. He was beginning to get drowsy when he his ear twitched, hearing the muted sounds of footsteps, just before the door opened. After a moment, he opened his eyes a slither and saw Hutt slinking into his room. Hutt stood back and eyed Likea.

"They say that you are a great hero and a fine warrior. Hutt said brazenly.

Likea looked fully at the boy standing before him. He took in the slight frame and the thick, unruly thatch of red hair. There were no visible signs of his Majority,

"You are human!" Exclaimed Likea; quite surprised.

Hutt edged closer to the bed. "They say I am the one that was Vidal. The King is my guardian, but my father was a woodsman."

Likea stared at the boy's face. The features were without any sign of a totem and only Hutt's yellow eyes gave lie to his life form. Likea blinked away a stray tear. Vidal shone only through Hutt's eyes.

"You are definitely human, Boy." Likea said.

"You said that before. Are horses prone to repeating themselves?"

Likea thrust out his arm and grabbed Hutt by the leg. Hutt struggled but Likea pulled him effortlessly onto the bed.

"You are impertinent Boy, if I had the time, I would colour your rear with my hand." Likea said sarcastically.

Hutt scowled but when Likea released him he took many hurried steps backwards.

"The King would forbid you." claimed Hutt.

"The King would help."

Unsure now, Hutt changed tack. "Are you a hero? They say you are, and the old females are saying prayers for you."

Likea shrugged. "I am a soldier - no more, no less."

"You are going into the Proto Forest to find the Lady Aria. I heard you say so."

Startled at Hutt's admission, Likea tensed and scowled at the boy, "How do you know that Boy?" he snapped at him, face darkening.

Hutt grinned. "I listened. I was outside when the King was with you." He confessed, unabashed.

"They say that humans are odd. Spying is a hafling practice. Are you a hafling, Boy?"

Hutt was indignant, and he threw Likea a contemptuous look. "I am no mutant. I am human just as you soon will be."

"Do not repeat what you have heard, jackass ears. Understand this - you do not know what is at stake."

"You roar like the old King. Tis odd for a Horse."

Likea scowled menacingly and he threw off the blanket covering his legs. Hutt turned, ready to run.

"Stop," he yelled. "I want to go with you."

Likea swung his legs over the edge of the bed but at Hutt's words he stopped.

"What?" he asked.

"Deaf too." Murmured Hutt

He retreated a couple of steps when Likea stood up.

"Wait. I'm sorry Likea," he said worriedly.

Likea sat down again. "Why do you want to come?"

Hutt frowned as if he was puzzled. "I know not. I feel I have to go. I have been waiting for you – waiting for so long." he confessed.

Likea stared at him and motioned him to approach, but Hutt hung back and eyed him suspiciously.

"Come here Hutt."

"No for you will grab me again. I'm no fool."

"Word on my totem, I will not. Come closer," Likea coaxed.

Hutt inched forward, keeping a careful watch for any sudden movements from Likea.

"Sit down," said Likea and pointed to the end of his bed.

Warily Hutt sat down. Likea slowly reached out and gently grasped Hutt's jaw.

"Tell me – what do you mean 'waiting for me'? Have you been waiting since you heard I was being brought back from the Badlands?"

Hutt shook his head slightly for Likea's grip was firm and strong.

"Before that." He said. "When I was first with Citor and Jayca. I knew you would come. I want to go with you. I am human, so the Forest will not affect me. There will be no danger for me."

"I will speak with the King, but Hutt, the mutants are in force and we could be in danger from them."

"I understand that, but I…"

Likea interrupted him. "Alright, I give you no promises however, I will speak to the King."

Hutt smiled and said. "You will be in more danger if we have to go into the Hiatus Forest, you know."

Likea looked pensive, finally he nodded. "The Lady must be found. Go now Hutt, I will talk to the King, but I warn you, I guarantee nothing."

Likea was invited to sit beside the King for the last meal to be partaken before the dark time. As assured, he asked if Hutt could accompany him.

"No. I have his maps for you, but he can't go. Why do you want him? He will only hinder you; you must know that."

"There is a passion within him. I don't know how to tell you, but I feel it. He believes he must accompany me." Answered Likea, lamely.

"He cannot go. He is too young, and he doesn't know nor understand the Covenant. If he transgressed the laws, then he would be in great danger. The Hiatus will allow no-one to go outside the law if they are within in Forest.

There are no exceptions. I command you in this – he is not to go."

After the meal, Likea bowed his head and withdrew from the table and started to make his way back to his bed. Hutt emerged out of the soft night and silently walked with him. Likea glanced down, a half smile on his face. "No doubt you heard." He said. "I will not disobey him Hutt."

The boy sat on the end of the bed. "I heard. The Queen convinced him that I was too young."

Likea patted the boy's knee. "She is right though. You are too young, and the Covenant is dangerous."

"Do you know the readings of the Covenant?" Asked Hutt.

"Only in part. Few of us know it completely. All within the Forest is mostly unknown. None save the King has any idea of the true scope of the Light. When I return with the Lady, I will have to complete my learning. Only then can I live with the humans on the edge of the Forest. If I do not pass the tests put before me, then I will be relegated to live among the humans in the far colony. I will never be allowed out of their boundary. The King knows this and that is why he orders you to stay here and study – sooner or later you to will have to leave because humans are forbidden to live in the Kingdom of Sway. There is very little adult happiness to be had in the far colony for they failed the tests put before them. You see, only in the Hiatus can adults find the Light. It is sad. Anyway, so you will study and when I return I will too. Agreed?"

Hutt nodded and grinned. "Agreed. The King is my guardian as well as my Monarch. Safe journey Likea and I will see you soon."

He lightly touched his forehead to Likea and without another word he left the hut. Likea looked after him thoughtfully. "Now I wonder what he meant by that?" he murmured softly. He sighed as he lay back onto the bed. His heart felt heavy. He couldn't shake the feeling that the King was wrong not allowing Hutt to accompany him.

The King had prepared a litter made from bamboo and vines for Likea to travel on until he reached the Forest. Beside the litter, stood Jayca and at attention, stood a squad from the Kingdom's leopard brigade. These warriors were his escort and behind them the King has assembled an honour guard of horsemen. The sight of these brought a sudden wetness to Likea's eyes, but as he made his bow of allegiance to the King, he betrayed no sign of regret.

"I trust you will be strong enough by the time you reach the Forest, for once you are there you must walk. You understand that you cannot force the animals that dwell within both Forests, to help you. If they offer assistance, then you may accept it."

Expressed the King.

Likea bowed low. "I understand. The Second Life is theirs and not mine to command." Likea replied. He looked around. "Where is Hutt?" he asked.

The Queen smiled. "He threw a tantrum and refused to join us. Brave Heart - he will get over his disappointment. Have a great care Likea and rejoin us soon. You will be missed." She said.

Likea again bowed low as she placed a hand on his forehead.

Two leagues away from the ceremony, Hutt climbed a large tree. The leafy canopy was huge, and Hutt had no trouble concealing himself amongst the branches and leaves. He established himself comfortable on a large branch and settled down to wait for the small party to pass beneath his perch. He didn't have long to wait. Grinning in great mirth, he saw Likea travelling in the litter. Once they passed, he slid down the tree trunk. Noting carefully which fork in the road the squad had taken then he hurried to the valley that ran parallel to the road. His saddled horse was still quietly grazing near to where he had left him. Grasping the trailing rein Hutt led the horse to a fallen tree. He held the reins tightly while he climbed onto the trunk and then he clambered into the saddle and set off after Likea.

He followed them all that day and when they settled for the dark time, he did too. Although they were still in the Kingdom and the soldiers close by, Hutt spent an almost sleepless night. At first light he was back in the saddle waiting for the squad to eat and then to move out. He had one scare. The King's search party caught up to Likea's squad, but the Forest was too close now. He circled the guard and galloped his horse to the Forest's edge.

Overhead, Torbay the Raven, circled lazily in the sky. He spotted Hutt and followed him, all the time cawing at the top of his voice. Jayca looked up and Torbay knew he had been seen and heard for Jayca could be seen pointing to the Forest.

Torbay watched as Hutt unsaddled the horse and enter the Forest. He continued to watch until the denseness of the Forest hid him from watchful eyes.

Torbay returned to Jayca and reported what he had seen.

"What now, Advisor?" Likea asked.

Jayca shrugged. "Now we trust in the mercy of the Light. It is beyond our power to help him now."

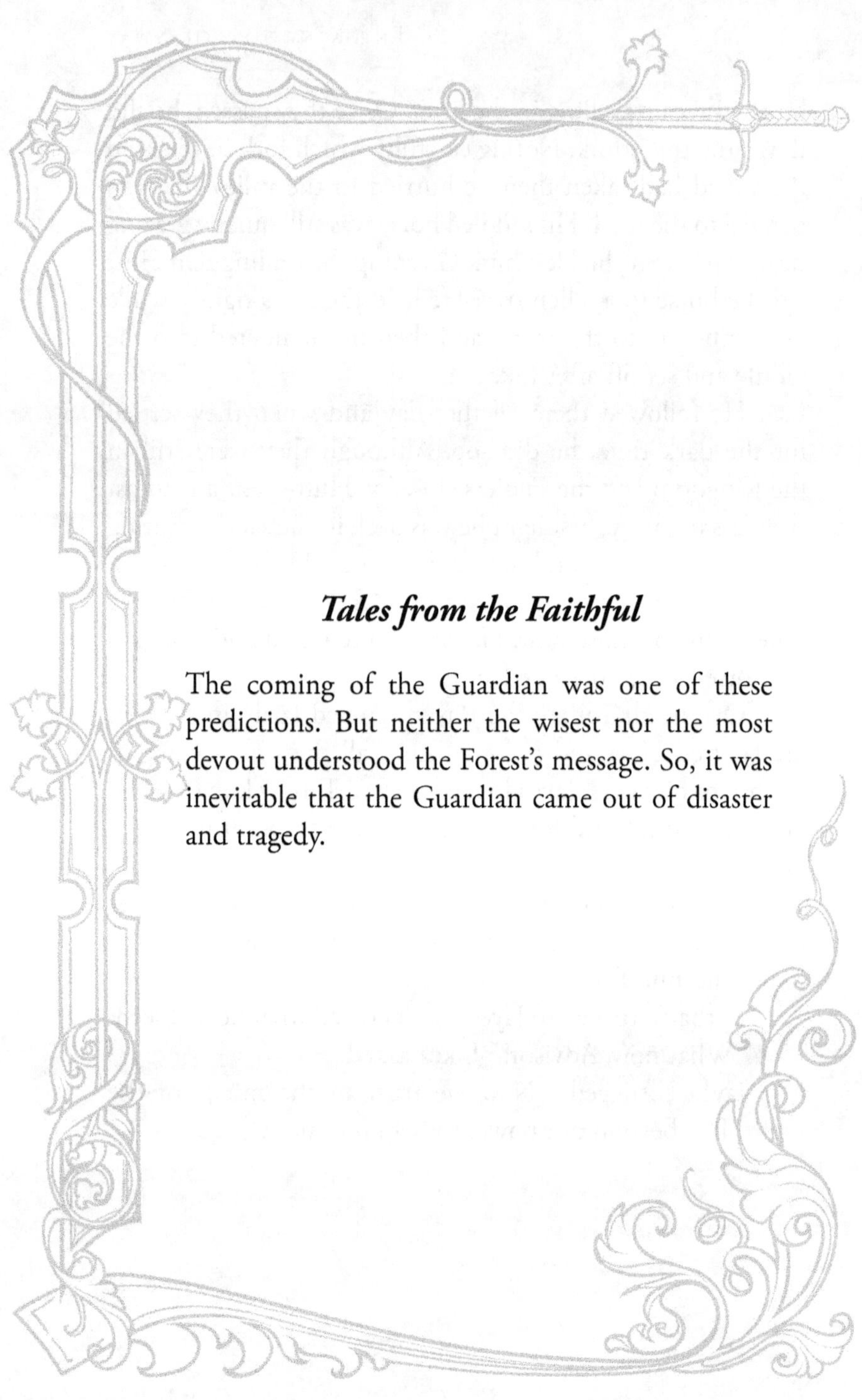

Tales from the Faithful

The coming of the Guardian was one of these predictions. But neither the wisest nor the most devout understood the Forest's message. So, it was inevitable that the Guardian came out of disaster and tragedy.

Chapter 7

ARIA

Aria remained unconscious. A thin trickle of blood ran down her cheek. A warm shaft of light filtered through the trees and dried her clothes and warmed her. As the soft night began to close in, a gentle breeze picked up the fallen leaves around her and covered her body from the cold dark time air.

Sometime during the night, she regained consciousness and slowly opened her eyes. The darkness frightened her, and she struggled to sit up. She groaned involuntary as the muscles in her leg pulled against the embedded arrowhead and moaned at the pain her movements caused.

As her eyes became accustomed to the darkness she quietened. The night birds were cheerfully chirping as the wispy breeze played with the leaves; you could almost hear them say "Be still, be calm." Her keen eyesight picked out a squirrel gnawing on a nut and a hedgehog picking its supper out of the leaves on the Forest floor. Sensing no immediate danger Aria slowly she relaxed, laid back and once more, fell into sleep. Once more the wind left the treetops, picked up the leaves and covered her body. Aria instinctively felt their warmth and continued to sleep. The gentle breeze left her and again went to play with the trees.

The sun was high and warm when she woke. She sat up, placed a hand on her forehead as she remained momentarily disorientated. For a moment, while trying to gather her thoughts, she panicked. When she tried to straighten her stiff legs, Aria groaned loudly. Looking down, she saw blood stains on her clothes. With deliberation, she leant forward and tentatively moved the tunic and looked at the deep wound – it was swollen and inflamed. Slowly, she reached out to touch it gently and grimaced. Again, she eased the tunic back to cover the wound. Her arm was painful and stiff. Carefully, mindfully aware of the bump on her head, Aria managed to turn her head. She scrunched her eyes up as the pain in her head started to throb even more. Refocusing her attention, she turned to look back at her arm and saw at the wound. The blood had stopped but the flesh gaped opened.

Exhausted from the effort and the pain, she lay back down and closed her eyes. Not long after, she drifted into a troubled sleep for she tossed and turned.

When she again woke, she had a raging thirst and knew she must find water. Listening carefully, she could hear the faint trickling of running water as it passed over stones and pebbles. By attempting to stand her legs could not hold her weight and she fell again. The wound on her arm reopened and the blood started to flow freely again. Feeling a little frustrated and not wanting to have her wounds get the better of her, Aria tried once more to carefully stand . She dragged herself up using stones and tree branches, whatever was in reach, pausing now and then for the pain was intense. Within a few minutes, she was on her feet and standing awkwardly. After a moment of deep breathing to breathe through the pain Aria set off in the direction of the sound. She was limping badly and tears ran unchecked down her cheeks.

Arriving at the stream, the source of the trickle sound she noticed a large tree branch had fallen across and was partially submerged into the stream. Aria struggled across to the end of the trunk that remained on land and cautiously sat down. Her wounds felt as though they were on fire. She whimpered as the log shifted from her legs. When she regained some balance, she leant forward and managed to scoop some of the cold, sweet tasting, water into her mouth and swallowed gratefully. Once she had her fill, Aria wiped her wet hands over her face. The coolness of the water seemed to revive her a little and it took away some of the lethargy that had crept over her. She tore away a piece of her tunic bottom, soaked it in the water, and patted the cloth to her arm. She winced a little as the injury stung. She tried to do the same to the arrow wound on her leg, but the slightest touch invoked a pain that was too great, and she involuntarily cried out.

Breathing heavily, she sat back to relax and tried to regain her composure. Hearing the patter of footsteps behind her, she struggled to return to her feet. The unexpected weight on her injured leg couldn't hold her and she fell. She strained to regain her feet, terrified, as the footsteps came closer. Somehow, she managed to turn and saw a vixen with two young kits trot past her to the water. The vixen looked at Aria curiously as she waited for the kits to drink, and when they had finished, she quietly led them away.

Beginning to sob openly in pain, Aria lifted herself back onto the trunk. Gradually the pain in her leg subsided to a dull, persistent ache. Gingerly she touched her head and felt the lump. Wetting the cloth once more, she applied it to the lump. The coolness of the damp cloth seemed to soothe the sharpness of the pain. It worried her a little that the cloth came away coloured with blood.

Feeling a little calmer, she looked at the surrounding area. She realised she was resting in a quite a beautiful glade.

The stream really was little more than a brook, but the water ran clear and pale blue. Further down the brook she saw a family of otter, busy in the water and taking no notice of Aria at all. Intent on their work they seemed to have no time for casual onlookers for they also ignored a lynx that passed them to drink. The lynx looked her way and seemed to smile at her. Aria marvelled at the animal's beauty and gave a small smile in return.

Go deep. You must go deeper into the Forest. The words echoed in her head. Startled at the sudden voice in her mind, but instinctively knowing she could trust it, Aria slowly stood up and looked about her. Unsure of the way she entered the Forest, with a puzzled expression reflected on her face, she asked the lynx which way was the deepest part of the Forest? The lynx watched at her for a moment before nodding and look to her left.

"That way? Should I go that way?" she asked.

The lynx looked at her again, then once more turned his head and looked to her left.

Aria thanked him and slowly moved in the direction the lynx had indicated.

Her pace was slow, every step she took jarred her leg, causing the pain to intensify. After travelling for some time, she was forced to stop and rest. She found a log and gradually eased her herself down. Sweeping her gaze around her once more, this part of the Forest was even more beautiful and lush than the little glade. The warm light filtered through the green canopy in columns of coloured light. There weren't any harsh colours, everything had a soft, slight golden glow. Even the crystal water in the stream, as it washed over the stones in its bed, had a touch of gold. The tall trees rode the light to the sun.

Aria no longer had any fear of the Forest – now, she felt warm and comforted. The animals took no notice of her and she took joy from watching them in their peace.

A large odd-looking bird came walking towards her. The species were unknown to her and she stared at the long legs and little wings. As it picked its way past her, she asked for directions. The bird looked to the left and Aria went in that direction. A little red fox joined her at some stage and walked with her for a way. The fox stopped to eat, and upon watching the little fox eat its fill, Aria suddenly felt hungry too. She found a bush loaded with fat, juicy berries and ate some. Before walking on, she put more berries into a pocket on her tunic, saving those for later. She resumed walking, but her pace had slowed considerably, and her movements little more than a shuffling action. Aria walked until she was forced to stop by the intense pain in her leg. The pain was agonising, as though her leg was burning.

Too ill and tired to seek shelter, Aria slowly sank to the Forest's floor of coloured leaves. Still wearing Likea's coat, she pulled it closer around her shoulders and scooped some leaves over her legs. Grateful for the respite, she lay back and mercifully sleep overtook her.

During the night several curious animals came to her. Even when a clumsy possum ran across her sleeping body she didn't stir. The red fox returned and sat with her for awhile. He sat beside her until he caught a scent that interested him. He lifted his head and sniffed at the fragrant air. The odour that caught his interest was too strong to be ignored and he trotted off.

Aria slept on – unaware that for a while she had a guard watching over her and the trees continued to whisper their lullaby.

Meanwhile, some distance away, the fox found the source of the smell it sought. Cautiously, the fox approached a huge, grey wolf. The wolf opened his eyes and growled a warning, but the fox ignored the hostility and came close enough to gently lick at the gaping wound on the wolf's leg.

Satisfied with his work, the fox scrapped some fallen leaves over the wolf and then it lay beside the wolf and slept.

Aria woke; thirsty and felt extremely hot. She removed the coat from her shoulders and sat up to brush away the leaves. She tried to stand but the injured leg wouldn't support her, and she fell back. Waiting a moment until she felt calmer, she reached down and peeled back the cloth she had covering the leg wound. Aria grimaced as the cloth had stuck and she had to pull harder.

The wound was badly inflamed and hot to touch. Holding her breath, preparing for the agonising pain, Aria pulled the cloth free of the wound. No sooner had she did that it had started to ooze a bloody, yellow pus. Aria tore another strip from the tunic and after several attempts managed to wrap it around her leg. Next, she tried to stand and after much effort struggled to her feet (although she had to lean heavily against a tree to remain upright) Aria began to cry uncontrollably. The physical pain, the catalyst, for the true pain hidden in her heart. Through her wracking sobs she offered a prayer.

"Forgive me, Light. Forgive Vidal. I am unworthy. Forgive me." She whispered tearfully. She grasped the tree trunk and pressed her tear stained cheeks to the cool, silken bark. "I trust in your Light, but I am unworthy. I am weak when you demand strength. Forgive me."

Her grip on the bark slipped and she slid to the ground at the base of the tree. There she lay, unmoving, for several minutes before she stirred.

"For Vidal and for the Kingdom I must go on," she said softly. "Likea said that you were lost to me, my Brave Lion but I feel that you are with me. The Forest has you now and the Forest is my Light. "

The prayer seemed to strengthen her resolve. She pulled herself up and with the aid of a stout stick she began a slow walk.

When she came across another shallow stream she stopped. Sinking to her knees, she crawled the last few paces to the water's edge. Cupping her hands, she dipped them into the water and then drank deeply. Although food was in abundance, she ate nothing. After a short rest she again drank. Moaning, she struggled to her feet and continued walking, going deeper and deeper into the Forest. At the onset of the dark time she collapsed, face down, to the Forests floor. Too sick to even try to shelter from the cool night air she lay as she had fallen.

The red fox found her as the darkness set in, he yapped softly to scare away a curious badger. The badger gave a disdainful looked but wandered away when the fox nudged him. The fox sniffed loudly and ran around Aria's still body twice before running off at speed. The grey wolf heard the fox coming and struggled to his feet. The fox was barking excitedly but when the wolf gave a low growl it fell silent and waited. The wolf made some odd rumbling sounds in his throat and the fox cocked his head and listened. When the wolf had finished and was silent, the fox approached the wolf, touched the wolf on the nose and disappeared into the night.

Following the fox's scent, the wolf slowly limped the way the fox had come. He rested several times along the route. Twice stopping to drink and once to eat. The darkness of the night was still upon the Forest when he finally reached Aria. He smelt her all over and briefly touched his nose to hers.

Aria felt warm for the wind had once again covered her with leaves, but her sleep was troubled as she tossed restlessly and mumbled incoherently. The wolf left her side and circled the immediate area until he found the bush he sought. He lifted his head high and using his teeth began pulling the small, bluish coloured star shaped flowers from the limbs. When he had gathered a small pile, he closed his mouth over them and carried it back to Aria. With his sharp teeth, he delicately pulled the petals away from the black centres. The petals were discarded but he lay the centres on a piece of bark. When he had finished separating them, he took two of the centres and chewed them carefully before swallowing. He then took another centre and laid it against the wound on his leg. Then, he slept. When the badger returned the wolf opened one eye. The badger moved on.

It was high light in the sky when Aria stirred. The wolf still lay beside her, paws outstretched and tongue lolling comfortably out of the side of his mouth. Aria's eyes narrowed as she squinted at him.

"You look like Helment," she said croakily. Her voice was scratchy and barely audible.

The wolf woke; he stood and walked the short distance between them. He licked her face and she tried to smile. She started to lift her hand to stroke him, but the effort was too much, and she fainted.

Now that the head and arm wounds were revealed. The wolf picked up, one by one, the black centres from the flowers. Very, very gently he dropped several of them onto the exposed wounds. When he had finished, he left, returning some time later carrying a mouthful of ripe figs which he dropped beside Aria.

Later that day Aria stirred. Slowly and painfully she opened her eyes, blinking at the brightness and closing them again. Time passed and eventually she woke, frowning, as though she was puzzled at her surroundings. Turning her head, she noticed the wolf was busy plucking more petals from the flowers. Aria watched, curious over his actions until she noticed the black centres on her arm. She brushed at the withered centres and they fell away at her touch. The wound, although still opened, had lost much of the redness and was no longer as painful. She raised her hand to her head and brushed her forehead. The flowers fell into her lap, cautiously she pressed her fingers against the bump. She grimaced as a sharp pain stabbed at her, but the lump felt considerably smaller.

Aria returned her attention to the wolf. He was delicately placing some of the flowers on his own wounds. She wriggled closer and picked up one of the flowers and raised it to her nose. It smelt peppery. She touched it to her tongue, frowned at the bitter taste. Curiously, she placed the flower on the wound that lay across the wolf's back. The wolf panted, and it seemed to Aria that he smiled.

Within her reach, Aria gathered more of the flowers and placed them on wolf's opened wound. She pressed down gently so that they wouldn't fall when he moved.

She wondered if the flowers would reduce the agonising pain in her thigh. Gingerly she pulled the tunic down exposing the injury. Her thigh was inflamed with a reddish streak beginning to rise towards her hip. Around the actual puncture the flesh was turning a darkish blue and deep yellow. The wolf saw and seeming agitated he growled.

"It doesn't look good, does it?" she said and bit back a sob. "Maybe your medicine will help."

She plucked some of the flowers and set them against her skin, then wound a makeshift bandage around her leg to hold the black flower centres in place.

The wolf growled again, and Aria glanced at him. He picked up one of the figs and chewed it. Once he swallowed, the wolf with his nose, nudged another fig towards her. She picked it up and started to nibble on it. When she had finished the wolf pushed another one towards her. She shook her head and the wolf gave a low growl.

"I'm not hungry," she protested. The wolf continued to growl, only stopping when she had eaten that one too. Seemingly satisfied the wolf laid back and rested.

Aria lay back too, but she didn't sleep. Her mind remained occupied by replaying all the good memories she had shared with Vidal. She began to weep and call Vidal's name over and over. The wolf crept closer until his head touched her arm. Aria touched his head with her hand, still crying until she eventually fell asleep.

She continued to sleep as darkness fell. The wolf helped the wind cover her and he laid beside her. The only time he stirred was when the badger returned. All the next day the wolf stayed close to her, only leaving her side to collect food and more flowers.

The leg wound on Aria looked worse but the gash on her arm was healing. The skies threatened rain. When water begun to softly fall from the sky, Aria was well protected by a thick covering of leaves. The rain continued to fall on her uncovered face, and it revived her enough to eagerly swallow whatever moisture fell into her open mouth. The wolf watched calmly but later when she began tossing about and moaning, he became agitated and started pacing, sensing what was to come.

The physical change began gradually. First the soft downy hair on her body slowly shrivelled and fell away, leaving her flesh smooth and soft. Then, the coarser hair on her head became finer and tended to curl slightly. The Change became more rapid as her powerful leg muscles started to shrink to half their original size while the legs stretched in length. The muscles in her arms lessened and extended. Aria's cat like eyes became rounder and the amber colouring changed to a deep, rich brown. Her strong jaw line softened. Her nose altered, losing its width and became smaller in size but longer. Her ears shortened, the taper disappeared, and they elongated at the bottom to become ear lobes. The fingers on her hands lengthened and the nails blunted. With the metamorphosis complete, Aria settled into a dreamless sleep.

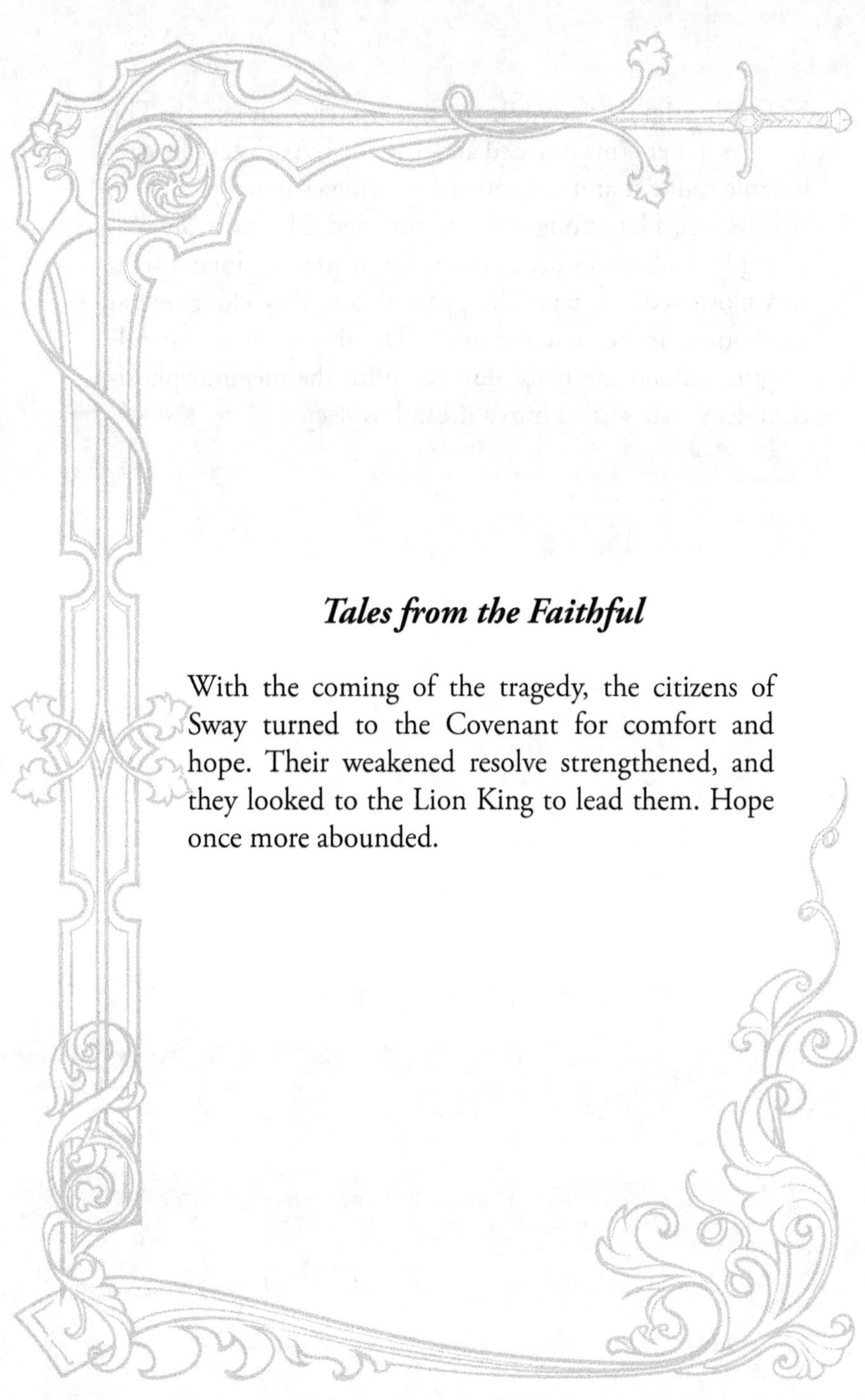

Tales from the Faithful

With the coming of the tragedy, the citizens of Sway turned to the Covenant for comfort and hope. Their weakened resolve strengthened, and they looked to the Lion King to lead them. Hope once more abounded.

Chapter 8

NADIR

"Tell me why I follow thee, Fox? Tell me why? I have left a warm shelter and a comfortable bed which I should be enjoying, to follow thee. Thee wake me from a sound sleep and bark continuously until I follow. I followed, and thee take me leagues from where I should be – where I want to be."

The fox turned and barked furiously.

"Thee bark incessantly. Thee are noisy, and the Forest is allowing thee to be so. Tis strange. Quiet noisy Fox! Rest I must. If thee is unhappy then take thee four legs and run away. Leave me to rest." Nadir said irritably.

She sat down in the long grass and rubbed her aching calf muscles. The fox continued barking but when Nadir refused to acknowledge him he too sat down.

"Thee are tired too, Fox. Should I carry thee?" She tilted her head and inspected him. She pursued her lips. "I know thee not – thee are a stranger. But thee know of me I think."

She shook her head as though to clear it and then she opened her straw travel bag. From it she removed a large baked seed pancake which she tore in half and offered a piece to the fox. The fox took it daintily from her fingers and bit into it. Nadir took a bite from her piece and chewed methodically.

"I cannot understand any of this. Humans don't know of me, so they don't seek me. Animals only come to me when they are sick or injured. Thee are neither injured nor sick and yet they want me to come. This is all very odd."

She finished her slice and offered another piece to the fox. The animal refused. Instead it stood up and ran a few feet – stopped and looked back at her. It started barking again and stopped only when Nadir rose to her feet.

"I would feed thee forever if only to stop the noise. Thee have only recently been granted the Second Life or thee would not behave thus. Soon thee will have no memory of your other life and will just be like all the other animals in the Forest.' "Which," she added tartly, "Will be a blessing to both my ears and legs?"

She walked after the red fox, who was keeping a steady gait. Nadir frowned. "East. We are heading east - the haflings are this way. Oh, little Fox, I will refuse thee if it's a mutant thee mean me to attend. Nor will I travel in the Badlands. That way is no safer to me than any human."

Nadir kept up a steady stream of chatter while they walked. They came upon a stream and the fox paused to drink. Nadir stopped too, cupped her hands and drank. With her thirst sated she sat down on the bank. The fox began to bark furiously. His sharp voice stopped the birds singing and a nearby rabbit fled.

"Quiet! Quiet! The darkness will soon be here, and I am tired. I will eat and rest here. If your mission is still urgent on the morrow then I will accompany thee. Now enough!" The fox wouldn't stop barking and Nadir's eyes narrowed as she began to feel anger well inside her.

"If thee were human I would tie thee brush in knots," she threatened. However, beyond her anger was curiosity.

Reluctantly, she rose again and followed the fox. As the darkness deepened, she was forced to slow down and pick her way around the hazards. In the faint light she could see the fox run on ahead and then disappear. Nadir stopped.

"A joke! Thee have led me several leagues for a joke!" she angrily exclaimed. "Tis an unkind act and one I will not forget!"

A huge grey wolf suddenly appeared beside her. She jumped, hand to her heart as she uttered a stifled cry. After a couple deep breaths, in the weak light she could see that the wolf did not move an inch as it watched her. Looking closer, Nadir could see that the fox stood silently beside the wolf.

"So, this is your friend. Yes, I see that he is injured." She glanced at the fox. "Lucky Fox for I was about to call down the wrath of the Light on thee head. Come Wolf – sit here and I will look at thee."

Nadir made to sit upon a fallen tree but was stopped by the low, menacing growl from the wolf.

"Oh no! Not another one that talks. The Fox was bad enough, but a Wolf is bigger and makes more sound." Nadir groaned. "What now?"

The wolf limped across to her and gently took the sleeve of her jacket in his teeth. He tugged on the material. Nadir was puzzled.

"Follow thee – but why? Thee are also new to the Forest for I do know you. Since thee wounds are not healed then that tells me that thee are a very recent arrival. Who is thee friend that warrants this much devotion? Thee must know that once you enter the Forest that thee are set free, but both of you are acting as though thee are under an obligation. Tis odd – I said so before - tis odd."

She allowed the wolf to lead her across the way. Together they pushed though the undergrowth and then into a small clearing. On the edge of the clearing Nadir saw a leaf covered mound. The wolf stepped to the side and allowed Nadir to make her own way across. She brushed away some of the leaves from Aria's face. The light was too dull to see her features clearly, but it was enough for Nadir to see the girl was human. She laid a hand on Aria's brow and felt the radiating heat.

"Tis bad. The Forest's medicine should have worked but the child is burning," she muttered. "And the dark doesn't help either." She grumbled.

Reaching once more into her travel bag she extracted a small gourd and two pouch bags. With the aid of what light there was she poured a portion from each bag into the pot. The gourd glowed briefly and then a small flame shot up from the neck.

Nadir moved her makeshift torch closer to Aria then rummaged through the straw travel bag again and brought forth a small, dark bottle. She uncorked it and with her other hand and forced Aria's mouth open. Nadir poured a little of the mixture into Aria's mouth. Most of the liquid trickled down the sides, but Nadir continued to pour. "Just a little more, a little more child," she murmured soothingly.

Holding the torch aloft Nadir brushed the rest of the leaves away and inspected Aria's body. When she saw the inflamed thigh and the wound she hissed through her teeth.

"So, this is the one. The enchantment of the Forest has not been able to help. Well never mind, Child, am I Nadir, and does not the Forest allow me to stay. Come the morn light we will begin to repair the damage." She raked the leaves over Aria again then beckoned the wolf forward.

"Now for thee Greybeard. Would that thee could talk for I am sure there is many a tale that could be told.. Not least the mystery of this girl." She ran her fingers over the wolf's coat. "Old scars, new scars. A fine or foolish warrior thee were, Greybeard. These wounds are not the usual wounds I treat; thee have been warring with ungodly weapons. Hmm. The haflings, perhaps?"

The wolf growled and Nadir chuckled. "So, haflings. And not so long ago for thee wounds are new and the girl still has your trust." Nadir set about wiping clean the open wounds then gave him a drink from the gourd. "There now thee will sleep. I can do no more until we have true light."

She turned to the little red fox who was calmly sitting beside her. She run her hand over the wiry hair and gently gave his tail a little pull. "Such devotion." She said quietly shaking her head. "At least thee are now silent." She gave a small smile. "Sleep now – sleep little one. The Forest is now the Guardian of us all."

The wolf woke her at first light. His method was simple. He pressed his cold, moist nose against her cheek.

"Drat, thee four-legged oaf. Look to yourself and not me." She complained bitterly, wiping at her face. She glared at him, but she rose and brushed the leaves from her clothes.

She turned her attention to Aria and gave her another dose of the liquid from the small bottle before setting about clearing the covering from Aria's body. When she removed the cloth covering the leg wound Nadir shook her in despair. "Something is lodged deep inside her body. This is more of the haflings work," she muttered as she reached for the bottle. She uncorked it and forced the opening between Aria's lips and poured. "It is a bad wound, but she will feel no pain."

Nadir once more dove into her straw bag and this time pulled out a, small, well-pointed, bamboo knife. The wolf rushed forward and stood, bristling and growling, between the two women. Although Nadir was momentarily surprised by the wolf's action, she showed no fear. She lay the knife down.

"Greybeard, that she is important to thee I know, for thee actions have told me so. She will die if I don't remove whatever is lodged, it is certain - for the Forest tells me so. Believe me, Greybeard I mean her no harm. The Forest would not keep me safe if I speak false. Now Wolf, stand aside. I must cut the corruption out. Thee have no choice but to trust me for I am the only human within many leagues of this place and a human must wield the knife. So, stand aside, Wolf and let me work."

As she finished speaking, she gradually picked up the knife. The wolf hesitated a moment longer then walked back two paces. Nadir smiled.

"Trust is earned. So be it. She will feel no pain for my elixir is strong. Now, guide my hand, Keeper of the Light."

Nadir began to cut away the flesh around the arrow shaft and blood began to freely flow. The wolf gave a low, rumbling growl but Nadir ignored him. The fox averted his head away from her bloody work. Nadir worked swiftly and silently although her lips moved constantly in prayer; then suddenly she smiled. Her deft fingers plucked the arrowhead from the wound and she flung it away in disgust.

"Tis bone. Made from some animal. Repulsive. I heard that they used air borne missiles. They are truly abominations." She looked back at Aria. "Now I shall clean the wound and the Forest will heal."

She wiped the injury clean with water and a cloth and then packed in some crushed seeds. She wrapped large, green pallor leaves around the leg and tied them in place by twine cut from a vine. After checking and gazing at her handiwork, Nadir turned to the wolf and the fox. "Well?" After no reaction Nadir raised her eyebrows and repeated the question. "Well?"

Subsequently, the wolf slowly sank down and lay with his front paws stretched out. Nadir smiled.

"I will give her some water later but now I take a look at thee."

Aria stirred while Nadir was still attending to the wolf. Nadir looked across to her.

"So, the beauty awakens. Lie still girl and soon I will bring thee water."

Frightened, Aria struggled to sit up and move away.

"Stay, thee stupid girl. Would I harm thee? I took the time to cut the contamination from your leg and to see to thee four-legged friend. I could have easily cut thee throat!" Snapped Nadir.

"Who are you?" Aria whispered.

"I am one, Nadir – a human like thee. Now be still until I finish here."

"Human?" breathed Aria softly that Nadir didn't hear the disbelief in her voice.

Aria looked down at her hands and noticed the change. Tears welled and threatened to fall but Aria forced herself to remain calm. She tore her gaze away from her hands and looked at Nadir who was still bent over cleaning the wolf's injuries.

Nadia was indeed fully human – without a single trace of her original Majority. She was also the most beautiful creature Aria had ever seen. Although she was kneeling Aria could see she was tall and her body slender. She was some years older than Aria, but her face was unlined. She had a wide mouth and lips that looked like they could smile easily and they matched perfectly with her firm chin. But it was her hair that made Aria stare. Nadia's hair was pure white. Long and silken with a slight curl graced with a strange, single thin black stripe running down the right-hand side. Nadir had tied her hair back with a strip of cord.

"What was your totem? I know not your colour." Curiously asked Aria.

Nadir glanced at her briefly and Aria saw the brilliant blue of her eyes.

"That information is not for thee girl," she replied not unkindly, but in a voice that brooked no argument. "I see thee were Lion." She added.

Aria nodded and once more looked at her own body. Again, she felt a momentary pang of despair, but she forced it away before she could dwell on it.

"The remaining characteristics will fade quickly now. Thee were a Lion of some significance, since I have noticed that thee still command the respect of these two animals."

Aria didn't reply. Her mind was in turmoil and she didn't know whether to trust Nadir. Her gaze wondered to the wolf for guidance, but he just stared steadily back at her.

"I was the daughter of a Plains Lion,' was all she said.

Nadir smiled and nodded as she offered Aria a gourd filled with water.

"And thee name?" asked Nadir.

Aria took the gourd and eagerly drank some water before she replied.

"Aria."

Nadir stared at her for a moment and frowned.

"Thee are from the Kingdom?"

Aria nodded.

"The Princess Royal?"

"Yes."

"Tis a shame that thee did not have time to begin the metamorphosis." Nadia said kindly.

Aria sadly shook her head. "Tis no matter. The haflings killed my mate while he was human. I care for nothing anymore."

Nadir tilted her head. She appeared to be thinking rapidly but her voice was non- committal. "Vidal is dead?" Nadir probed.

Aria nodded, and her eyes began to fill with tears as if to cry, as though her heart would break. Nadir set the gourd aside and wrapped her arms around her. Nadir cradled her close and let Aria cry without any attempt to stop her.

"We will speak of it no more," was all she said.

With many tears shed Aria fell asleep and Nadir left her to gather food and more water. The wolf accompanied her. She looked down at him and smiled. "The Fox is forgetting. Soon he will have no memory of Aria. What of thee, Greybeard? The fire in your eyes tell me that thee devotion runs deeper - but thee too will forget. It is the way of freedom of the Second Life. When the memory is gone then thee will be truly free. Sometimes thee have an unreasonable desire for human company, when thee do come and visit me. Thee will be welcome."

Nadir idly stroked the wolf's soft ears.

"The Lady Aria trusts me a little, I think, but she knows nothing of me, I cannot tell her lest she be distressed. It is really no matter because she cannot stay within. When she is stronger, I will take her to the human colony. She must live out her life among humans and not animals. I will be concerned for her a little for some humans have also been contaminated, but I will take her to the strongest and most devout part of the colony. There she should be safe."

Nadir sighed, and the wolf turned his head and nuzzled her.

"Yes, yes, I know, but I have no choice. The Forest is forbidden to humans. She must leave."

Two days passed before Nadir even thought of moving Aria. On the third morning Nadir set to work with stout limbs and stronger creeper vines and fashioned a litter for Aria to travel on. With the stretcher completed, she gathered more food and water and gave them to Aria to consume. Satisfied with her work Nadir disappeared into the Forest. She was away for many hours and upon her return, she was leading a horse.

"I travelled far before I found one willing. This fine beast will give us the strength I lack to pull thee carriage," she said.

Aria smiled a little. "It is strange, but it feels right. In the Kingdom the animals that stay with us are willing to help us. In here we must always ask."

Nadir agreed. "That is the joy of the Second Life. If those in the Kingdom remain within the Forest for more than the fourth day after Hiatus, then they would not serve thee. Servitude within the Forest is their choice. In the Kingdom it is otherwise to a degree."

"The Monarchy never mistreats those who choose to stay with us," replied Aria, offended.

Nadir smiled at her. "There speaks a Royal. No. No. Do not take offence. The Kingdom animals are those who failed to fully understand the Covenant. They are happy enough or else they would return here for the days of Light. Very few do although there has been an increase since the haflings became stronger. As for any mistreatment of the Kingdom animals – the Covenant has placed that trust to the King. The penalty is harsh, and it falls to the King to administer. He is a good King and has worked well."

"I understand the Covenant," said Aria softly. "What will happen to me?"

Nadir helped her onto the litter and made her comfortable. She looked pensive.

"Thee will need a lot more rest – when you are stronger I will take thee to a human colony. It is out of the Forest and to the north. I will escort thee to the most lawful region and there you will make your home."

Nadir asked the horse to move and they set off. The wolf and the fox walked behind, and Nadir walked along side Aria.

"How is it that you stay within? I have never heard of humans allowed to stay."

Nadir didn't answer immediately, and Aria thought she hadn't heard. "Why are you here? It is forbidden for humans to dwell within." She repeated.

"I heard thee child. I was trying to think of an answer that would not offend thee. Suffice it to say that the animals know of me and they can't talk."

"But you are human and all that was taught to me was humans are forbidden in dwell here, and yet it is obvious that you have been here for many, many seasons."

"The Forest has granted me a special life – I can never leave the Forest for more than a few days at a time."

Aria's glance to her was filled with compassion. Nadir smiled.

"Do not pity me – tis all I know of life. I was born within and I know of no other way. Now, enough, I cannot, nay, I will not tell thee more."

The journey was long and for Aria, very tiring. She slept a good deal of the way and slowly Aria's strength returned. Each morning Nadir would clean and dress her wounds and allowed Aria to walk a little. On the third day of travel Aria had fallen asleep early in the noon time. When she woke, the shadows were lengthening. Nadir knelt beside her and untied the bonds that held her still on the stretcher. The horse was already free and grazing contently nearby.

"The litter is too wide for this part of the Forest. Can thee walk? It is not far for I know the way." Nadir said gently.

Aria looked about her. All she could see was thick, impenetrable Forest. Nadir saw her disbelieving look and smiled.

"Tis a maze – my home is inside. This is no longer the Proto Forest but the centre of the Hiatus. So, can thee walk?"

With a nod of acknowledgement, Nadir assisted Aria to stand and held her firmly as Aria tepidly tested her weight on her injured leg.

"It is not very painful." Aria responded amazed.

"Good, then let thee goal be a warm bed and hot food."

Nadir guided and helped Aria to the wall of green where Aria stopped and looked back. The wind had picked up the leaves and covered the drag mark left by the litter. Of the litter, there was no sign. Some loose pieces of wood lay about but that was all.

"There are no markings of the trail – see! The wind covers the marks and the litter is gone!" she exclaimed.

"There isn't a need for a trail – the animals know the way."

"But, I, I," began Aria and stopped.

Nadir smiled. "No human comes this way. The centre is protected and only the most cunning and the wisest come even close. Then they are stopped by the maze."

She noticed Aria's shocked expression and whitened cheeks and frowned.

"Were thee thinking that the King would seek thee? He cannot. He is our Protector and will not violate the Covenant. If his reason for removing a human from the Forest is valid – if he could find a human to volunteer to come. If that human could find the centre and then if that human could penetrate the maze, then the Forest might relent and allow the humans to leave. Has the King a valid reason for searching for thee?"

Aria thought quickly.

Vidal, Helment and Likea knew she was pregnant. Her mate and Likea were dead and Helment achieved his Second Life. Nobody knew.

With eyes cast down, looking at the ground, "No," she whispered. "No valid reason."

"Then think no more of returning to the Kingdom — think only of the human colony. No one will search for thee." Nadir advised sternly.

"Would it be possible for me to live in the Kingdom?" Aria asked.

Nadir pulled a face. "Possible? Yes — but not practical since thee would be the only fully human. Thee would long for your own kind. The place that I will take thee is close to Sway but not within."

"You could take me back to the Kingdom."

Nadir shook her head. "Even I am banned. I could take thee no closer than that of five days travel. Thee would never be able to find thee way out. After the allocated time the Forest would claim thee for its own and thee would never be allowed to leave in a lifetime."

Aria fought back the tears that filled her eyes.

No-one knows that I carry the Heir. No one will come. Vidal, forgive me. Please forgive me.

Now she couldn't stop the tears from falling. Nadir patted her hand.

"Thee are tired and grieving still. My house is not far now."

Aria made the effort to compose herself and wiped her tears away.

"How long do we stay before I must leave?"

"Since the Forest granted that I find thee alive then I am allowed one new moon to escort thee from the Forest. By the time thee are strong enough and with the distance we must travel to reach the colony, we will need all that time. There. At last – my cottage."

Aria obediently looked ahead but could see nothing but trees and grass.

Nadir chuckled gleefully.

"The Forest hides its secrets well. Look closely child – the house is a regular shape and there are no straight lines in nature."

Aria squinted and stared ahead again, suddenly she could see the outline of a small cottage. An unexpected flush of warmth touched her, and she looked at Nadir.

"The cottage is welcoming thee," she said.

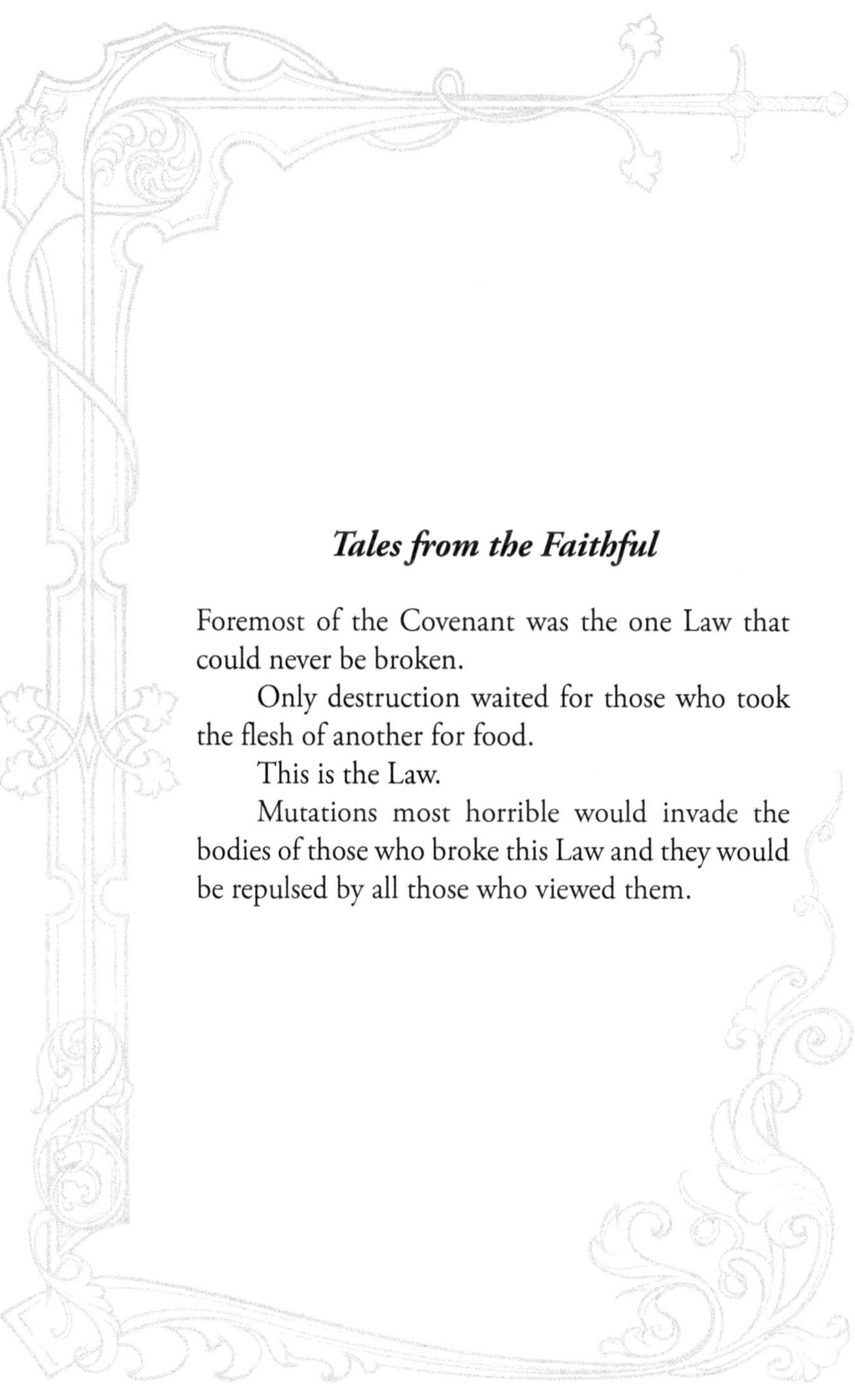

Tales from the Faithful

Foremost of the Covenant was the one Law that could never be broken.

Only destruction waited for those who took the flesh of another for food.

This is the Law.

Mutations most horrible would invade the bodies of those who broke this Law and they would be repulsed by all those who viewed them.

Chapter 9

NADIR AND HUTT

At the entrance to the cottage Nadir turned back to both wolf and fox.

"Come. Come in, thee are welcome here." She said, gesturing with her hands the sign of invitation.

The fox looked at the doorway and then at the wolf. It touched the wolf on the nose, turned and disappeared into the maze. Nadir nodded in satisfaction.

"It is time and the Fox has chosen."

"I am sorry to see him go," Aria said sadly. "He was my friend."

"Yes, but the Second Life has called him. The Wolf will one day go too Aria so do not become too attached." Nadir replied, shaking her head. "No – he is worthy of his freedom."

Nadir settled Aria comfortably on her bed and then set about preparing a meal. Aria was amazed at the array of containers and gourds that lined the trestles along the walls. She watched with interest as Nadir poured a fine, silver coloured powder onto a stone tray. The tray began to radiate a soft yellow glow of light and emit heat.

Nadir then set about to ground some pearl seeds and add some mushrooms that she had picked earlier on their travel. Kneading all the ingredients together Nadir then rolled the mixture into a thick pancake. She placed the pancake on a wooden frame and set it over the stone tray. Soon the delicious smell of cooking bread invaded the room. Nadir set bowls of fruit and berries on the bench and added a gourd of wine.

"There, soon we will eat. I confess I prefer my meals heated," she said with some inflection of guilt in her voice.

"What is that?" asked Aria pointing to the stone tray.

"It's a preparation I have made from the things the Forest has supplied. There isn't a use for fire among the animals and I rarely have much need. This serves the purpose for my cooking and light."

"Are you a magician?"

Nadir laughed loudly. "Magician! Ha! Stories the woodsmen tell their children. No. I have some power but that is because the Forest and I are one." She looked searchingly at Aria. "Do not seek the answers for there are none – faith is all thee needs."

Nadir took the pancake from the frame and cut it into slices and passed one slice to Aria and another to the wolf. "Eat." She commanded them both and sat down herself.

Aria nibbled at her food, but she was more interested in the room. It was large, and Nadir had kept half for her living quarters. The other half was her laboratory for gourds, vials and equipment lay everywhere.

Nadir looked up from her plate and caught Aria's perplexed look.

"Most was my fathers, I studied too – it helps to pass the time when the rains come." said Nadir nonchalantly.

"But, what do you make?"

Nadir expressed a 'how-do-I-explain' face. "Anything. If I find a new plant or seed, I experiment with it until I find a use for it."

Aria gasped. She looked horrified. "Do you practice on the animals?"

Nadir gave her a contemptuous look. "Would the Forest keep me if I experimented on the animals? I test it on myself," reminiscing she gave a sudden chuckle. "The sleeping seeds were the worst. The first time I tried it I slept for days until I finally found the correct measurement."

"Surely that is dangerous? I mean, to use unknown plants – what if they were poisonous?"

"Nothing in the Forest is dangerous – everything is edible. Some are tastier than others but still edible. I am more careful now. I only use smaller portions until I fully understand the plants use. Now eat, we can talk later."

The days past quickly but for Aria the dark times seemed endless. In the quiet solitude of the night, Aria's thoughts returned to Vidal. During the day light hours, Nadir gave her no chance to brood; she talked constantly. Aria only had amusement and genuine interest in the activities which were ever changing.

Several animals came to visit, and Nadir would invite them inside and introduce her house guest to them. Aria watched with interest as Nadir treated the wounds inflicted on them and sometimes, she assisted in treating them if Nadir was in a generous mood.

Finally, the second half of the moon came and passed. Nadir told Aria that they would be leaving on the following day. Aria hardly slept that night and as dawn began to light the Forest, she climbed out of bed and prepared herbal tea.

The wolf had been sleeping at the base of Nadir's bed, when out of her periphery vision, Aria saw him suddenly stand. Without moving an inch, she observed silently as he walked with stealth towards the closed door of the cottage.

Aria tensed, suddenly afraid. The wolf stood motionless only his nose twitched eagerly as if he caught an interesting scent. Aria cautiously crept across the room and shook Nadir awake. She held a finger to her lips to indicate silence.

Although just woken from her peaceful rest, Nadir looked puzzled but remained obediently silent. She quietly flung back the woven bed cover of silken cobweb and swung her feet to the floor. The wolf still hadn't made any further movement, but his attention was fixed on the door.

Now annoyed, Nadir stalked to the door and pushed it open. The wolf leapt past her and was outside before she could take another step, but she moved quickly to follow him. Outside the cottage Nadir abruptly stopped. The wolf was calmly sitting beside a young boy. Nadir was momentarily speechless.

"Who are thee, Child?!" Nadir demanded.

"I am called Hutt. I am the son of a woodsman."

"But why? Why are thee here?"

Hutt shrugged and continued playing with the Wolf's ears. "I am not sure – I think to guide you out of the Forest."

Nadir scowled angrily and shook Hutt by the shoulders. 'Enough of this nonsense. Where is your parent, Boy?" she snapped.

"I haven't any parents." replied Hutt.

"Do not lie to me. A fool can see that thee are at least a second-generation human. Lie not to me for I have the means to extract the truth from thee." She threatened him.

Hutt shook his head. "I do not lie – my parents are no more."

"Then who sent thee?" she demanded.

"No one sent me. I just had to come."

Nadir threw up her hands in disgust as Aria pushed past her. "Shame, Nadir. He is just a boy. Why he isn't even at the age of enlightenment."

"Perhaps not but he shouldn't be here." She snapped and glared at Hutt. "How did thee get into the maze?"

Hutt lifted his thin shoulders. "I searched for two days but I couldn't find the way. This morning when I woke the way was revealed and so I followed."

Nadir frowned and sat down on a wooden stool as she stared at the boy who was still playing with the wolf. "The Forest opened to him," she murmured. "But why? Why?"

Aria held out her hands to Hutt. "I was just about to make something to eat. Come inside where it is warmer." She said softly, gently.

Aria smiled as Hutt took her hand and led him inside. The wolf waited with Nadir. He looked as if he was smiling. Nadir looked at him. "What does it mean, Greybeard? He shouldn't be here and yet here he is."

Without an answer to her question, Nadir stood up and walked to the others inside.

Nadir kept a closely guarded watch on Hutt as Aria prepared the food and drink. She impatiently waited until Hutt began to devour his meal before beckoning Aria outside. Nadir closed the door behind them and with her hand she hurriedly grabbed Aria above her wrist and pulled Aria away from the cottage.

"Do thee know that Boy? Do not speak false for he is in direct violation of the Hiatus!"

Aria shook her vigorously. "No, I have never seen him before." Aria gazed at the disbelieving look on Nadir's solemn face and again said, "by the law of the Covenant – I don't know that Child!"

Nadir satisfied of Aria's answer, she released her grip on Aria's arm and nodded.

"That's what I thought. He is too human and so young, but even so, he shouldn't be here. What is strange is that the

Forest allowed him access into the maze. That way is only open to me and the animals. I don't understand." Nadir said crossly.

"Will you question him more?" asked Aria.

"Of course! We will not delay our departure a second longer than we must! We will leave as soon as we have eaten."

"What about Hutt? Will you leave him here?"

"No – I cannot. He must leave the Forest, so he will travel with us."

"He claims to be our guide – do you think it is a trap? Perhaps he is a hafling."

Aria suggested.

"No. He is not contaminated," Nadir shrugged. "I do not understand. I don't need a guide for I have travelled to the settlement many times and he is hardly worthy of the title bodyguard. I cannot fathom this puzzle. The Forest should not have allowed him entry into this region."

Aria looked sceptical. "Are you saying that he has the blessing of the Forest?"

"He must have, otherwise the entrance to the maze would not have been revealed. Tis very strange and what's more, the Wolf seems to be attracted to him and yet the Boy knows not the Wolf."

"How can you tell?" Aria asked.

Nadir made a noise that sounded like a snort. She gave Aria a contemptuous look. "Because I have eyes and I use them. The Wolf knew thee and thee recognised the Wolf."

Aria started to protest but Nadir held up her hand and stopped her.

"Do not deny it. I am aware thee haven't made up thee mind to trust me. So be it – but do not think me a fool."

Aria hung her head for a moment then looked up defiantly.

"I wasn't sure before, but I am now; I have seen the trust the animals give you. So, I will tell you – the Wolf you call Greybeard he was known as Captain Helment. He was my mate's bodyguard."

Nadir smiled; her blue eyes sparkled. "Helment! I should have guessed. I have heard of him. Yes, I have surely heard of him. My King will miss him for they were young together." She gave Aria a stern look. "Now, what else should I be told?"

Aria forced a smile. "What else can there be?"

"I do not know, Child, but there have been some strange happenings here this day."

Nadir gave Aria a penetrating look but didn't probe any further; instead she turned and walked back to the cottage.

Within the walls of the cottage, Hutt was feeding his scraps to the Wolf. He stopped when Nadir sat down beside him.

"I am called Nadir," then Nadir pointed to Aria when she re-entered the cottage and said, "She is Aria. Have you heard of us?"

Hutt carefully chewed a piece of crust before he answered. "I have heard the King speak of the Lady Aria, but I do not know her. You are not known to me. Father did speak of a human living within, though."

"And what did he say?"

Hutt shrugged. "It is forbidden to speak of the one they call the Guardian. He told me and my brothers and sisters to stay away."

"Do thee know why he said so?"

"He said the tales of the Guardian's origins were shrouded and that the old people speak the tales in whispers. I am not afraid," he said and did not boast.

"No, thee are not afraid. But I think thee should be, just a little, for I am the one they call the Guardian."

Hutt gave her a wide grin as he scooped the last of his meal into his hand and offered it to the Wolf. "I am a woodsman's son and we know the Forest." He boasted.

Nadir's hand snaked out across the bench and grabbed Hutt's hand.

"And do thee know me?" she hissed.

Hutt jumped in fright but still he smiled. "No, but you are the Guardian and I trust in you."

Nadir released him and stood up. "Do not take me for granted for I am more powerful than the King." She warned him then added. "Now tell me Hutt, the woodsman's son – who knows that thee are here?"

"Several from the Kingdom saw me enter and there is one more within by name Likea. He was Horse, so his journey will be slower because he must wait for the Forest to take his Second Life."

"Why, is he a hafling?" Nadir asked sternly, the question directed to Aria not Hutt.

Aria's cheeks lost colour, the news clear to see it both frightened and pleased.

"He was the guard of the Lady," answered Hutt.

Aria strived to keep her voice neutral. "Yes." She nodded. "I had a guard of that name."

Nadir nodded slowly. "Thee told me there wasn't any reason for the King to search for thee. Now I find that there are two within the Proto Forest who seek thee. Why do they search and why did thee lie?" Nadir's eyes narrowed, cat like, as she focused on her. Aria gripped the edge of the bench. She swayed slightly but didn't answer. Nadir allowed her gaze to wander from Aria's face and down her body. Her eyes widened in surprise, as she noticed the slight bulge of Aria's midriff.

"Thee are with child!" she gasped! "Fool that I am! Of course - thee could have chosen the Second Life, but thee did not. Thee carry the Heir."

Aria shook her head in denial, but she couldn't speak.

"Do not deny thee child and the Kingdom's Heir. Do not!" Cried Nadir.

Startled at Nadir's outburst, Aria started to cry. Hutt stood and helped her into a chair. Nadir slapped at her thigh and began pacing, rapidly, up and down the room.

"Of course – a blind fool – unworthy of brains. That is why Hutt was sent. He is needed to guide thee through the woods of his former home. Not the Forest. That is why he is here."

Nadir became aware of Aria's distress and knelt beside her and took her hands in hers. Softening her face Nadir said comfortingly, "Cry not, Child. Now I know. Now I know. I will not harm thee. The unborn is the rightful Heir. I am his Guardian as he will be mine. It is written in the Covenant. Do thee not understand – the Child will be the protector of the Forest of Light and thereby I am his Guardian."

She shook Aria gently. "If only thee trusted me. Now your babe is in danger."

Nadir jumped up and began throwing food into her straw bag. "We must hurry – time is almost gone into the danger level of our existence. Hurry!"

"I don't understand. Likea said I would be safe within the Forest," disputed Aria through drying tears.

"Soldiers are fools. They know little and think they know a lot. Thee are safe, but the Child – the Child. Come on girl! We must not tarry. Dress warmly and gather some food."

When Aria still didn't move Nadir firmly gripped her shoulder and shook her impatiently.

"Even the unborn are influenced by the magic and chemicals of the Forest. It is inevitable for the Forest is so strong. We should have been gone from here two days past. If we hasten we can reach the outer Forest, to the west. The distance is shorter. Now hurry!"

"What will happen if I stay too long?" Aria asked, fear heard in her voice.

"The Child will not be granted the Second, the most important, life."

Aria still looked dubious and Nadir clapped her hands together sharply.

"Fool! Dolt! Look at me! I am the result of a mother who carried full term within. I have no Second Life, but I was lucky for the Forest has taken me. As a human the Heir must have the choice, or He can't rule the Kingdom. Every creature in the Kingdom, the Plains, wherever we are is dependent on the chosen King. That Lion must understand and live both lives or He cannot protect us. The Forest gave us the gift but if we break the Covenant then we lose the First Life and have only the Second and we dwell only within the Forest, as it was before. Now do thee understand?" Nadir lectured.

Aria nodded dumbly and began to pack. Fear made her move quickly. Nadir ordered Hutt outside to bring in some of the smaller pots she had been drying while she sorted through some of her potions.

"Yes," Nadir mumbled to herself. "Yes. That is why Hutt was sent. The western side is the closest and the way is known to him."

"But you can take me – you were going to do so anyway."

Nadir stopped her frantic rummaging and looked sadly at Aria. "Child I was taking thee to the human colony. It is on the boundary of the Forest. I do not know the woods and so we have a need of Hutt."

"Then you aren't coming with us?"

"Only a part of the way unless it is granted. I am forbidden to leave the Forest for long periods and must never go beyond the river in the west. That is the price I pay for longevity and peace."

"You are speaking in riddles. You have the Faith – even more than the most devout I have ever known. Yet you are bonded here."

"I am bonded by fear."

"What is there to fear? What frightens you? You are kindly and gentle, and all the animals trust you implicitly. What is there to fear?"

Nadir gave a bitter sounding laugh. "I fear nothing, but others fear me. Now, enough. If thee are ready, then we leave now." Ending that conversation completely.

Nadir stalked outside, yelling for Hutt. Aria followed more slowly. At the doorway she stopped and looked back fondly. Nadir shouted at her to make haste and she hurried after them. Nadir walked at a cracking pace. The only one of the odd quartet to keep up with her was the wolf. Aria and Hutt were too far behind to hear what was said but it appeared that Nadir was talking incessantly to the wolf. She halted her long stride twice – both times to yell at them to keep up. Aria stumbled twice but Hutt was always there to offer his hand.

Sometime early in the afternoon the wolf disappeared. He had not returned by the time they stopped for the evening meal.

Both Aria and Hutt gratefully sank to the ground. Aria sighed in relief as her leg muscles relaxed.

"I am stiff and sore," she complained.

Nadir handed her a bowl of nuts and berries.

"Enjoy this respite for as soon as we have eaten we walk some more." Nadir said grimly.

"You must be joking! Aria exclaimed. "It is too dark."

"Is it darker than the Badlands?" asked Nadir with a gentle lift of her eyebrows.

Aria blanched and shuddered as she recalled the two dark times she had spent out there with Likea.

"No," she said softly." It is not as dark."

Nadir relaxed a little. "Thee will feel better after some time. Eat child." She turned towards Hutt. "Thee too, Boy."

"I am called Hutt. I told you so," Hutt replied as he stuffed the ripe berries into his mouth.

"Thee will feel the back of my hand if you keep opening thee mouth for other than food," Nadir tartly replied. "So, eat Boy for thee need all thee strength for the immediate future." As she spoke, Nadir passed him more berries and a slice of cold pancake.

Hutt grinned at her and chewed rapidly. "I will rely on my brains,"

Nadir snorted. "What brain?"

Hutt started to reply but was interrupted by Aria.

"Where is the Wolf?" she asked, looking around.

Nadir hesitated. "No doubt he will turn up," she answered.

"Do you know where he is?" Aria persisted.

Nadir shrugged. "How should I know? I told thee he would not stay. Forget the Wolf and eat."

Aria stared at her. "You are lying. You spoke with the Wolf earlier and he gave no sign of leaving."

Nadir slammed her bowl down and began shoving the drinking gourds back into her bag. "I do not lie. I never lie. Since thee both have energy to waste in argument, we will resume our walk again."

Nadir hastily picked up her bag and stormed off into the gloom. Both Aria and Hutt stared after her, but as she gave no sign of ceasing, they rose to run after her.

"She has a worse temper that the tutors in the Kingdom, Hutt puffed.

"She lied. I am sure she lied."

Hutt smiled at her. "The Guardian doesn't lie. Next to my Liege she is the most powerful agent of the Covenant. Trust her, Lady Aria."

Aria smiled at him. "You are a youngster Hutt – your trust is universal."

"I know not what that means but I am not a fool. The Guardian is your friend," replied Hutt with a strange dignity.

Aria saw that she had somehow offended him but before she could utter an apology with a burst of speed, he left her and ran ahead to Nadir.

Nadir looked down at him. "Frightened, Boy?" she questioned.

Hutt grinned. "No. The Lady is angry with you."

Nadir grunted. "She asks too many questions and yet trusts no-one."

"I ask all the time too – where is the Wolf?"

"Where does thee think he is, Boy?"

Hutt laughed engagingly. "I think you sent him to find Likea."

Nadir stopped walking and looked at him. "Do thee indeed? And why would I do that?"

"Because I am not a warrior and that you think we might have need of one."

Nadir laughed and touched his forehead with her hand. "What else does thee think?"

"I think that you didn't tell her because you didn't want her to be worried."

"Thee is very clever and what else does thee know?"

Hutt shrugged. "Not much. There are many questions, but I don't think you will answer them. I know that I trust you."

Nadir smiled. She turned her head and glanced back at Aria, and without a second thought she swung the bag from her shoulder and rested it on the ground.

"Does the Lady know of your origin?"

Hutt shook his head. "No, I felt it wiser not to say. I don't know if she would understand and I don't want to hurt her."

"Thee are wise beyond your years." Nadir said as she nodded soberly and clicked her tongue. "That's what I thought too. We will sleep here."

"Guardian?"

"What?"

"How did you know my origins?"

She smiled. "Am I not the Guardian? The Wolf was devoted to thee and I already knew a sleeper had awoken – the rest was easy to guess."

"You are indeed wise," said Hutt.

Nadir grunted as she swept leaves over her legs. "Not wise enough. I should have seen Aria was with child. What of my origins? Do thee know?"

"No, I only remember the rumours that my father had told me but nothing else. Will you tell me Guardian?"

With a shake of her head Nadir replied, "No. I cannot. The prophesy is in the Covenant. When thee return to the Kingdom - read it."

As Hutt was settling down to rest Aria had finally caught up to the secretive duo, but she didn't speak. Ignoring her companions, she made herself a bed and laid down. Hutt lifted himself onto one elbow and looked across to Nadir.

"Who in the Kingdom knows the full Covenant of Light?" He asked curiously.

"Only myself and the King. Some advisors know a great deal of it. Thee see, Hutt, the citizens believe so they don't question. They cannot understand the Covenant because they don't ask. Their way of faith is imperfect, but their trust is complete."

She reached over and patted his hand. "Thee will become a part of the Covenant. The King will write thee into it and that will be thee reward. Sleep now little warrior, for the morrow is not far away. Sleep too, Lady Aria – dream of the future."

"I have no future."

Nadir snorted. "Self pity. The cub thee carry are thee future. That too, is written."

"Guardian." Hutt said sleepily with a yawn.

"What?"

"You forgot yourself. You called me by name."

Nadir laughed.

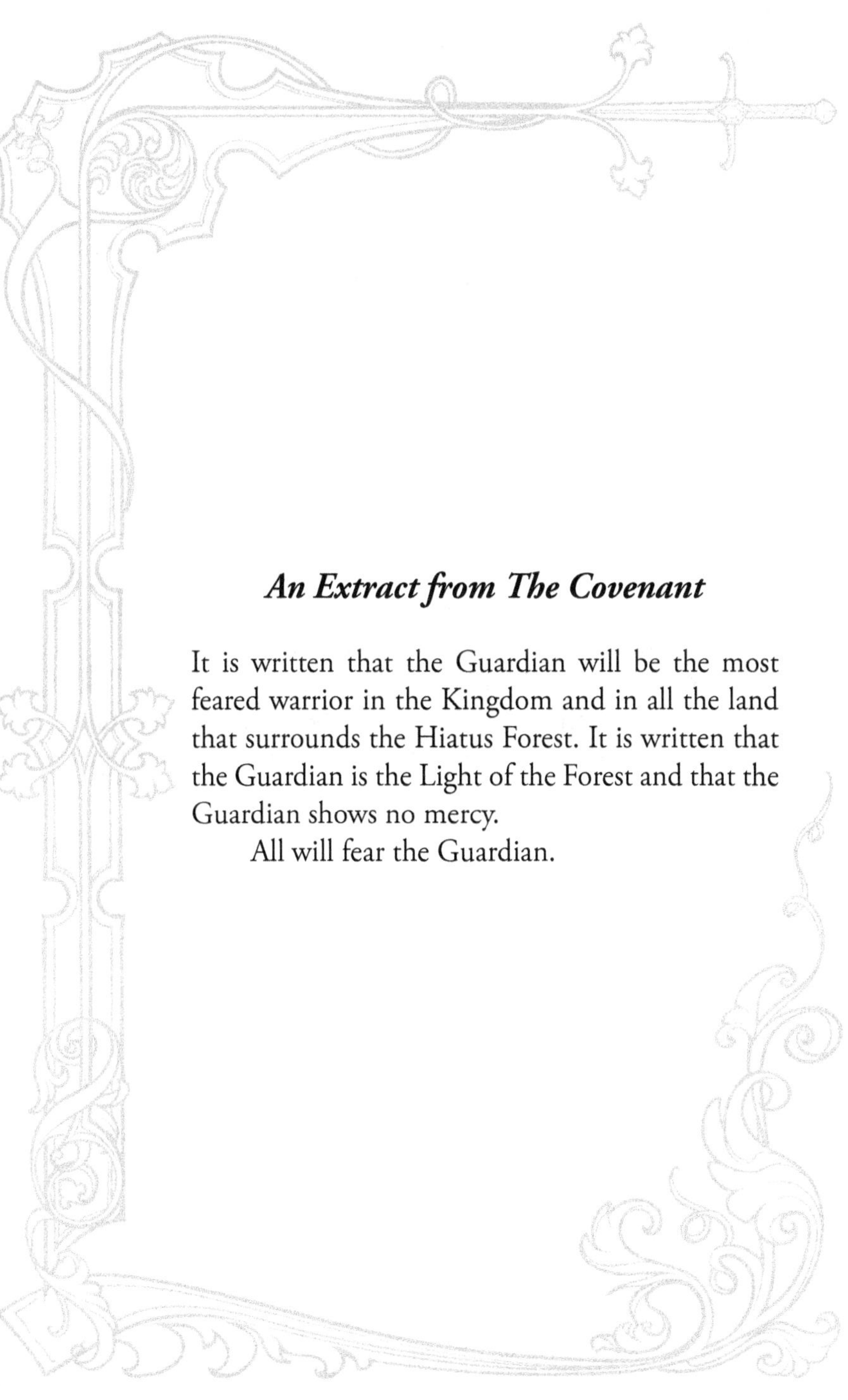

An Extract from The Covenant

It is written that the Guardian will be the most feared warrior in the Kingdom and in all the land that surrounds the Hiatus Forest. It is written that the Guardian is the Light of the Forest and that the Guardian shows no mercy.

All will fear the Guardian.

Chapter 10

THE WOODLAND

There was no gradual change from the Forest to the Woodland. In one moment, Nadir's party was trekking through dense Forest, and in the next, they are all walking into bright sunshine with good visibility.

Nadir stopped walking and offered a prayer to the Light. Hutt watched her keenly – intoning the segments that he remembered. Aria stopped and observed them dispassionately while walking away before Nadir had finished. Hutt saw Aria turn away and then he threw a quick glance back to Nadir before following. When Nadir had finished her prayer she easily caught up to them – it appeared that they were both delaying themselves while trying to appear to hurry.

When Hutt saw her, he dropped back to join her." Did you see Likea?" he asked.

"No. He must have been further away than I thought. He will come, boy, do not despair."

Nadir stopped just before night had arrived. She chose a secluded dip in the ground that was surrounded by large boulders.

Hutt and Aria lay out the fruit and berries they had picked and sat down to eat. Nadir eyed the meagre fare and dipped searchingly into her bag. She removed the stone tray and the bag of silver powder. Once she had the heat, she selected a large bowl, poured in some water and added powdered mushrooms. She placed the bowl on the tray to heat. While they waited, Hutt chatted away happily but Aria pretended to be more interested in the coming nightfall.

When Nadir offered her a cup of the soup she refused. Nadir looked annoyed and Hutt was wary.

"The stubbornness of the Plains lions is renown, but their stupidity is not," she snapped. She cupped Aria's hands around the bowl. "Eat then for the Heir."

Aria glared at her, but Nadir was unmoved.

"Tis the best way the haflings have of causing mischief – disharmony amongst the faithful."

Aria flushed and turned her head away, but she did sip some of the soup.

Nadir sat down and took up her bowl.

"Tell me Hutt, is this way known to thee?" she asked.

"No. It is not familiar." He paused, then added. "It feels wrong, not right, but I haven't seen anything."

Nadir nodded in agreement. "Nor I but I feel..." She stopped and grimaced. "Perhaps it is because we have come from the safety of the Forest into the unknown."

"There is no need for you to come any further. Hutt can escort me," spoke Aria.

"No, I will stay longer." Nadir finished her soup and looked up at the sky. "I have time." She added, mused.

Aria gave a hollow laugh. "I should think that you would be missing the animals."

"I do. I have always found them to be better company than humans." Nadir's voice suddenly grew cold and menacing. Hutt shivered with apprehension. "Now hear me girl. Thee have never been in more danger than thee are now. Use the aid that is offered and do not offend me further. I am not of thee Royal court and I will not stand thee tantrums. I begin to doubt Vidal's capacity to choose a fitting bride."

Aria hung her head. She didn't speak so instead she curled up to sleep. Hutt breathed a sigh of relief and he too lay back.

During the night Nadir woke. Aria was intoning the prayer of unworthiness. Nadir smiled.

The route they were following was rough and they made slow progress. A thick blanket of fog covered the area and visibility was reduced to a few paces. A strong smell of smoke came with the fog. Hutt came and walked abreast with Nadir. She looked down at him and touched his hand.

"Eerie, isn't it." She said.

Hutt nodded and walked closer to her.

Halfway through the morning the fog disappeared, and they made better time. In the distance they could see the source of the smoke. Hutt pointed, and Nadir nodded grimly.

"My people would not do that. Guardian I am afraid."

"Courage Hutt. The smoke is still some distance away and it is only the first real sign that we have seen."

As the smoke slowly dissipated and the air once again smelt fresh, Hutt's anxiety faded. He began to ask questions to the point that Nadir deliberately ignored him.

Aria was repentant. She didn't speak much and when she did it, it was without rancour. Nadir was also very quiet, and an unaccustomed frown creased her forehead.

Nadir became aware that Hutt was tugging at her sleeve. The frown disappeared, and the smile returned.

"You aren't talking to me." He complained.

"That is because thee is talking enough for us all."

Unabashed, Hutt grinned, "You talk a lot." He said.

Nadir's eyes twinkled even though her expression was stern. "I am very old and I don't see many humans so I am excused." She replied.

Nothing loath Hutt continued to talk. His good humour was infectious and eventually Aria joined in the conversations.

When they stopped to eat, Nadir had Hutt draw a map of the woodland area that he remembered. He did so, and Nadir bade Aria to pay close attention.

"This map is for in case we are separated," she said. Then she turned to Hutt. "Is this area familiar to thee?" she asked.

Hutt nodded. "It was so long ago but I have been here. Just the once as I recall for my home is closer to the Kingdom. My parent brought me here. There is a village close by and another this way." He pointed to the west. "We could make that village by nightfall if you wish."

Nadir frowned "I would prefer to avoid habitation if possible. Word had reached me that some humans had been contaminated. As this is not the most devout region of the colony I would rather not meet any humans."

She glanced at Aria. "Thee are tired and are limping a little. A rest will do thee good, but I..." but she didn't get to finish as a strange expression shadowed her face for a moment.

"What is it, Guardian? "Asked Hutt, in some concern.

Nadir shrugged and gave a little laugh." An old woman being fanciful. Tis nothing."

Aria looked at her sharply. "Do you have the insight?" she asked.

Hutt looked puzzled.

Nadir shrugged again. "A little, child, a little."

"Then we will avoid the village," said Aria decisively. She began to repack their bags. Hutt reached over and touched her hand.

"What are you talking about?" he demanded. "I don't understand."

Arai looked at Nadir who nodded. "Nadir can see her own death. That is the insight. Only those most devout and of Royal blood can do so."

Hutt swung around to stared at Nadir, his mouth dropped open.

"Are you a royal?"

Nadir smiled at his question. "I was many lifetimes ago – now I am just the Guardian."

"What was your origin?"

But Nadia ignored him and spoke to Aria.

"Then thee trust me, Aria?" She asked, seeking clarification.

"Hutt trusts you implicitly and I feel safe with you," she smiled at Hutt. "I offended him - I will not do so again." She glanced at Nadir then looked down at her hands. "You told me not to be stupid, so I have spent this day thinking." Aria looked squarely at Nadir. "Do you think the wolf found Likea?" she asked.

Nadir chuckled. "He would have done so by now, but they must have been too far away to catch us, and they will catch us."

"Why don't we wait here for them?" Hutt asked.

Nadir shook her head. "'Tis too dangerous. It would look suspicious to those who observe us. Better that we keep moving."

All the afternoon they walked, seeing neither animal nor human. They finally arrived to a large area of the woodland that had been burnt. The smoke still rising from the smouldering trees.

Hutt raised a fist to his lips and he pressed his knuckles hard into his flesh, misery etched into his face. Hutt tried to be brave but at the sight of such intensive destruction he broke down and cried. Aria wrapped her arm around him, in comfort but he was inconsolable. He broke free from her comforting arm and walked through the dark grey ash and scorched timber. One sapling had escaped the fire, a stark emerald green colour against a backdrop of black and grey. Hutt gently touched the bark on the trunk and then lifted his face and the leaves brushed his wet cheeks.

Aria went to him and again slipped her arm around his thin shoulders. He turned in her embrace and she enveloped him in her arms and held him while he wept. He whispered repeatedly. "My people would not do this."

Nadir's eyes were bleak as she surveyed the mutilation. Her jaw seemed to harden, and her breathing became more rapid. She went to Hutt and tugged gently to release him from Aria's grasp. She wiped the tears from his cheeks.

"Enough. Enough now. They will pay for this – but not now. We have been given a task and we must not be swayed. The Lady must be made safe and we are only here to ensure that it happens."

He stopped crying and made an effort to control himself. Nadir looked at him with compassion. "I understand Hutt," she said softly. "I really do but the trees and the grass will grow back. The birds and the animals will return if they are allowed too. Hutt, we can't stay here. Look yonder for thee eyes are younger than mine. See, in the distance, that is a reflection of light striking something. What is it? Can thee see?"

Hutt wiped his eyes and squinted through the smoke haze," It looks like a village," he finally said with his voice sounding thick. "I know of no village here."

"Tis many seasons since thee were here. Likely it has been erected between times." Nadir paused. "It bars our way. If my reckoning is correct, then there is a deep ravine across our direct path and to detour will take us very close to that village."

Nadir thought carefully. She could sense the rising fear and alarm in the others and she knew of their weariness.

"We will go to the village and rest there," she said decisively.

Aria grasped her arm. "Are you sure?"

Nadir nodded. "I feel uneasy but nothing more. We cannot cross the ravine and we must press on, so we have a very limited choice. A rest on a comfortable bed will restore us for the journey on the morrow. Come, thee and Brave Heart."

Nadir straightened her pose and set off on a brisk pace. The others followed but travelled slower until they were close to the village – then they hurried to catch up to Nadir.

The village was clearly visible and there was some sign of habitation.

"It looks normal enough," Hutt said but he closed his grip on his staff.

Nadir entered the village first and she slowed her pace so could get a good look at the layout.

It was more than a village for there were plenty shelters for housing but there wasn't any true layout. Buildings were erected any-which-way and the alleys and tracks ran in all directions. They passed what appeared to be an inn. Nadir hesitated but walked on. A couple of old men were sitting nearby on a log. They looked at Nadir's travelling group without interest and a cluster of young individuals, playing in the street, they didn't even look up from their game. Some of the primitive buildings had been damaged by fire but

Nadir could see from the cracked charcoal that the fire had been some time ago.

Aria took Hutt's hand and they hurriedly caught up to Nadir.

"Are we to rest here or go on?" Aria asked Nadir, looking around her.

"I do not know – there is something amiss, but I cannot tell what. The people, what there is, look calm and perhaps that is the problem. It is almost as though they are without fear – but they should be fearful because in their backyard there has been mass destruction. Even some of their own buildings have been burnt."

They continued walking along the path until they came upon another inn; Nadir looked at the long shadows.

"It is too late to travel. We will rest here. Wait with Hutt while I seek a bed." She instructed.

Nadir pushed open the door and entered. It took a minute for her eyes to become accustom to the dim light emitting from the burning twists of wrapped bark. Nadir approached the only occupant in the room. A large man, tall and thickset. Nadir looked him over with a feeling of wariness but apart from one quick glance from his dark eyes he took no notice of her.

"I am seeking accommodation for myself, son and daughter." She said.

The man set down the cup he was holding and poured more wine.

"What payment have you got?" He demanded.

Nadir's facial expression was contemptuous. "I have a gourd of fine wine – the best that thee will ever taste."

He emptied his cup in one huge swallow and then held it out.

"A taste then." He said.

Nadir pulled a large gourd from her bag. She poured a little of the wine into his vessel. He tasted it first with his tongue and then drank it. He licked his lips and nodded.

"It is good enough. You look unfamiliar are you from these parts?" he asked.

"No. We have just arrived," she said shortly. She rested the gourd on a barrel.

"Ahhh," he said and motioned her to follow. He led the way to a room just off the one they had been standing in. Nadir looked inside and pulled a face of distaste. She counted five straw filled sacks and if it weren't for them, the room was bare. There wasn't a window and the room was dark.

"No. This will not do. My son is young and the noise from the drinking room will disturb him. Show me another."

"The other room is more expensive. What do you expect for one jug of wine?" the man protested.

Nadir walked back into the other room and over to the barrel. She picked up her gourd and replaced it in her bag.

"My wine is the sweetest that thee will ever taste. There are other inns."

The inn keeper barred her way. Nadir fixed him with a cold, unblinking stare.

"There is a room upstairs," he muttered and avoided her eyes.

"Then I will look at it and if I find it acceptable then the price is still one jug."

The room was smaller, but it had a window. A cool breeze drifted in through the opening and it blew away a faint musty smell.

Nadir nodded and passed the gourd over. The innkeeper took it without grace. "Your tone is such, woman, that a beating wouldn't go astray." He said, leading the way downstairs.

Nadir snorted.

At the door she beckoned Aria and Hutt inside. The innkeeper was busy with his jug of wine, but at the sight of Aria he lowered the jug and leered. Aria didn't even look at him as she pushed Hutt towards the stairs. Nadir gave the inn keeper another look that came close to a sneer. He flushed angrily, but Nadir turned and followed the others upstairs.

Aria closed the door and leant against it. "There is no lock." She said.

Nadir nodded. "No, I noticed. Hutt get my stone tray from my bag."

Hutt rushed to oblige and soon Nadir had given the room some light.

"This better than their smelly brush torches. We will eat shortly but first pay attention. Hutt can you see from the window? From this room we have an escape route. Climb from that window onto that building below and from there to the ground. Aria that way is for thee too. It is a dangerous descent but better than nothing."

"Do you think we are in danger?" asked Aria.

Nadir shrugged. "I do not like the inn keeper." She frowned then went on. "There is something else and I cannot quite grasp it, but the smell of this place is strange, and I wonder..." She did not complete the sentence. She smiled at her companions instead. "We will eat now and be away at first light, by then my overactive imagination will rest."

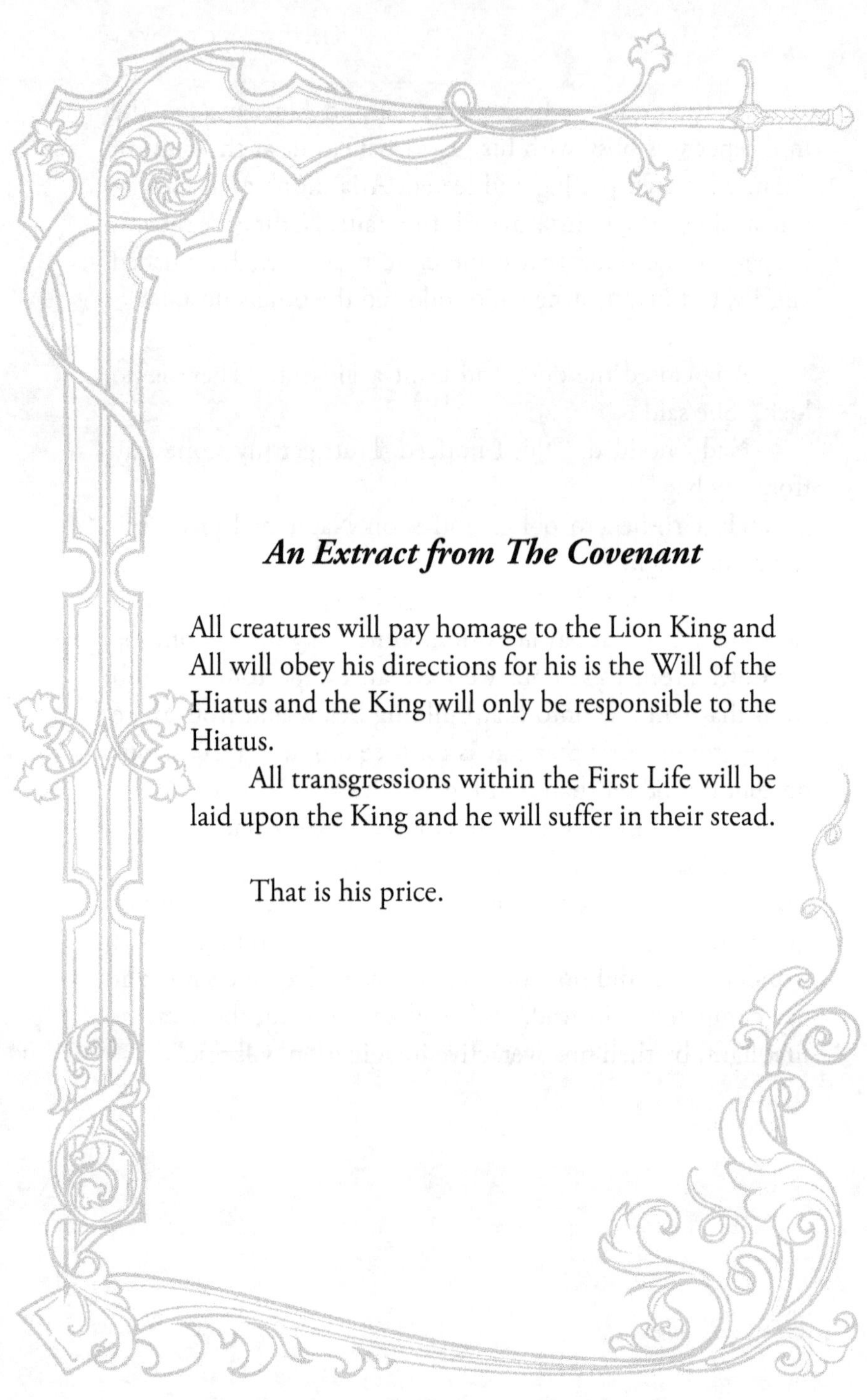

An Extract from The Covenant

All creatures will pay homage to the Lion King and All will obey his directions for his is the Will of the Hiatus and the King will only be responsible to the Hiatus.

All transgressions within the First Life will be laid upon the King and he will suffer in their stead.

That is his price.

Chapter 11

THE CAPTURE

A noise emanated from the bar room and filtered through the thin floorboards. The longer the night stretched, the louder the noise became. Wild shrieks could be heard from the women as the shouting, slurred voices of the men gave the weary travellers no respite. Not long after, Nadir, Aria and Hutt overheard of a large crowd of people entering the village. Some of the travellers stopped at the inn for a while, but the main group continued to walk past the door.

Nadir tossed and turned restlessly until finally giving up on her rest she got up and walked across to the window. A strong smell of burning wood was being carried on the breeze and she wrinkled her nose at the acrid smell. She poked her head further out the window and on the outskirts of the village she could see huge bonfires. In the pale light from the illuminated grey her cheeks were ashen.

With one eye open, Hutt was watching her closely, but it was Aria who spoke. Her voice trembled.

"What is that smell?"

Nadir's blue eyes blazed, her nostril flared so deep was her anger.

"Child get up!" she said, and they sensed her urgency. "Listen carefully. The insight has been with me all day. It was weak and now it grows stronger."

Aria shook her head numbly and her shaking hands grasped Nadir's.

"No! No, Nadir, please no!" She cried as her voice decibels gradually became louder.

Nadir pulled her hands free and grasped Aria by the upper parts of her arms. She shook her roughly and her voice was harsh.

"That smell is burning flesh. The meat eaters have arrived. Obey me and argue not! Obey me!"

She released her grip on Aria and with no time to spare, Nadir snatched up her straw travel bag and began to desperately rummage where she brought forth a small, grass bag, "Take this powder – it is the root of the Talbough tree. It will help thee to be strong if thee are captured. Eat it."

Aria took the sack but made no attempt to eat it, instead she stood there, numbly staring at Nadir.

"Thee have a whisper of a lion's roar. Eat it! There isn't time for thee stupidity."

Aria's eyes flashed angrily but she tipped the contents into her mouth and swallowed.

"Hutt, I have nothing for thee. Remember who thee once were. Vidal was the finest warrior in the Kingdom. Remember that and it will serve thee well."

Nadir bent and briefly touched her head to his forehead. Hutt sunk to his knees and pressed his face into her smock.

"Guardian you speak as one about to die." He whispered tearfully.

Nadir gently pulled him to his feet.

"There are many forms of death. Hutt, the Light is stronger and now our time is short. Remember thee origins – woodman's son – and take the Lady Aria away from here."

Nadir again faced Aria who remained standing still beside the window with a stunned expression. Nadir slipped her arm around her shoulders. The tears rose in Aria's eyes as she looked from Nadir to Hutt.

"Vidal?" She whispered.

Nadir nodded. "He was and now he is not. Your mate couldn't live but Hutt could. I am sorry thee had to find out in so cruel a manner. Aria, there isn't time for gentle words and soothing hands. Thee must save oneself and all that is Vidal, do thee understand? Do thee?"

Aria nodded, and Nadir pushed her closer to the window.

"Hutt the way below is barred – this is thee only escape. I entrust the Lady to thee care. Be swift - be strong, Brave Heart."

"What of you Guardian?" asked Hutt and his voice trembled.

Nadir smiled "My life was decreed many seasons past. Fear not for me for I have prepared myself."

Hutt nodded. He gave her a lingering look then held out his hand to assist Aria through the narrow window. She snatched her hand away. Hutt looked impassively to her and again reached for her.

"I was but I'm not. All Vidal was – I am. Come with me Lady. We are strangers, but you know me."

Nadir gave them both a little push. "Make haste! The Light sent him Aria. Trust him."

Nadir watched them climb down and onto the adjoining building. She saw Hutt wave when they reached the ground, then nothing as they disappeared into the shadows of the night. Nadir returned to her bag and sorted through her various potions. She removed corks from four vials and drank from each. Now, she could hear heavy footsteps on the stairs. She hastily grabbed her bag, hurriedly returned to the window and threw out her bag just as the door burst open.

A milling bunch of both human and hafling poured inside. One jackal hafling roared in ecstasy and grabbed her, imprisoning her within his strong arms and forced her to the floor.

"Heh, we have the old one," He laughed loudly, and the others laughed in unison too. Nadir grimaced in pain as another hafling grabbed a handful of her hair and yanked her head back.

"The little ones have fled. Never mind for they will not get far. This one is for Tonka." He shouted.

Ignoring the pain that shot into her pinned arms, Nadir listened carefully to their conversation. Tonka! He must have circled around the Forest and into the human colony. Her heart cried for the innocent victims who had lost their lives to Tonka's evilness.

The hafling who held Nadir pinned lifted her effortlessly to her feet. He shoved her, and she stumbled into the crowd. She felt their hands pawing and touching her; she didn't struggle but choose to submit to their disrespect.

"Take her to Tonka. We will search for the others." Ordered the jackal hafling.

Eager hands grabbed at her, one of the humans picked her up and slung her over his shoulder and carried her down the stairs.

Aria could feel the Talbough powder warm her stomach. She walked behind Hutt barely noticing her surroundings. As the warmth spread through-out her body she began to feel stronger and less afraid.

Hutt stopped suddenly, turned, and pushed Aria into the darker shadows.

"Back! There are haflings everywhere. Lady if we get separated then go back to the Forest. The King will look for you there and Likea will not be far behind us," he whispered urgently.

"I understand. Tell me true, Hutt. Are you really Vidal?"

In the dim light she could see his face turn towards her.

"Lady, I am Hutt but within my heart I knew that I had to find you. That was my mission. I know not your Vidal for I have no memory of him."

Aria smiled and squeezed his arm. "Vidal sent you and this I know." She said with a smile.

"Careful now," he hissed. "The voices are close."

They pressed themselves as far back as possible into the shadows of the ally way. A hafling walked past the entrance carrying a burning torch that lit up their hiding place. The hafling yelled and running feet sounded out.

Hutt grabbed Aria and dragged her away from the hafling. She screamed as the hafling caught her and her hand slipped from Hutt's.

"Run! Hutt. Run! There are too many, run!"

He hesitated but now the mutants were rushing into the allay way. He turned and ran into the darkness.

The haflings brought a subdued Aria to the bonfires. She didn't struggle against her captors; instead she laughed and joked with them, choosing to do whatever possible to keep herself safe. Deep in her stomach, the warmth from the Talbough root spread and grew stronger. By the time they reached the fires the hafling who had held her so tightly had slackened his grip. Aria was sharing a sack of wine with them while the smell of their cooking meat made her nauseous, but she forced herself to remain calm.

Her companion called out when he found their way barred by a mob.

"Ho, what is this? This is supposed to be a great feast in celebration of our great victory. Why are you standing and staring when you should be eating and drinking?" he shouted.

One of the humans came closer, his eyes aglow with excitement.

"They have caught the Witch from the Forest. Tonka has her now." He cried with enthusiasm.

Aria felt numb, but she laughed in delight. The hafling sniggered and pushed through the crowd, towing Aria behind him. The sight of the humans and haflings gorging themselves on meat made Aria dry retch and the smell of roasting food caused her to gag. The hafling laughed.

They managed to reach the front of the crowd and Aria had to bite back a gasp of shock at the scene. Nadir lay unconscious, at the feet of a huge hafling lion. Her head was bloody, and her clothes torn. The hafling lion was sitting in an enormous chair. One of his legs was draped over the arm of the chair, swinging nonchalantly. Occasionally his boot would strike Nadir's body.

"Who is that?" Aria shouted above the cheering.

Her captor bent his head a little so that she could hear him.

"That is the witch."

"No, not the woman. The lion."

The hafling roared with laughter. "You must be a stranger, woman. That is the warrior, Tonka."

Aria felt of chill creep over her body. *Tonka. Tonka.* Her brain kept repeating the name and for an instant she felt true fear.

Tonka raised his hands above his head and the crowd immediately fell silent. Aria retreated a pace but as Tonka looked around the mob his eyes seemed to seek her.

"Wake the Witch," he ordered, and his men ran to obey. They poured water over Nadir until she finally stirred. Tonka stood and placed his hands on his hips. He slowly walked around her, nudging her with his boots. Nadir struggled but she managed to sit up and look about her. Two haflings dragged her to her feet, and she stood, swaying unassisted before Tonka.

"Do you know me, woman?" he asked her.

"I know thee Tonka. Tonka the Mutant. Tonka the Destroyer."

Her voice was unsteady and soft, but it carried to the crowd who hissed and jeered.

Again, he raised his hands for silence.

"I know you too, woman. You are the one the fools call the Guardian."

The crowd hissed.

"See! See! My people – my army." He waved his arms around, indicating the crowd. "They would harm you. But not I. No. Not I. I would honour you."

The mob laughed, and Tonka grinned mockingly. "No, but I am serious. I would honour you." He roughly pushed Nadir to the huge chair he had vacated and pressed her shoulders down until she was seated. "I would honour you and why not? Are you not the Guardian of the Forest and of the Light? See - I too know my scriptures. I also know my enemies and that is how I will destroy them."

"If thee know the Covenant then thee will also know that thee will fail." Replied Nadir with an air of defiance.

"Oh, no, no. I am an unbeliever, see; The Covenant is only for fools."

He leant forward and poked her with a finger.

"Are you a fool? Nadir, daughter of Ambrose," he sneered.

The crowd instantly fell deathly silent. Tonka laughed out loud at their reaction. He pivoted to face the crowd and pointed to Nadir. "Nadir, daughter of Ambrose!" he shouted. "Daughter of the Princess Royal, Valrama. Do you see what I know! I said we should honour you – you are the direct descendant of our idol, Ambrose. The one who set us free and onto the true path of life."

He bowed mockingly but Nadir showed no emotion.

"Ambrose knew not what he did – but still he suffered for the rest of his life for his one mistake. Thee death, Tonka will be swift and that is a blessing that you do not deserve for thee have caused more suffering and misery that is comprehendible." Nadir said dispassionately.

Tonka's face darkened, and he bared his teeth. "I offer you life, Nadir, daughter of Ambrose. Do not spurn me," he strongly warned her.

Nadir grinned. "Ambrose took his punishment. He saw his family destroyed by the Light. He saw his offspring cursed, but not once did he show bitterness. Instead, he took the animals of the Forest and made them well when they were sick. He spent his whole life in atonement. He gave me, his only surviving offspring to the Light to be kept forever. Ambrose made a mistake, but he did not make the mistake of losing his faith. Thee did not know Ambrose. He was never as thee make him to be. You have twisted his error to suit a twisted mind and belief. Thee own weakness condemns and now the Light will extract your life." She paused, stood up from the large chair as steadily as she could, narrowed her eyes to pierce over at the now silent mob and spoke in a loud voice, "Tonka will not be remembered, nor will any of you. Thee will perish by the King's sword; thee bones will bleach and be crushed underfoot. There will be no trace of thee or offspring. Make the most of this life, mutants, because as for thee there will be no other."

Some of the crowd murmured to themselves and to the companions beside them all the while shuffling their feet uneasily.

Tonka threw back his head and angrily roared. He drew his sword and roared again as he raised his arm. Nadir smiled – as the moment seemed to play out in slow motion. She slightly staggered, as the sword fell against her body and blood spilt messily, the mass howled in exaltation. Nadir fell forward and two haflings knelt beside her, they shrugged and looked at Tonka.

"Get rid of it – leave it open for the birds to pick. I will feed them a meal of Kings. I give them the Guardian." He lifted a gourd and toasted the body then drank greedily as the two haflings carried the body away.

Aria fought back her tears as she laughed and clapped with the crowd. Her captor took her arm and led her to a fenced compound where he bound her with rope. "Tonka has an appetite for women, but I would have you first, woman. On the morrow you will submit to the feeding and then you will be freed." He lifted her chin and admired her. "You are not as beautiful as the witch, but you will do me well." He said as he stood. He reached for the bag she still carried.

"Leave the bag, warrior." Aria said coyly. "How else can I make you the sweetest wine you have ever tasted if I haven't got the ingredients?"

The hafling laughed. "You will do me well." He said leaving the bag and staggered off.

Aria watched him leave and felt herself relaxing a little. Now in solitude, she cried openly and prayed for clear passage for Nadir to join with the Light. When her tears slowly subsided and dried, Aria managed to compose herself. She took in her surroundings and tested the strength of the ropes. Across the other side of the compound she could make out the shapes of other prisoners. They too were bound. Some of them were talking softly and Aria strained to hear what it was they were saying.

Their voices sounded shocked and scared. Aria listened closely, and then she heard of one mention Nadir's name.

"They killed the Guardian." Someone said.

The story kept repeating down the line. Some of the prisoners cried; others laughed and said that the Guardian was only a tale used to frighten babies. Eventually, they stopped talking and they returned to the misery of knowing what the tomorrow would bring. Aria settled back against the post that held and waited.

Aria puzzled over Tonka's words. Ambrose's daughter he had said. How could this be so? Nadir would've been so old that she would've struggled to move around the Forest. He must have been lying to impress his soldiers. The King would never allow the daughter of Ambrose to keep the Forest. Aria frowned in concentration. Nadir wasn't old enough, but she certainly had a place of power and even some special powers of her own; witness the insight and the way she made heat. What was it Likea said? The old King was heartbroken when he ordered his daughter to accompany Ambrose. She had been dyed white for her royal blood and was given a single black stripe to denote her disgrace. The King could not forgive the parents, but he forgave the child – Nadir. Nadir.

The raucous sounds from Tonka's wild party grew louder as each new convert was made and the crowd cheered wildly. The hafling guards brought them food and drink which they left at the prisoner's feet, but they didn't linger but hurried back to the fence to watch the debasement.

Aria's gorge rose at the smell and sight of the roasted meat. Most of the prisoners averted their eyes from the food but Aria noticed some were watching covertly. A terrible anger engulfed her, and she rattled the stones on the ground around her legs; making enough noise to attract the prisoner's attention.

"Do not touch that abomination they have placed before you. Do not submit!" She exclaimed.

The other captives looked across the compound at her.

Aria shook her head vigorously. "Do not be tempted!"

One human male sneered at her. "Easy talk when your belly is full. We haven't had food for three days."

"Then be stronger. The Guardian curses all who weakens." In the weak light from the brush torches she could see their disbelieving looks. She shouted at them.

"Fools! I was there when they killed her. I saw her die and I heard her words."

"If she is dead then what good can she do now? How can she help us?" Called out the human male.

Aria curled her lips in contempt. "Nadir the Guardian will live. She lives even now; kick the abomination from you and out of reach. If we must die, then let it be under the Laws of the Covenant of the Light."

"What hope is there for us? If we don't eat, then on the morrow they will force feed us." Yelled the human and this time there was an audible murmur of agreement.

"There is no Heir so there will be a war. Tonka has planned it this way. The armies will destroy each other, and only Tonka's will be intact. Do you not see – there is no hope?"

Aria laughed confidently. "You have so little faith. There is an Heir. A true bloodline of Vidal's. Tonka is so wise that he is stupid. There is an Heir."

The prisoners eyed her with suspicion. "How do you know this? Vidal was killed and his mate, the Lady Aria fled to the Forest." Called out a wolf human. "The news is all over the colonies, but we have heard nothing of an Heir."

Aria sneered. "Captain Helment would chastise you for your defeatism. Who do you think Nadir brought from the Forest?"

She could sense their doubt and thought hard to say something that would convince them.

She opened her mouth to speak but the wolf interrupted her.

"Who speaks of the warrior Helment with the ease of intimacy?"

Aria smiled. "Kick that abomination away and renew your faith. Believe in the Guardian who says that Tonka will be destroyed."

The wolf stared at her for a long time before he extended his leg and sent the bowl of food and drink spinning into the sand. He turned to his companions and nodded his head towards Aria.

"This lady – she speaks the truth. Destroy the foulness that they have placed before you."

There was muted murmur of agreement and the prisoners kicked at the bowls.

The wolf turned back to Aria.

"You are in danger, Lady." He warned her. "For your own safety, speak no more. I will keep these citizens pure. I am one, Velma and these woods are my home."

"How much has Tonka destroyed?"

Velma looked both angry and sad. "Too much. He brought his army around the edge of the Plains and through much of the human colony. On his march he contaminated much of the human population. His methods are crude but effective and he has made many converts. His army is without parallel; more than twice that of the King."

He smiled at her. "Rest Lady for you look tired. Bound as I am, I cannot free you, but I will stand fast with my faith and I offer it to you." He said.

"I cannot ask for more," she said simply.

Aria laid back as far as the ropes allowed her. Without conscious thought she looked towards the direction of the Forest. Far in the distance she could see the gathering of a massive storm. It appeared to be forming over the Forest. Aria watched as the lightening illuminated the darkened sky. For an instant the noise from the bonfires stopped – the woods were silent – deathly silent.

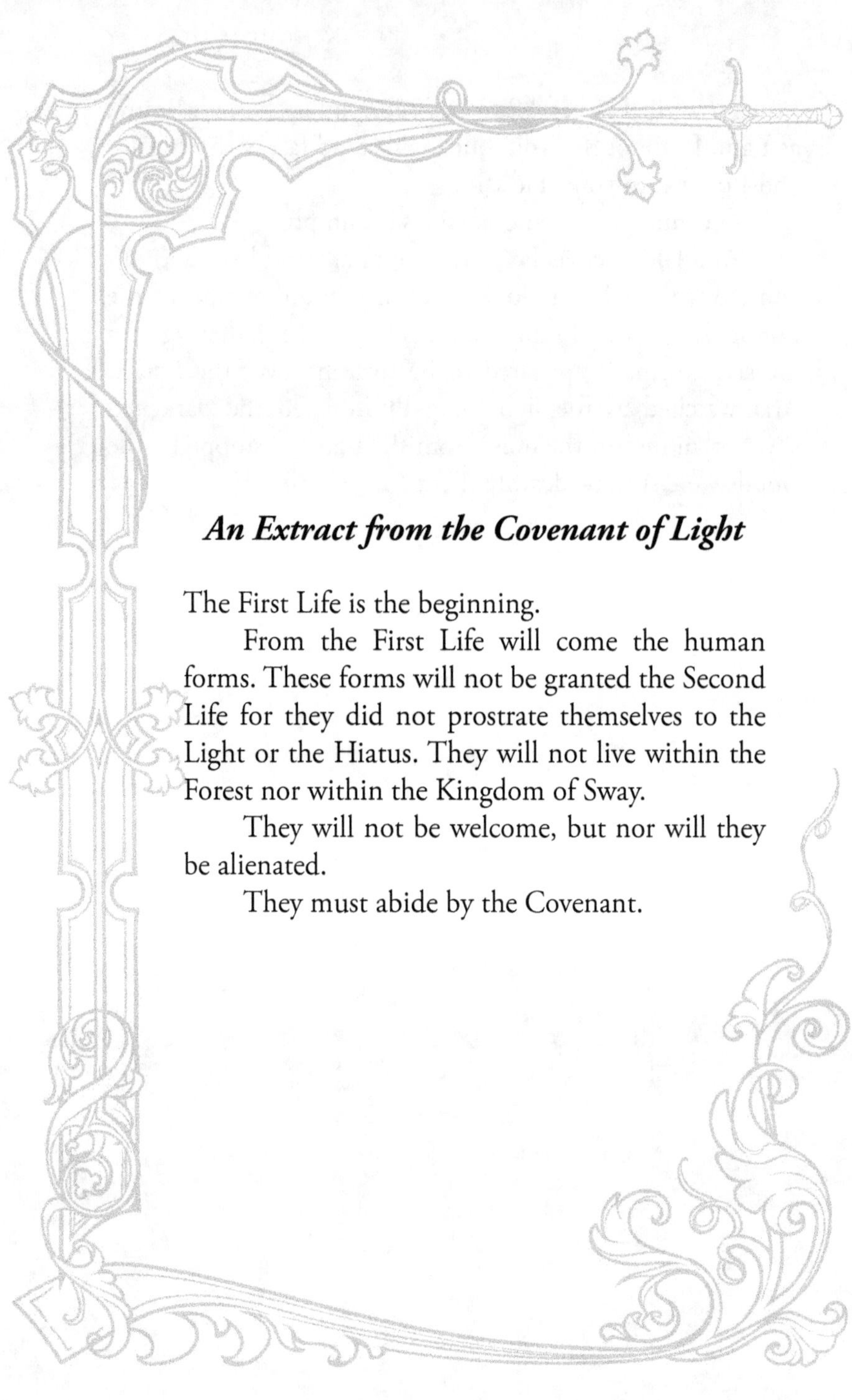

An Extract from the Covenant of Light

The First Life is the beginning.

From the First Life will come the human forms. These forms will not be granted the Second Life for they did not prostrate themselves to the Light or the Hiatus. They will not live within the Forest nor within the Kingdom of Sway.

They will not be welcome, but nor will they be alienated.

They must abide by the Covenant.

Chapter 12

HUTT AND THE SINGING WOLF

The noise from the mutants and haflings heightened as they danced and cavorted around the bonfires masking Hutt's arrival. He moved swiftly and silently from shadow to shadow until he was inside the compound. The hafling guards had long deserted their posts so although his stealth was wise it seemed unwarranted.

He stood in a shadow and stared at the prisoners. With the aid of the light reflected from the bonfires his gaze identified Aria. Slowly, and silently, Hutt inched his way closer making his way to Aria. Without warning, out of the darkness a voice carried across the yard.

"Ho hafling, are weakened women your size? Your totem is cowardly and your valour excrement."

Hutt stiffened and glanced over his shoulder. A wolf human was sitting up, watching him.

"A midget coward at that," provoked the wolf.

Hutt's eyes gleamed. "A wolf by name and a dolt by another. I have known wiser rabbits and the offspring of such."

Velma flushed at the insult. He rocked his head a little as if amazed. "The runt looks human."

"A wonder! The wolf has eyes," Hutt hissed.

"Are you touched?" the wolf demanded.

Hutt quietly snorted. "Only by loud mouthed wolves."

Velma chuckled softly. "What is your business with the Lady?"

"No business of yours," Hutt retorted.

With the final word said, Hutt continued his way over to Aria. When he reached her, he knelt beside her and firmly, but gently, touched her shoulder. She stirred to wake and sat up frightened before she recognised the young boy in front of her.

"Hutt!" she exclaimed.

"Hold still Lady. Brave Heart you will soon be free of these bonds."

Aria felt confused and embarrassed by Hutt's presence, but he didn't appear to notice. She watched him inspect the knots on her bonds. She cried silently for Vidal but all she saw was Hutt.

He looked up at her and as she looked into his dark eyes, for a moment, she saw Vidal. In that instant Vidal renewed his love for her and she returned his love with hers. Hutt smiled.

"The Guardian thought of everything," he said cheerfully.

He extracted a small knife and a gourd from the inside of his jerkin. He uncorked it and sprinkled some of the powder over one of the knots. The rope fizzed, foamed then broke apart.

"She is dead, Hutt. Tonka struck her with his sword." Aria said gently, sadly.

Hutt's eyes welled with unshed tears. "I know. I saw him do it. I wish I had a sword for Tonka should not live."

"Oh Hutt. What can we do?" Aria sobbed quietly.

"We will do what the Guardian said. We will make for the Forest."

Aria nodded as she untied the rest of the rope. "How did you find me?"

"After we were separated, I returned to the inn, I found the Guardian's bag and I removed this gourd. I then followed you to the fires and then to here. Tonka must die for his treachery," he promised, anger clear in his voice.

"Did you know she was Ambrose's daughter?" asked Aria.

Hutt shook his head. "She didn't tell me. She probably thought we wouldn't trust her if we knew. I wish I had brought some of her food."

"Oh Hutt!" Aria laughed softly through her tears. "When I doubted – you trusted."

Hutt gave a small smile. "I lay covered by the Forest for many seasons. In my comatose state I knew someone was caring for me. I eventually remembered it was the Guardian. How could I not trust her?"

He held out his hand and assisted her to her feet.

"We must leave. We will need a good head start." He started to walk towards the entrance.

"Wait!" Aria looked at Velma and the other prisoners.

Hutt waited impatiently. "We have no time to idle." He said.

"We cannot leave them." Without a second thought, she took the gourd from Hutt and hurried across the compound and poured a little of the powder over Velma's bonds. Following her lead, Hutt drew his little knife and cut the ropes on some of the captives while Aria continued using the powder. He freed a few more before returning to Aria.

"Lady, there are too many. We will move swifter and more silently by ourselves..." he whispered.

Aria nodded in agreement, she used the powder once more and as the rope fell away, she spoke to those she had freed.

"Forgive me but I must leave you, will you help free those I cannot?"

A stout woman stepped closer and bowed her head. "I will free these and it will be my privilege to do so. Leave us Lady and go swiftly and may the Light guide you well." She said.

Aria smiled her thanks and allowed Hutt to pull her into the shadows. Velma followed them to the outskirts of the village. Hutt turned to face him, drawing his knife.

"Whoa, bantam," he yelled and raised his hands." I desire only to serve. Bid me your will."

Hutt paused and shot a quick glance at Aria who smiled and nodded.

"One Likea – a human is coming this way. We have need of his strong arm and sword. He will need directions." Said Hutt, returning his knife to his pocket.

Velma grinned. "Tonka will not have me twice, Hutt is it? This, Likea will have his directions." He bowed low in deference to Aria. "His sword and mine are at your back, Lady. Go with speed for the morrow is soon and Tonka will call for his prisoners."

He gave a brief wave and disappeared into darkness of the night. Hutt and Aria turned east for the sanctuary of the Forest.

Dawn broke clear. In the distance they could see the storm that had begun to develop the previous night. It held stationary over the Forest and continued to build – sucking in every cloud that dotted the sky.

To Aria, Hutt seemed to recognise this area of the woods for he led her over the ground swiftly until she called to him to rest. Hutt stopped and looked back impatiently.

"We cannot tarry," he said.

"I know, I know, but we must eat, and drink or else out strength will sap."

"We will rest for a moment, but no longer. It is not safe here, not yet."

Hutt's gaze moved restlessly over the lay of the land behind them.

"We must go." He said gently.

Aria agreed, and they set out again, walking faster as the faint sounds of barking dogs could be heard behind them.

"There is a deep river not far from here. It has a rope foot bridge. If we can get across, I'll cut the ropes and that should give us a little extra time. The next crossing is some leagues downstream, he panted.

Aria could only nod in agreement for she too was breathless. Her well- muscled legs carried her well and soon the bridge was in sight.

They had to slow to an unsteady walk to cross the bridge. Halfway over Hutt stopped and listened. His eyes widened, and he glanced back at Aria. She too was listening attentively. The dogs were no longer barking instead they could only hear a melodic but haunting song that was being carried on the wind.

"What is that beautiful song?" whispered Hutt, captivated.

"I don't know. I have never heard anything like it before," Aria replied, equally awed.

"Perhaps it is a hafling trick?"

Aria shook her head. "No abomination could make such a beautiful sound. Whoever is singing it is not a hafling."

The singing ceased, and Hutt urged Aria on. They reached the far side safely. Hutt drew his knife and began to saw at the thick ropes, a few strands parted just as the first haflings appeared. Aria gasped as one rope snapped back across the river. The weight of the haflings caused the remaining ropes to stretch and snap, moments after, the bridge collapsed. Hutt grinned in triumph.

Suddenly the air around them crackled and a ball of white light streaked past them. Aria looked towards the Forest, but the storm was still stationary. She frowned, with a puzzled expression, and looked at Hutt.

"Lightning?" she asked.

Hutt shrugged. "I don't know. It didn't look like lightning."

"What was it then?"

"I don't know but we can't stop and wait for it to return. Come-on we haven't gained too much time."

Aria still looked troubled. Just as they began to make their way, they heard the singing once more. It was louder, the sound clearer, and the wind became increasingly stronger.

Hutt looked uneasy. He gripped his knife tighter and walked on. Aria followed.

All that day they walked or ran, when they could. Darkness had begun to fall when Aria stumbled. She grabbed at a tree for support. Hutt wasn't in any better shape for he too rested against a tree trunk.

"I cannot run any further Hutt," she gasped.

Hutt sobbed for breath and he slumped to the ground. Not long after, they could hear the baying of the dogs.

Aria lifted her face to the night sky and a cool breeze touched her heated cheeks. She breathed deeply until she could control her breathing. A flash of light caught her eye and for a moment she stared and then looked at Hutt. She twitched his sleeve. He slowly raised his head and Aria pointed ahead of them.

"A fire," she whispered.

Hutt pulled himself up straighter and peered into the deepening gloom.

Someone had lit a campfire and it they judged it was close by. Slowly and quietly, they both inched their way closer until they could see a small hut made from straw and brush. A faint smell of cooking bread reached them. Hutt looked for guidance from Aria who gave a tired shrug.

"Haflings don't eat bread and we must rest. The mutants will probably rest too since the darkness is almost here."

Hutt motioned Aria to stay where she was. He boldly stepped from around the tree and walked towards the hut. He stopped some distance away and stood deathly still – staring at the ring of stones that circled the hut. Aria could see him shrug then he stepped over the stones and approached the entrance.

She watched him enter, her heart pounding. Her heart hadn't settled when she saw him again reverse his steps. In the faint evening light, she could see his ashen cheeks and the shock etched onto his face. Without thought, she ran forward and pulled at his arm. He looked stunned and he couldn't speak. Aria hesitated and stepped up to the entrance – she looked inside and froze.

A young woman, no older than Aria knelt over a cooking tray. She looked up from her task and beckoned Aria inside. Aria couldn't hold back a gasp of surprise. The young woman had pure white hair except for a single black stripe which ran through one side of her hair. Aria gripped the sides of the entrance, fingers digging into the wood and her mouth wide open.

"Thee know me Aria; come forth and bring that fool, Hutt with thee."

"No! No! This cannot be. I saw you die by Tonka's hand."

Nadir chuckled gleefully. "Then my legend will grow even stronger."

"I do not trust you. This must be a trick. I saw you die."

"Stop behaving like a fool and come in." Nadir said irritably.

Aria shook her head. "No! Prove to me that you are the Guardian."

Nadir grinned. "Proof? Why now let me see - I can tell thee exactly what thee carry in thee bag. I can also tell thee that on the first day at my cottage we were visited by a cheetah, a monkey and six assorted birds. The cheetah had torn his pad on a rock and the monkey was lonely. Proof enough?"

Aria remained at the entrance shaking her head with complete disbelief, "I don't know. I saw you die."

Nadir stood up and went to her. "Come child, thee are tired and hungry. The mutants are close by and still more come. Eat and be safe for a while."

She brushed past Aria and went outside to Hutt. He retreated from her until he fell backwards over a large stone. Nadir stood over him.

"Thee who I kept warm for many seasons. I fed thee and looked after thee – surely your small brain hasn't failed ." She chided him. "Come inside and rest."

Aria went to him took his hand and led him into the shelter. Nadir looked around at the gathering gloom. She could hear faint sounds of movement. Aria had moved closer to the fire while Hutt position himself near the opening.

Nadir looked amused as she ladled out soup and cut the bread she had baked.

She set the bowls down on the floor, then picked up her bowl and commenced to eat.

"We both saw you get struck by the sword. We saw your blood flow." Aria commented, and the disbelief was strong in her voice.

Nadir smiled grimly. "I saw thee there. Did thee think me so unprepared? I knew that the inn was a mistake almost as soon as we arrived. I also knew that if there were to be trouble, we could not all escape. After thee left I drank from four small jars that I carried. One mixture was to heighten my awareness so that when the blow was struck, I could avoid most of the power behind it. The second jar was to slow down my metabolism to near standstill. The third was to staunch the blood and the fourth was to aid my recovery. I had to take a chance that the haflings would not mutilate me."

She pulled the scarf away from her neck to reveal a long, thin scar. "Tis his mark I carry,"

Hutt, stared, eyes agog. "You were old," he stammered.

Nadir smiled. "The Forest gives me my life – for each death I live, but my age diminishes by some years. I am still Nadir but now I appear as your grandfather might have seen me."

"Will you truly never die?" Hutt asked.

Nadir's eyes softened as she looked at the boy. "I am the Guardian – who else is there but me. I am mortal and if I am careless when I am away from the Forest than I am as thee."

Her voice strengthened, and she looked from one to the other. "Make no mistake we are all in grave danger. The haflings are close and unless I can find aid from some other quarter then we may all perish here - this dark time."

Aria put down her bowl and spoon and made to rise. "Then we should leave here now before they arrive in number." She said, defiantly .

"Tis no use. Both thee and the boy are too tired to travel far. Even if it was possible, two leagues from here we will be stopped by swamp and marsh land."

"No Guardian." Protested Hutt. "The way is clear."

Nadir gave him some more soup before she answered him. She put down the spoon and looked kindly to him. "No Hutt – the way is impassable. Tonka has flooded the Plain with sour and evil water. The roots of the trees are exposed and grow above the soil. The water is stagnant and putrid.

Tonka has caused the insects to change and now they sting and spread poison. The way is impassable."

Hutt began to cry, and Nadir lightly rested her hand on his curly hair in a gesture of sympathy.

"He will be destroyed Hutt. As we speak his time grows nearer. We must pray to the Life Tree that the rot has not gone too deep and that our world will recover from his madness."

Nadir fell silent. Each seemed pre-occupied with their own thoughts. Aria glanced through the open doorway then jumped at a movement outside.

"I saw movement – out there!" She cried and pointed towards the door.

Nadir calmly cut herself another slice of bread. "Yes, they are here and more arrive every minute." She replied calmly and continued eating her meal.

Hutt sprang to his feet, pulling his knife from his belt. Nadir glared at him.

"Sit thee and rest." She ordered him. "There is nothing to be done now."

"I have a mission or else my life. He retorted angrily.

Nadir's hand snaked out and grasped the knife. "Go beyond that circle of stone and it will be thee life – foolish boy! Your brain is the size of the peas that grow on the Plains. I am not finished with Tonka."

"Nor he with you," Hutt retorted.

"Had I known that thee mouth would have been used for other than food I would have sewn your lips together and fed thee through a grass straw."

"Ho! Old woman and I would stuff your eyes with potatoes and tie vines around your head," snapped Hutt angrily.

After a moment, Nadir laughed merrily and with her free hand she casually clipped Hutt across the side of his head. "Sit. Thee have shown that thee have courage now; show some sense and be guided by an older, wiser head."

As she spoke, she released the knife blade then pointed to the ground. "Sit," she said in a milder tone. "I came here on the wings of Light to build thee this sanctuary. I am not the only one working to keep thee safe. We are in grave danger, but help is coming, and we cannot do anything until then."

"Why should we believe the daughter of Ambrose?" asked Aria softly, carefully watching Nadir.

Nadir looked mockingly at her. "Because I have not failed thee yet." She picked up an olive and chewed it daintily. She waved the spoon at Aria.

"Ambrose was a great scientist. Even the old King knew that which is why he was allowed to study the haflings. Ambrose made one mistake and it cost the Kingdom dearly – but his heart was pure, and his faith never waned. He never forced the haflings on the road they chose but he was the cause for awakening the dark side of their brain. For his mistake the Hiatus demanded his life in servitude and the King banished both him and his family into the Forest. Neither he nor my mother was offered the Second Life and eventually they died. While he lived Ambrose was the first Guardian but as the reports of the haflings violations reached him he died a little each time. After his death the Hiatus relented and gave me freedom. They offered me the Light and I became the second Guardian. I am the oldest and the wisest being within all the Kingdoms and not just Sway. On your return I suggest thee read the Covenant – the prophecy is in it."

Aria studied her closely and marvelled at her serenity. "How much power do you have?" she asked curiously.

Nadir laughed and her beautiful eyes gleamed. "See for thyself. I passed thee while thee were on the rope bridge. I plotted the path and built this shelter. I gathered and lay a circle of stone, I taught a wolf to sing and still I had time to find my carry bag, I even prepared a meal…"

"I built stone walls in play. One good kick and they fall." Said Hutt, smartly.

"Ah - but my stone walls are impenetrable until Tonka and twelve of his top satellites arrive. Until then we are safe."

"Is it Tonka, himself that is following us?" asked Aria.

"Yes," said Nadir. "He recaptured some of those that you released. Under his torture they told of a woman who carried the child. It is Tonka who follows."

"Then we are lost for his army will come with him."

"Nay, child. I sought to divide his army and therefore I shall win. On the way here, I came upon a wolf human by name Velma. I gave him a voice to carry on the wind and now he sings of the Heir to come. His voice will carry, through to the free animals and birds, to the Emir and all the other colonies. Fear of unity will cause the haflings to quake; some will turn and hide. Tonka will find it more difficult to recruit and those he does recruit will be more difficult to train for I have planted doubt." She stopped and pointed through the opening. "See – yonder that storm? That is the soul of the Forest. Never have the Plains or the Woodlands witnessed a tempest of such fury. In the period between my death and life, the Forest built that storm."

"How will a storm help us?"

"The citizens will feel the fury and think, quite rightly, that it is the Light in anger. It will weaken the haflings resolve." She tilted her head to one side. "Not that their running away will do them any good. I have sworn that they will all die." She added with a slight smile.

"Now sleep. I must prepare for Tonka's arrival."

Hutt eyed her balefully. "They party and you say sleep."

Nadir extended her hand and gently covered Hutt's eyes. "Not say – mouth that gurgles like a brook. I really mean sleep."

She removed her hand and gently pushed Hutt into a prone position. He was sound asleep.

Nadir's face etched into tender lines and her eyes gleamed with love as she watched him sleep. She turned away and looked at Aria who smiled at her. Nadir raised her eyebrows in a silent question; Aria smiled again and laid back. Nadir looked at the sleeping boy once more then turned her attention to her straw bag which was considerably thinner. She took a container filled with a pinkish powder and sprinkled it around the inner edges of the shack. Next, she mixed some of the same powder with water until it became a sloppy paste with which she spread over the walls and roof. Satisfied with her handiwork she repacked her bag and settled back to wait.

The noise from the haflings grew more excited as the night wore on and the wine they drank began to take effect. Occasionally there would be a single, shrill cry of pain when a hafling touched one of the rocks within the circle.

"Thee do not sleep, Aria?" said Nadir.

Aria sat up and rubbed at her eyes. "Do you know everything Guardian?"

"No. Thee breathing is too rapid for one that sleeps. Thee cubs will be watchful and restless for their parents set their example."

Aria touched her swelling stomach, "Perhaps it is as well. The legacy we leave will not be as I knew it."

"It will be safer than now," replied Nadir placidly.

"If they survive what will be their future?"

"The King will lead the faithful. Do not ask for more."

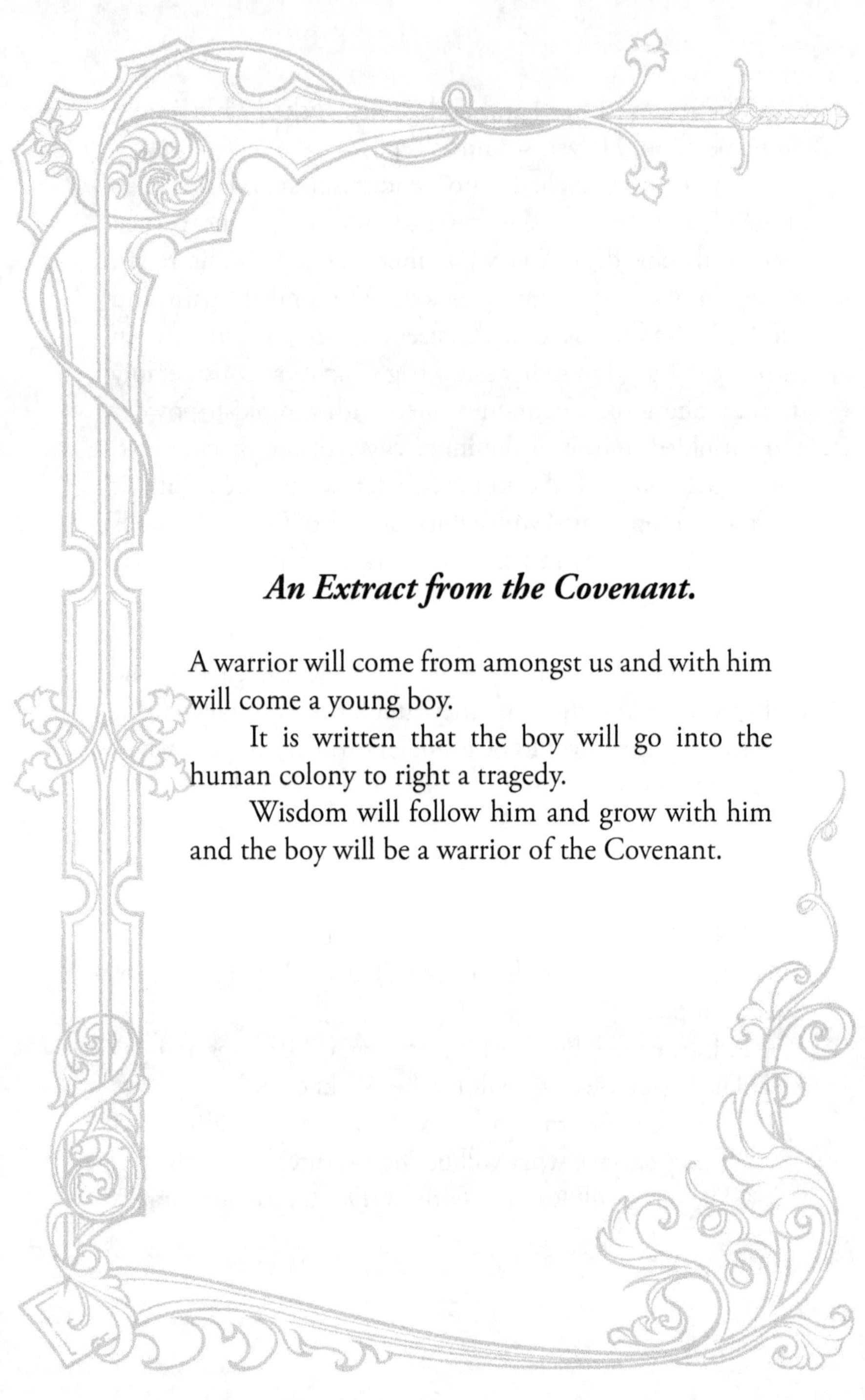

An Extract from the Covenant.

A warrior will come from amongst us and with him will come a young boy.

It is written that the boy will go into the human colony to right a tragedy.

Wisdom will follow him and grow with him and the boy will be a warrior of the Covenant.

Chapter 13

NADIR AND LIKEA

adir tilted her head and listened closely to the noise from outside. She rose to her feet and cautiously walked to the entrance and peered into the fire, with its light casting dancing shadows.

With widened-eyes, and without a moment to spare, she quickly glanced back at Aria and said urgently "Wake Hutt!" The moment Aria stirred him from sleep Nadir ordered them both outside with her in-front and close so she could protect them both at a moments notice.

The haflings had lit multiple fires around the shelter and now the night was almost as bright as day. Although the flames licked at the stones none passed over – even the smoke did not penetrate the shield.

Nadir stood her ground and watched calmly as the haflings parted to allow Tonka passage. He stopped at the stones and glared fiercely at Nadir.

"You live!" he exclaimed.

Nadir ignored him as she scanned the crowd that had accompanied him. Word of the sanctuary had obviously been passed on because with him he had brought twelve of his commanders.

"I told thee that it would be thee who died mutant, and not me." She said sweetly, sarcastically.

Tonka grimaced, exposing his long teeth and his eyes narrowed to slits in his anger and frustration.

"She witch! A cross breed of two species!" He gathered all the saliva in his mouth and spat at her.

Nadir gave a confident laugh. Some of the haflings retreated obviously shocked at seeing her alive.

Tonka saw some of them retreating into the shadows and he roared. The retreat ceased, and his attention returned to Nadir.

"You have trapped yourself. I have the numbers to force my way past your ineffective shield." He sneered.

"Thee do not listen to thee betters. I said thee have to die – not me," and she laughed again. Nadir deliberately turned her back to him and re-entered the shelter. Once out of his sight her pretence of nonchalance disappeared.

Both Aria and Hutt followed her in, not keen on wanting much empty space between them, she handed them both a small bottle of her cooking silver fire powder.

"He has a weakness in his chain. If I fail use this powder. Throw a pinch and they will be blinded for a few minutes. Go south – there are horses there for I heard them while I was within the Light. Seek them for thee legs will tire."

Hutt clutched at her arm. "What about you? What are you going to do?"

"To break my seal, he and his aides will concentrate all their power on one point. He has a weakness – one hafling woman has doubt in her heart. I will focus on her and redirect their force into this shelter. Come outside now for their strength is increasing."

Nadir walked past them to outside the shelter and pointed them to move closer to the far rim of the circle – and away from Tonka. She moved to the left of the group and stared at the hafling woman.

The air around the shelter crackled sharply as though charged with electricity. Nadir focused intently on the woman. The haflings perspired freely from the effort to focus; Nadir did too.

Suddenly a brilliant red light leapt along the line of haflings until it reached the woman. It channelled from her to Nadir. Nadir blinked and from her eyes, twin beams of the brilliant white light flashed and struck the shelter. The haflings screamed as they fell to the ground, terrified and instantly blinded.

The grass and brush burst into flames and it wasn't long before the flames found the paste that Nadir smeared on the walls. The whole of the night lit up from the searing white light. Huge fireballs flew into the air and hung, suspended, and burning fiercely.

Nadir blinked and shook her head to clear her vision. Tonka's army, those not blinded, fled from the terror that was Nadir.

She recovered quickly and ran to Aria and Hutt, pushing them over the stones, shouting at them run. Hutt regaining his sense of urgency, picking up a stout limb as he ran through the dazed haflings swinging the limb like a club, clearing a path for the women to follow.

On and on they ran until the flaming night was far behind them.

"How much longer will it last?" Asked Aria in between huge gasps for air.

"Not much longer. Only until they fall from the sky – save thee breath. Hutt turn more southerly – the horses are close."

Hutt obeyed and then as they all passed the tree line, they entered a small clearing where Hutt spotted the horses.

He glanced back over his shoulder and saw the balls of fire slowly waning and falling.

"They're falling," he shouted.

Nadir didn't answer nor looked back but both Aria and Hutt stopped.

"Come on!" Nadir shouted as she ran on.

They hastened to follow her, slowing their pace as they approached the horses. The herd took no notice of them but just simply continued grazing. Eventually a couple looked up and they to resumed eating.

Nadir slowed to a walking pace. "Keep back." She said quietly.

She touched the closest horse on the flank. Slowly running her hand over the horse until she reached the head. Hutt could barely hear her whispering and leaned forward to try to catch the words.

Suddenly a human figure stepped from the shadows of the hedgerow – his sword drawn. Nadir stepped away from the horse. Her lips peeled back in a snarl as she used a portion of her power to lock eyes with the human. The human sank to his knees in agony and collapsed onto the grass.

As she released her hypnotic stare, she became aware of the sounds of a scuffle behind her. She swung around, prepared to defend herself and burst out laughing. Aria was flicking the silver powder at the haflings and Hutt was clubbing each of the blinded mutants. Nadir laughed again and casually kicked her victim in the throat. She hurried to join her companions but as she neared, another figure brushed past her and flung himself into the pack of haflings.

By the faint night light Nadir could see his sword flash and the haflings fell before him. As the battle turned so did the haflings and they soon fled into the darkness. The newcomer watched them go before turning to face Nadir. He prostrated himself before her.

"Forgive me my Guardian I am late." He said.

Aria gave a cry of surprise and relief and clapped her hands together. "Likea! You are Likea!" she exclaimed, as she needed to convince herself that she was definitely looking at Likea.

Likea bowed to her and smiled. "Well met, my Lady." he said, sounding relieved.

He looked at Nadir. "Your wolf guided me, but he wouldn't leave the Forest and then I heard the wolf that sang, he guided me, but the way was long, and my progress was slow." He smiled at Aria. "The Light guided me this last distance. You battle well Lady."

"Ho! Horse Head. What about me?" demanded Hutt.

Likea's gaze found Hutt and appropriately pinched his ear. "The midget still crows. You are the finest warrior in the Kingdom. The finest." He said mockingly.

Hutt rubbed his ear and grinned broadly. "At last we have a warrior to join us. The women have only trickery and no skill," boasted Hutt.

Likea grinned and picked him up by the belt and shook him.

"'Tis a wonder that thee mouth hasn't been filled with straw."

Hutt struggled and Likea dropped him. Hutt sprang to his feet to attack but Likea held him off with one hand.

Aria watched their play with amusement, but Nadir spoke sternly.

"Oaf! We have no time for play; I can hear them coming."

She stalked off after the horses, when she was close enough, she whispered to them. Four horses broke away from the herd and came to her while the remainder galloped away in the direction of the Forest.

"Forgive me Guardian. My relief at finding you unharmed was too great to be still," pleaded Likea.

Nadir grunted. "It is as well thee arrived - my bag of magic is almost gone. Come, mount and we will ride."

Likea lifted Hutt and Aria onto their horses while Nadir's mount knelt, and she nimbly climbed onto its back.

"My brothers know you," said Likea in admiration.

She snorted. "My preference is for my own legs, but age does tell, and a horse is a fine a beast as any. They serve me well and I care for them."

"Which way do I go?" asked Aria.

"I cannot take thee to the Forest – that way is to destroy the Heir. The way south is barred by the swamp I have spoken of. To ride around the swamp is to ride through Tonka's army. Regardless of Hutt's brave words they are too strong and too many for us. That leaves only one option; to ride north to the human colony and the Plains. Tonka has been through the colony and I do not expect he has left much unsullied. We didn't cover much territory however." She shrugged. "It is the best I can think of." She added.

"But we came by the way – it is not safe." Hutt argued.

"When faced with no choices then thee will abide by my decision." Nadir looked at Likea. "I won't let thee take the Lady any other way." She added.

Likea grinned cheerfully. "North is good. I am of a mind to hear the singing wolf again."

Hutt scowled. "You are supposed to be a fierce warrior and leader."

Likea nodded kindly. "So it has been said, and I also live – wiser heads than mine saw to that and so I always listen to advise. You could do the same, Bantam."

"Don't call me Bantam. I am a woodsman son; Horse Head."

Likea laughed and urged his horse forward to catch the two women. Hutt mumbled something and glared at Likea's rear, but he too encouraged his horse and followed.

They rode without stopping until they reached the river. Likea led them downstream a-ways then reined in his horse.

"I crossed here. The water is swift but not too deep.' He said.

Both women encouraged their horses to enter the water, but Hutt hung back – reluctant to cross. Likea glanced back and returned to the bank.

"Well, woodsman son, it's a fine night for a swim."

Hutt glared at him. "Tis well known that horses are a mind to swim," he said sweetly. "Except their brains are so small that they cannot tell that they have legs and not fins."

With that he nudged his mount with his heels, and they entered the water. Likea, still laughing, followed.

Once on the other side of the river they rode again. Far to the right they could see dim lights belonging to a village, but Nadir kept the same rapid pace until Likea appeared alongside her.

"The horses cannot go any further. We will have to rest them."

"Yes. Keep thee eyes open for a haven that we may rest as well." She agreed.

Within minutes, Likia settled on a poorly vegetated hill. He found a small cave on the summit and escorted Aria to it.

"I will keep watch and Hutt can relive me," he said.

"Light will come soon but even Tonka must rest." Nadir muttered.

Nadir unknowingly dropped her guard for a moment and Likea clearly saw the worried expression reflected her face; Likea touched her hand.

"All is well, Guardian. Now rest. I will not be lonely – the wolf Velma is beyond for I hear him singing still."

Nadir gave him a small smile and settled down to sleep.

Nothing came close to them during the rest of the night. At first light Likea woke Hutt.

"I need to water the horses. There is a stream down there," he said pointing towards the far side base of the hill.

"Watch carefully Hutt. The light time is not friendly to us." He warned the boy.

"So, I have some uses then, Horse Breath?"

"I would need no other warrior beside me if you rode with me," Likea replied and Hutt blushed at the compliment.

Aria woke while Likea was away and she joined Hutt at his post. She greeted him easily and Hutt grinned. She sat on the hard ground beside him.

"Have you seen any sign of them?" she asked him.

Hutt nodded and pointed.

"A small party of haflings are down there but they haven't seen our tracks. I'm hungry. Do you think the Guardian has any food left?"

Aria laughed softly. "You have annoyed her so much she might not want to feed you."

Hutt grinned. "She will feed me if only to shut my mouth."

They sat in silence for a-while. Hutt watched Likea return with the horses. Hutt waved to him. Likea returned the wave and continued his way to settle down for deserved sleep.

"Lady, will the Guardian come with us to the Kingdom?" Hutt asked quietly.

Aria saw his misery and she placed an arm around his thin shoulders.

"She cannot Hutt. It is forbidden for her to do so." She answered him as gently as she could.

"But she has saved us both from Tonka. Won't the King forgive her?"

"I think he already has forgiven her family, but I am not sure that it is his decision. Besides if she leaves the Forest then there will be no one to be the Guardian." She paused for a moment – unsure how to phrase her next question.

"Will you miss her?"

Hutt nodded sadly. "I do not, of course, remember the comatose period when the Forest kept me, but I feel the same warmth from Nadir that I use to feel then."

Aria took his hands and held them tightly with her own. "If the Guardian leaves the Forest then all the others like you will never feel that warmth. You are special to her Hutt. Never would she have encountered one that she had nurtured, woken, and then met. You are the first of her own family that she has seen living but you cannot stay with her and she cannot leave the Forest."

Hutt wiped his eyes from the tears forming. "Do you really think she regards me as her son?"

Aria smiled warmly. "Yes. I do. Look she is awake and signalling to you. Go down now and I'll keep watch."

Nadir gave Hutt some food and then she carried a plate to Aria. She sat down beside her as she ate the meal.

"Thee do understand that he is not Vidal, don't thee, Aria? Thee understand that he is Hutt and that's the way it must be." Nadir asked her.

Aria nodded her understanding. "Yes – he is only Hutt."

"Good."

"And you Guardian, he asked if you would go with him to Sway?"

"What did thee tell him?"

"I told him that it was forbidden. I don't think he really understood why but he will. I will see that he learns the

Covenant of Light. I will look after him, Nadir. You have saved my cubs, so I can do no less then to care for one of yours."

"He is the first, thee know? I have seen others before, when I have gone into the colonies, but he is the first I have ever known."

They sat together, silently, each engrossed in private thoughts and memories until Nadir shrugged impatiently and stood up.

"I have work to do." She said, dusting herself down.

She turned to leave but stopped and touched Aria on the shoulder.

"See there," She pointed. "Thee eyes are sharper."

Aria stiffened. "Tonka," she whispered. "Tonka and his army. It is huge."

"Stay, hide, while I wake Likea," Nadir instructed and made haste. Likea heard her rapid approach because he sat before, she reached him.

"Tonka – he is coming!" Nadir cried.

Likea thrust his sword into his wide belt.

"Hutt! Gather the horses – Nadir pack!" he snapped. Likea raced to Aria who remained watching the group. He crouched beside her. "Tonka's army is now clearly visible. They're slowly making their way out of the woods and onto a wide belt of grazing land.

"We must run; there is no place for magic now." He said before glancing up as a cloud obscured the sunlight. The storm that had been threatening for the last two days was closing fast.

"The storm will slow them down but it won't stop them. He has many mounted troops, so they will still come even if the foot soldiers are slowed. We will also be slowed if the rain is heavy." He helped Aria to her feet, "Come Lady, there is nothing we can do here, and they have cut our sign."

He led their small party down the hill and Hutt brought the horses closer. Likea helped the others to mount and then he led the way north. Nadir galloped her mount to catch him.

"Can we outrun them?" she asked bluntly.

"No, our horses haven't had enough rest," he grimly replied.

"That's what I thought. We need time to delay them and still keep ourselves safe."

"Delay! Guardian? There is no other army save Tonka's between here and freedom."

"Do not give up. We only need time so pray for some." Nadir said sternly.

"The storm is close maybe that will help a little," replied Likea.

Nadir looked up at the clouds. "The storm will save us this day, but we need one more night. Use your head warrior – find us a fortress that can be defended by four."

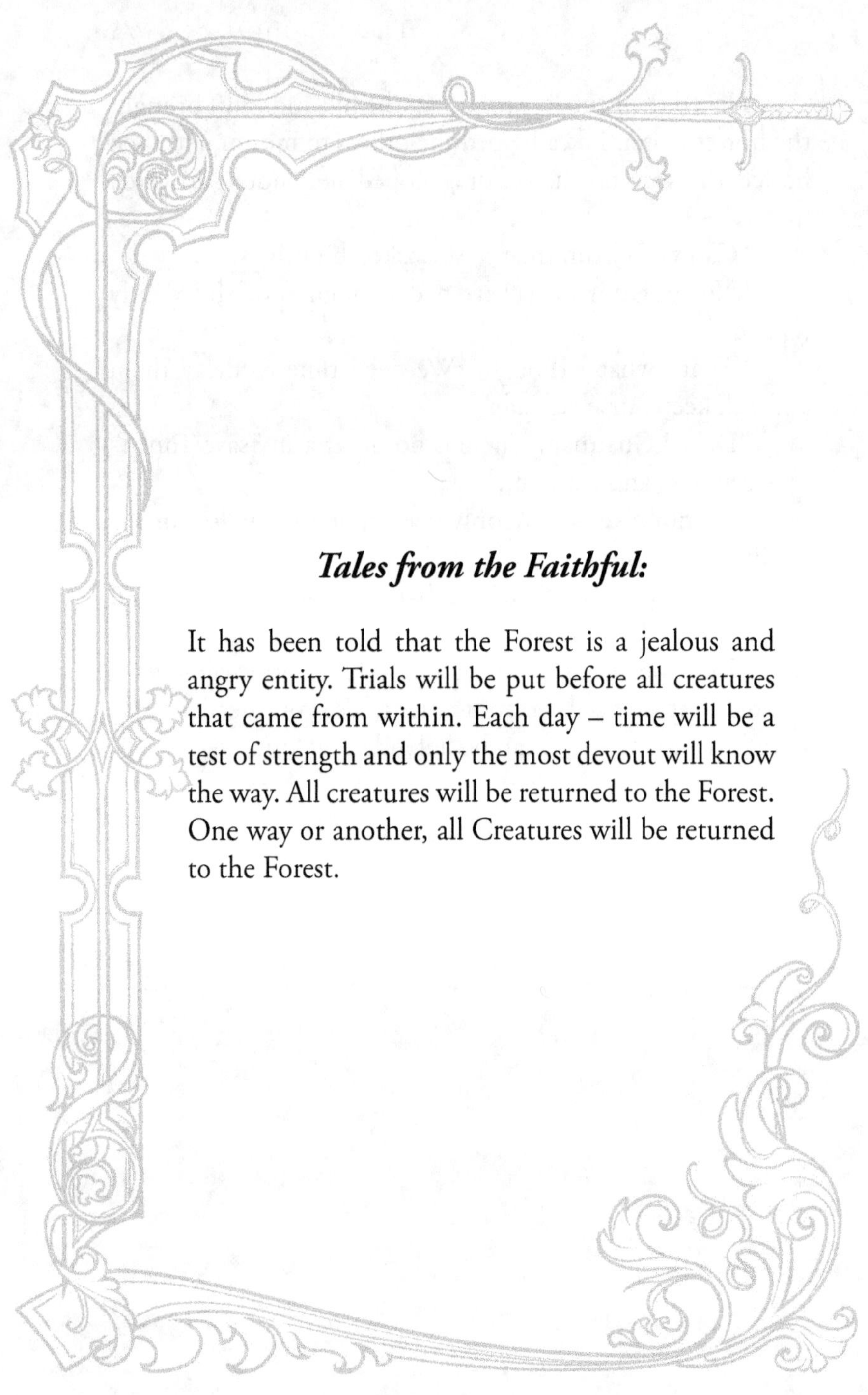

Tales from the Faithful:

It has been told that the Forest is a jealous and angry entity. Trials will be put before all creatures that came from within. Each day – time will be a test of strength and only the most devout will know the way. All creatures will be returned to the Forest. One way or another, all Creatures will be returned to the Forest.

Chapter 14

THE PROTECTOR OF SWAY

"**S**ire! You cannot leave the Kingdom! To do so is to invite war," pleaded Jayca.

"What would you have me do then, Advisor? I cannot remain idle when I have not received any word from Likea!" Roared the King.

"Patience. You must remain patient. There are armies gathering on every border. If you leave, they will march on the Kingdom. You are the only being able to hold them out. Sire, none of them want war, but to protect the Hiatus and Proto Forests there needs to be a leader. They think they are doing the right thing but to fight amongst themselves is wrong. You have to stay."

"There hasn't been any word!" The King said angrily slapping his fists against the tabletop to stress his displeasure however, Jayca stood firm.

"Clear your head, My Liege, My Lord. You have some news; you know Tonka has marched. Reports of atrocities are coming in daily. Refugees have spilled over into the Kingdom. They must be fed and sheltered, and they need to be vetted, making sure none are contaminated. These are problems that we need to address and deal with now. Whatever happens to those pretenders who seek your throne isn't important. Your duty is to destroy Tonka and his mutants. Plan his demise but don't leave the Kingdom. Not yet Lord, not yet.

The King slumped into a chair and covered his eyes with his hands. Jayca waited a moment for the King had composed himself.

"My Liege – Likea and Hutt are not alone. All that is the Hiatus is with them," he said gently.

The King raised his head and looked at his Advisor.

Calmly and slightly nodding he responded "Yes," then with squaring his shoulders and sitting straighter in the chair the King repeated "Yes. Jayca, are we ready for war?"

Jayca nodded. "The woodsmiths have had most of the bamboo fields cut, and they are working two shifts to produce spears and swords. The armoury is full. We have sent two wagon loads towards the northern border. With the wagons we sent horses, donkeys and recruits. The recruits are pouring in, so many in fact that some other services have been left short-handed."

"Are they all volunteers?"

"Yes Sire. Likea's action has spurred a rush of pride and the horse platoons are filling rapidly."

The King nodded in understanding. "Send Essura to me – I would speak to him."

Jayca bowed and quickly left. He nodded to Essura who was standing outside the room giving silent instruction for Essura to enter as the King would speak with him. Essura acknowledged and entered the building. He stood and waited until the King turned away from the window to face him and respectfully bowed.

"Your word, Sire?" he said.

"Give me the latest reports," ordered the King and pointed to a map spread on the table.

Essura hastily made his way to the table and picked up the marker stick. "The Plains army has mustered on their border. The other armies are forming along these lines. Most of those armies are small and I don't think they are very well lead. The birds report that there is extensive activity out on the Plains. The Emir must have recalled all warriors. They have been raising dust for days now."

The King looked pensive. Using his index finger, he pointed to the woods north of the Forest. "Then the woods are clear – no armies?"

"So it seems, Sire, but there are strange happenings within that area." Essura frowned with deep furrows across his brow. He continued to stare at the map until the King commanded him to continue. "We have not received any reports from there at all and that is a problem. Nothing seems to be getting out of that area.' His scowl deepened. "It is only a feeling, Sire, but we know Tonka marched north of the Badlands. That is a fact but what if he circled the Forest and entered the human colony. By now he would be or could be in the woods." He tapped his teeth with a nail, a sure sign he was thinking. "We aren't getting any refugees from there, although they do have a way to travel."

The King closed his eyes. "Tonka. Yes, he could have bypassed the Plains army because it is only massing now. If he marched as soon as we left the Badlands, he could have slipped past Aria's father." He clenched his fists and hammered at the tabletop. "That would explain the silence from the woods." He stalked over to the window and looked at the mass actively outside. "What is the state of the Kingdom's force?" he demanded.

Essura smiled, his dark eyes glinted. "Full strength, Sire." He said proudly. "And more arrive each day. We even have more than thirty wings assembled."

Jayca re-entered the room and stood silently beside Essura.

"Where are they deployed? I know they aren't all here." The King turned and gave his full attention to Essura. "What have you done with them?"

"Two days past I ordered three squads of twenty soldiers to each of the sections where the pretenders have massed. I have sent ninety cheetahs to the Plains border." He looked at the King.

"Why?" asked the King.

"Sire, I have no reason except a feeling that Tonka is or has been to the human colony. This is based only on the lack of information coming from that area."

The King glanced at Jayca. "You tell me to wait so what did you tell Essura?"

Jayca shuffled his feet, eyes downcast. "Essura is very persuasive."

For the first time in days the King smiled.

"Essura we must wait. We must wait. Tonka is not going to escape me this time. Take your army closer to the river that separates the Woodlands from Sway. Tonka is your target. If he attacks the Kingdom, then he is yours. Understand me Essura, he is not to breathe one minute longer than the time it takes your sword to strike his neck."

Essura bowed low.

"That will be my pleasure, Sire."

He departed with a spring in his step. Before the doors firmly closed the King and Jayca could hear him shouting for his commanders.

The King stared at the map. "Where is Likea? Where? Where?" he muttered.

Jayca watched in silence.

It was Jayca who woke him. He touched the King on the shoulder and the old warrior was instantly awake.

"What is it? Is there word of Likea and Hutt?" demanded the King.

"I'm sorry, Sire. There has been no word from them but there is a message from the Woodland." He paused long enough for the King to glare at him. "Speak!"

"The word has come from Essura. I cannot be sure that he didn't misunderstand as the message is strange. I questioned the messenger, but he swears the message is accurate..." He stopped again, looking worried and puzzled.

"Am I to wait all night?" Demanded the King.

Jayca collected himself – he stood straighter as though on parade.

"The message is odd and according to Essura it was carried on the wind. It came from a wolf human from the Woodland."

The King tensed, his manner suggesting that he was fully alert. "Did you say carried on the wind?"

"Yes, Sire. Essura said it almost sounded like a song. But the distance was great, and he apologises if the message is misleading."

The King smiled and gave a short sigh of relief.

"This message is from one that I know. You dolt, Jayca. The message is from the Guardian."

"The Guardian! Why is the guardian in the Woodland? It is forbidden."

The King shrugged. "What is the message? Her reasons must be sound for she has not contacted me for many seasons. The message, Jayca."

As he spoke, he flung aside the rug and swung his legs from the bed. He strode to the table and stared at the map.

"Well?" he demanded.

"Essura said that it is incomplete – all we have is – a child, a mother and a Royal." That is all...apart from a rough idea of a location." He added.

"Show me the location."

Jayca marked the map with a piece of chalk.

The King nodded. "Yes. Yes! I see it now. They are here, and Tonka is closing. Pray that we are in time."

"Tonka?"

"Yes Tonka. The Guardian is with her. Good. Good! She will give us a little time. Good."

The King began pacing up and down the length of the room. Jayca watched fretfully. He was still puzzled, and it was shown by the deep frown that etched his forehead.

"What to do? The Guardian is there, and she has much power, but she is only one. What to do?" mumbled the King. Jayca did not respond to the rhetorical question.

After some minutes, Jayca cleared his throat noisily. The King awoke from his thoughts and infuriatingly glanced at him.

"Do you have a suggestion?" he asked.

"Sire, I am concerned, I don't know what has excited you." Jayca complained. "What does the message mean?"

The King laughed and slapped him on the back. "Old friend thee age is showing. The Guardian has brought Aria from the Forest and into the Woodland. Tonka is after them, the message is plain, the method of delivery is different. But the Guardian was probably hard pressed at the time she passed it."

"Then we have to go into the Woodland and rescue Lady Aria." Replied Jayca with understanding now dawning.

"Yes, and without delay. The Guardian has never asked for help before, so their plight must be serious."

The King began to pace again while Jayca studied the map and marked in Essura's new position. Abruptly the King ceased his pacing and Jayca could see that he had made a decision.

"Send a message to Essura and inform him to make haste over the river and beyond as he is needed out there. Send me the air patrol leaders now and wake the army for we march. This night we march." Ordered the King.

Jayca left at a run and could be heard shouting orders both near and far. He returned minutes later and entered with some of air wings. Minutes more passed, and the rest raced into the Kings' rooms.

"I have need of all your flights. The Lady Aria is found but she is in danger from Tonka. The Lady carries the Heir to Sway and thus the Kingdom has a rightful Heir."

He held up his hand to stop the cheering. "Nay. Do not cheer. She is in danger and our way is not yet clear. I want all your squadrons' air borne. I need the fastest to fly to the map reference Jayca has marked. In that vicinity you will find and protect Lady Aria, the young boy Hutt and one other. Likea too, maybe, if he has caught them. Now go." The warriors raced from the room without delay. The King waited for the noise to abate and addressed the rest of the bird wings." The slower birds need to carry the most important message of their lives. Carry the message of the Lady, of the Heir and their peril. Carry it to all parts of the Kingdom. Carry it to the Plains, to the colonies and beyond. Tell the message to the armies that mass on our borders. Tell it to the women who stay at home. Tell it to all you see. Go now and fly." Ordered the King.

The commanders bowed hurriedly and almost ran from the room so great was their urgency.

The King called one officer back.

"Preston stay – for you I have a special mission." The King beckoned him to the table. "Jayca order the army to rise. Don't wait for the stragglers we must march tonight. Make sure the food wagons are hitched to strong beasts for the army must be fed. Then you leave and find Essura and send him about his mission. Tell him to have the cheetahs move at best speed to relieve the Lady Aria."

"Yes Sire. What of you – do you stay?"

The King smiled and his eyes gleamed. "First I will see my bride. I ride but a few minutes behind you and if you tarry then I ride ahead of you. Tonka is mine."

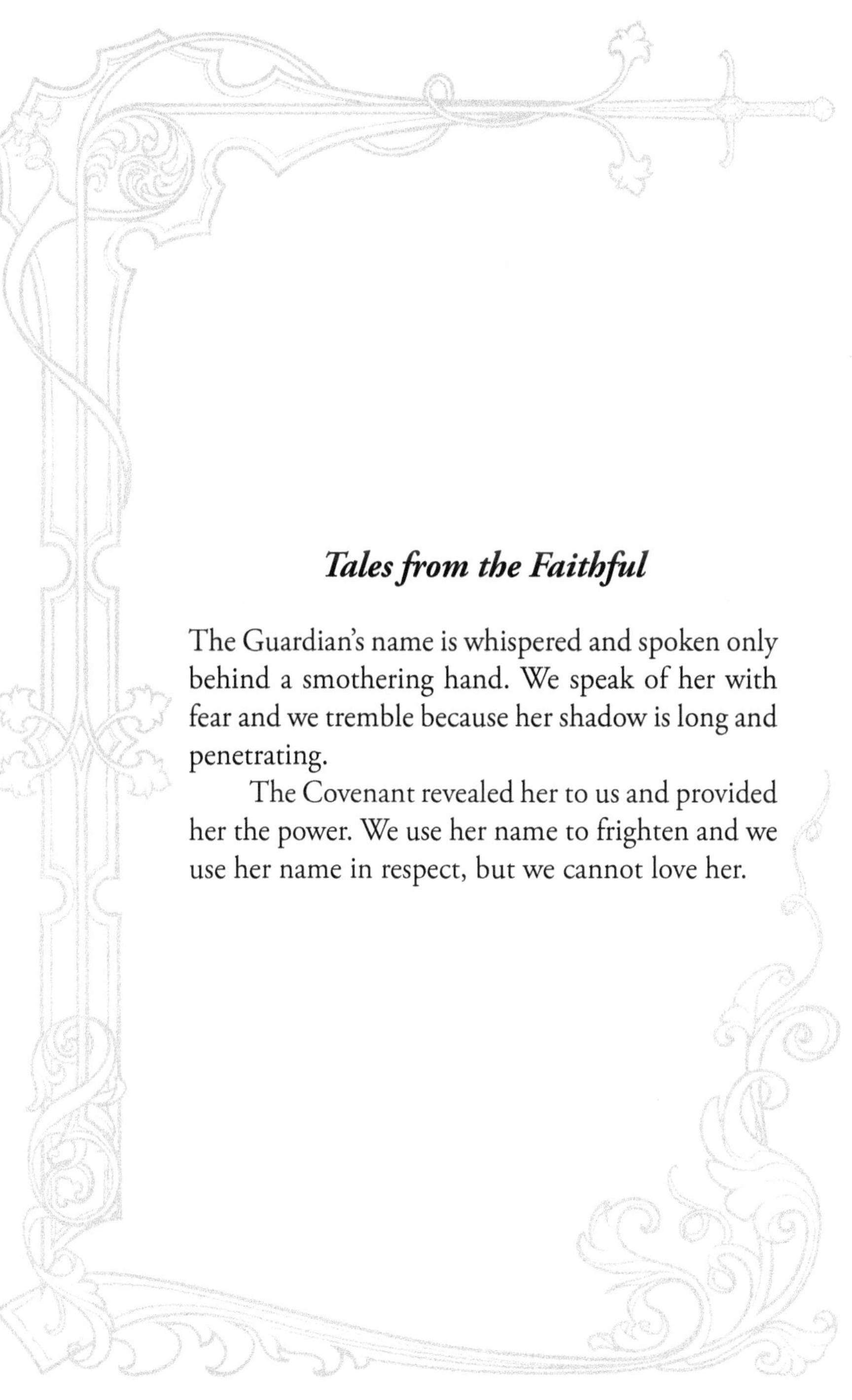

Tales from the Faithful

The Guardian's name is whispered and spoken only behind a smothering hand. We speak of her with fear and we tremble because her shadow is long and penetrating.

The Covenant revealed her to us and provided her the power. We use her name to frighten and we use her name in respect, but we cannot love her.

Chapter 15

SANCTUARY

All that day the storm remained a few leagues behind them. Hutt stared in awe at the spectacle that was the black sky that chased them but never caught them.

Likea pressed on until he was forced to call a halt. Reluctantly he dismounted and signalled the others to halt.

"We cannot travel any further on these mounts." He said and helped Aria down while Hutt simply slid off his horse. Nadir too dismounted. She gave thanks to her horse and freed him from their bond.

She glanced behind them to look at the storm. "Has thee a plan for although the storm has slowed them – still they come?" she said.

"I haven't a plan, but I think I have found a fortress. We won't be able to stop them for eventually they will overrun us in numbers, but we will gain some time while they force us out. See over there?" He pointed to a steep rocky outcrop. All but one side was unclimbable. The side that they would have to climb was covered in thousands of loose stones and pebbles.

"With those stones we fight. They will have to climb to reach us, but only a few of them at a time will be able to climb that narrow path. The other sides are sheer, so we should be able to defend ourselves for a while."

Nadir returned her gaze to the storm. "Yes, we will have one more night. Release these beasts Likea, send them home. They can do no more for us; they have served us well."

Hutt lead the way up the narrow path. At times he was on all fours as the loose stones slipped from under his feet. Likea assisted Aria with Nadir following. By the time they had reached the top all four of them were grazed and bruised from numerous falls. Just short of the summit, Nadir stopped and spread the last of the silver powder she used to illuminate the dark.

"This will give us light to see them coming."

Nadir grimaced as she tipped her bag upside down. "A little food and water are all I have left."

"Good," said Hutt. "I am hungry."

"When are you not?" laughed Aria.

"We will wait for the rest of the day before we eat and that way the night will not feel so long." Nadir decided for them, none complained. Likea nodded in agreement and Hutt looked dejected.

"How long will it be before the storm reaches us?" asked Aria.

"However long Tonka takes. The storm is not for us – it is all his." replied Nadir with satisfaction.

"Did you make that?" Asked Likea, but Nadir shook her head and laughed.

"Goodness no! The Forest did. My power is weak compared to the Hiatus. The Forest could sense that I needed help. When Tonka struck me with his sword, he enraged the Forest and the storm is the result of that anger."

She looked Aria. "Rest child. This time I do not have a potion to give if thee are captured. This time thee strength needed must come from another source. Likea and Hutt have a wall to build before darkness comes – then they too can rest."

"I don't need a potion. I am at peace. I can help them build for I am not tired."

"Then thee should be for I am," replied Nadir tartly.

Likea and Hutt worked swiftly and soon had a chest high wall built around the top of the hill. They made piles of smaller stones inside the barrier. The storm continued to encroach slowly as Tonka's army was completely shrouded in cold, driving rain.

Nadir watched the approaching tempest closely and once when Likea paused in his labour, he could see that she was intoning prayer after prayer. When the wall was complete, she prepared some of the little food she has remaining and after it was consumed, and everyone had their fill, she ordered them all to rest while she kept watch.

In the rapidly fading light, Nadir watch over Tonka's army arriving at the foot of the crag. She witnessed them set up camp for the night. They tried to make small campfires but every stick; every blade of grass was saturated with water. They were strangely quiet for such a large force.

The storm settled in around the hill and although no rain fell on the top of the crag, Tonka's army was still obscured by the driving downpour.

Sometime during the darkness Hutt woke and with sleep eluding him, he quietly stood up and made his way to Nadir where he joined her watching their enemies gather. He took Nadir's hand and she gripped his fingers with hers.

"Are thee afraid?" she asked softly.

"No." He smiled. "For you are here."

"Good. Son of a woodsman. With such faith, Tonka will be defeated and destroyed."

They sat together in comfortable silence until the others woke. Nadir left them to go rest and so it was Hutt who witnessed the second of Tonka's armies to arrive – this time they emanated from the west. They had not been hindered by the rain and approached swiftly. They were a smaller army than the one Tonka led, but they were more confident because their laughter rose over the noise of the storm. They had made their camp outside the rainfall area and they successfully lit fires, soon the smell of cooking flesh drifted to the crag causing Aria to awaken and Hutt to gag.

"That is where the danger will come from, Hutt, they have not been exposed to the elements," said Likea.

"Perhaps we should gather a few more stones." Suggested Hutt and Likea laughed.

Although they kept watch all day, Tonka made no move to climb the hill. The rain fell incessantly obscuring the main army but even the second army made no effort to engage. The storm expanded slightly and now engulfed the second army. To the relief of Aria and Hutt the rain doused the fires and the odour of cooking meat ceased.

When darkness enveloped the land, Nadir rose and issued the last of the food.

"When will the storm clear?" Likea asked.

"On the morrow."

"Then Tonka will withdraw his soldiers until the ground dries. He will attack because he knows that we cannot withdraw and now he can wait."

The night passed uneventfully and when dawn came Tonka withdrew the bulk of his army to the plains. He moved the second army to the base of the hill. By midmorning the rainstorm began to clear. The rain slowed and stopped while the sun ate the clouds. That's when the haflings took the opportunity to begin their assault and started to make their way up the narrow path.

They climbed two abreast along the narrow walkway. Many slipped and fell on the loose gravel but still they came shouting and screaming until at last they were within meters to the stone wall.

Likea and Hutt pushed with all their strength at a temporary wall they created together. The wall shook and collapsed, causing a vast slide. Shouts of jubilation changed to screams of pain as the crumbled wall took the ground from under the haflings feet and sent the soldiers skidding to the bottom of the hill.

Likea watched in satisfaction at the chaos. He nodded in pleasure, but his words were dire. "We won't be so lucky next time." he warned.

He and Hutt set to work immediately building another wall. They had finished building it just in time as the second assault commenced. This time, the haflings commenced the attack by advancing in single file and slowly, carefully placing their feet.

Likea picked up his sword and Hutt pulled his knife from inside his jerkin. They lay side by side and waited until the haflings were close for shorthand combat.

When he judged the haflings were close enough, Likea stood up and kicked at the wall. This time the stones didn't slip as much and most of the haflings avoided rocks. The first three that climbed to the top were quickly dispatched by Likea's sword. He stepped forward a pace and met the charge full on, but now, the enemy numbers were increasing, and he was forced back. An arrow fired from the base of the hill and struck his arm causing blood to pour down his tunic.

Aria picked up a large stone and hurled it at the nearest hafling. He reeled and screamed in pain as the missile struck him in the face. Hutt, stayed crouched behind the remaining part of the wall, and stabbed with his knife as the haflings pushed past him. From his position he could only stab at their legs; he was very successful at this mode of attack for the haflings either fell to the ground or fell backwards. Aria and Nadir kept throwing stones while Likea used his sword to pick up the fire hardened spear he had made the evening before and stabbed at any mutant that passed Hutt. Under the pressure being asserted by the defenders, the haflings again withdrew from the missile range but some reached for their bows. Likea spotted their actions and pushed the two women behind a large boulder.

"Keep down." he shouted.

He made to move back to Hutt, but Nadir grabbed his arm and stopped him.

"Look!" She pointed to the south.

Likea glanced up and a sudden grin flashed wickedly.

"The King has sent the falcons!" he shouted. "Come on Hutt – we must give them time to transform."

He scooped up rocks the size of his hand and began hurling them down the slope. Several of the projectiles found targets but the haflings still managed to release their arrows. Most were ill-aimed and fell harmlessly but three found their mark. Two thudded into Likea's chest while one hit Hutt. Witnessing the exchange, Nadir ran from behind the boulder and quickly pulled Hutt to cover. Likea, ignoring his injury was joined by Aria and they continued to throw stones. Not long after, another pair of willing hands was beside him followed by another and another all throwing whatever projectiles they could get their hands on. Under the savage bombardment the haflings withdrew to the bottom of the crag.

Likea stood up from his crouching position when he coughed and staggered a step. Strong hands steadied him and helped him to sit. "Jaberill!" he cried and smiled.

"Must you always take on a whole army?" complained the falcon warrior.

Likea grinned. "Tis only a small part of an army." He protested.

Jaberill grunted and looked down the slope.

"Tis more than enough. Let us see to your wounds, there is more fighting to come."

"How did you know?" Likea asked through another attack of the coughs.

"A singing wolf told the King." Jaberill answered with a laugh.

He helped Likea behind the boulder to where Aria and Nadir were attending to Hutt.

Likea looked at Nadir." You sent a message, you didn't say."

Nadir shrugged. "The distance was great – it might not have been possible, so I said nothing." She replied.

Likea looked at Hutt. "How is he?" he asked anxiously.

"It isn't much more than a deep scratch – he will bear a scar as a memento." Nadir retorted but Likea could hear the relief in her voice.

Turning toward Likea, Nadir peeled open Likea's shirt and inspected the wounds.

"It is the fault of having such a broad chest," she said. "Thee make a larger target. No matter, the arrowhead is not in very deep, I'll soon cut them out."

Likea looked down at his chest. "Tis as well the haflings weren't any closer."

"They were close enough," said Nadir tartly. "Thee plaited coat took the brunt of the force."

She cut away the flesh that surrounded the arrow heads and wiggled them free. A look of distaste marred her face as she dropped them onto the ground and stamped on them. "Disgusting abominations." She muttered.

She took the cloth that Aria had smeared with a delicate blue paste and wiped it over the wounds. Likea winced. Nadir glanced at him and snorted.

"Aria tear his shirt and bind the cloth to his flesh." She said as she stood up. She smiled a little as she glanced down at him. "A word, after Aria has finished then refit thee coat. It seems to be good protection against arrow."

Likea laughed but his smile faded when he looked over at Hutt.

"The boy is comatose!" He exclaimed.

"No. I have willed him to sleep. Tis better that he rests a moment. We haven't any protection against the arrows. If we are overrun the sleep will be his reward."

"There will be no more fighting on this hillside this day." Jaberill uttered softly. "Look out there." He pointed. "That's Orthe, Booth and the cheetahs. Essura had them on the border as soon as he had word from the King. They have been coming this way these two days past. We flew over them some leagues back."

He looked at Likea. "Our turn now. Rest awhile, Warrior. We will see this crag free of haflings and defend our Queen and Heir." He grinned. "We will be back for dinner."

The cheetahs halted two hundred paces from the haflings. Half kept watch the other half transformed into warrior form. The weapons that had been fastened to the animals' bodies fell loose but were quickly regained by the warriors. They wasted no time and charged at the haflings, falling upon them furiously. Jaberill sent half of his warriors down the hill, instructing them to fall upon the haflings from the rear. The fighting ensued ferociously; the haflings fought in a mad frenzy while the Kingdom warriors were methodical in their actions. Once the second half of the cheetahs transformed it soon became apparent the Kingdom warriors were gaining ground. The haflings found themselves too close and were unable to use their arrows so the fighting resorted to hand to hand.

On top of the crag, the relief fighters were rebuilding the wall. Jaberill stood beside Likea as they watched the fury taking place below them. Jaberill grinned widely when he saw the haflings beginning to retreat.

Nadir came and stood beside them and sadly shook her head at the carnage and looked away.

"How much longer will they fight?" she asked.

"Not long now," answered Likea. "Why do you ask?"

Nadir looked at him grimly. "Because Tonka is trying to make his way back here through the mud."

Jaberill looked startled and jerked around.

Tonka was trying to advance but the viscous mud was causing havoc with both horse and warrior.

"What do you think Likea?" he asked.

"Some of the front ranks will reach here, but they will churn the mud so badly the bulk of the army won't get through until the ground dries."

"Likea I am going down. I have woken Hutt; keep him out of mischief." Nadir said.

"No, you can't go down!" Likea protested and made to grab her arm.

"I must. Some of the cheetahs are hurt and I must attend them."

"Nadir, you can't go. Tonka would give anything to have you."

She looked up at him and her lips twitched. "Likea thee can't stop me you know."

He scowled at her "Then I will come with you."

"No! What I need to do is not for thee eyes. Instead, find us some food and some wood and make weapons for the falcons. If Tonka decides to climb this hill, I think we will run out of stones to throw."

She glanced at Aria who had joined them.

"No Aria thee can't come either. More than ever your safety is paramount."

She looked at their sombre faces. "Oh, for the love of trees! I'll come back in good time if Tonka looks threatening. Don't upset Hutt; he's likely to follow."

Nadir clutched her nearly empty bag tighter and stepped over the opening in the wall. Both Likea and Aria watched as she gingerly made her way down the path and briskly stride over to a fallen cheetah.

"Thee name, cheetah?" she asked as she knelt beside him.

"Merrlah." He said bravely.

"Merrlah, I believe I can help thee. Thee wound is large but tis just a cut. With thee permission I will sew it together and then have thee taken to the sanctuary of the hilltop."

"Are you a healer?"

"Yes."

Merrlah managed a smile. "I hurt, make me better."

Nadir placed her hand over his eyes for but a moment and when she removed it the cheetah was sound asleep. Using thread from her bag and a sharp thorn Nadir quickly pulled the gaping wound together. Not stopping to admire her work she sprinkled a little powder from a small box over the wound then called to two cheetahs standing nearby.

"Carry him to the hilltop." She ordered. Not pausing to see if they did so she moved on to another. She bent over him, brushing hair back from his forehead.

"Cheetah, thee name, if thee please."

The soldier slowly opened his eyes. "Wivven." he gasped.

"Wivven, thee injury is severe. I might be able to help, or I can give thee to the Light.

The journey to the Light is painless and joyful but I cannot give thee the Second Life for we are too far from the Forest."

"My gut is open, isn't it?" he whimpered.

Nadir nodded.

Boldly, facing the truth of his situation Wivven said "Then give me to the Light, My Lady. I would look on your beautiful face as I go."

Nadir's eyes filled with tears as she prayed for the Light to take this soul.

The soldier smiled as he left his world.

Nadir held him a few minutes longer then slowly released him. She stood up, wiping away her tears. In the meantime, Likea descended the crag to stand beside Nadir. Likea took her hand briefly and shared her misery. She regained her composure and turned to face Likea. She opened her mouth to berate him but stopped when she saw him signal to two soldiers. The men picked up their comrade and carried him tenderly to the base of the hill where others waited to bury their friend.

"There are more wounded over there." Likea said gently.

"Thee must be hard of hearing." Nadir replied as she turned and walked to where he was pointing.

Most injuries were cuts or broken bones. Nadir attended to everyone with the same ease and compassion she had shown from the first. For the broken bones she had the uninjured moving in all directions to gather pieces of wood to be used as splints.

Those that had already died Nadir stood over them and spoke the buried lament. Likea didn't interfere but stood back from her while she worked. He kept a watchful eye on Tonka's advance and the distance Nadir was moving away from the hill. When Nadir would stand up, he would signal the soldiers to come and carry the wounded to the sanctuary.

Nadir finally stood up and rubbed her lower back. Likea came to her.

"Guardian, we are almost too far away to be safe." He said softly.

She nodded. "Are there anymore?"

"Just one. He must have been one of the first to fall, he has an arrowhead buried in his stomach."

"Where is he?' she asked.

Likea paused; when he didn't answer she turned to face him.

"Where is he?" she repeated.

Likea sadly shook his head. "'Tis not a man, but a woman."

Nadir stared at him. "A woman?"

Likea bowed his head. "They let females train in the cheetah squads. In the rush to move, the commander had forgotten to order her stay behind so she ran with males."

"Where is she?"

He pointed to small dip in the ground. "We lay her there."

Nadir handed Likea her bag and walked briskly to the woman. She knelt beside her and gathered her in her arms.

"Thee name, sister?" she asked.

"Veena." She whispered and groaned.

"I am the Forest's Guardian, named Nadir. I will try to remove the evil buried within thee but I might not succeed. Or I can give thee to the Light, Veena. What is thee wish?"

"Will I be able to breed?" she asked weakly.

Nadir looked at the exposed wound. The blood still oozed but she could see the broken arrow.

"No. The foulness is embedded in a part required for reproduction."

Veena gave a slight smile. "Tis well I have offspring then. I want to see them again, Guardian. They are so small and vulnerable."

"Do thee want me to try?"

Veena nodded. "My trust in you is complete, my Guardian. If I fail to be strong enough then I still have the joy of the Light."

Nadir signalled Likea to bring her bag. He hurried over and passed it to her.

"Will you cut it out?"

Nadir pulled a small knife from the bag. "Yes."

"Guardian, just know the light will fade soon and the enemy is approaching." He warned her.

"Then have Jaberill, wait, no, even better, the cheetah commander, push them back. This woman is a mother and should not be here. But she is and will die unless I defile her body and remove the abomination and all because he forgot to order her to stay behind." Nadir snapped. "I want a large fire for I must have light to see by. Then leave me for what I am about to do is not for thee. This time listen to me and obey."

While Likea set the fire, Nadir gathered Veena in her arms. With one hand she closed Veena's eyes and whispered words of prayer and so Veena slept, free from pain.

Nadir lay her back down and carefully removed the bloodied tunic. Using a cloth Nadir wiped the wound free of the blood and dirt, and then she packed another cloth around the wound and took up her knife.

Time passed slowly. Likea stayed back, behind the fire, which he attended to diligently. Mostly he looked at the crouched form of Nadir and the prone figure of Veena. As the night deepened, he could make out a very pale green coloured bubble that seemed to engulf both women. He observed carefully but the bubble neither increased nor got any smaller and since Nadir didn't seemed perturbed in any way, he accepted that whatever it was it was harmless. Occasionally he looked up to the hill. Jaberill also lit a large fire and Likea could see darkened figures moving but the distance was too far to make out who the figures were, but he hoped Hutt was safe and that Jaberill had the boy in hand. Likea smiled a little as he recalled the tantrum from the boy when he realised that he was going down to Nadir.

From there he looked to the base of the rocky outcrop; there he could see the cheetahs keeping watch for Tonka. Tonka's soldiers had moved closer but as darkness fell, their forward thrust seemed to halt and while they weren't silent, the voices and calls from the haflings remained muted and seemed to come no closer. Likea hoped the cats were alert. Instinctively, Likea tensed and cocked his head to one side. From overhead he could hear sounds of a bird in flight. The night was too dark, and he could see nothing but staring intently at the hilltop he could see rapid movements, indicating the bird had landed there. Likea looked at Nadir who was engrossed in whatever she was doing and wondered if he should leave her and go to Aria. Since there was no commotion coming from camp he decided to stay where he was. After few minutes he heard quickened footsteps. He gripped his staff firmer and faced the sound. Hutt abruptly appeared at his side and Likea heaved a sigh of relief.

"I was wondering how long it would be before you appeared." He said sternly and quietly.

Hutt just grinned at him. "Jaberill was distracted."

"I suppose so. Who was the bird?"

"An owl. I didn't wait to see,"

"You shouldn't be here, Hutt."

"I won't distract her, Likea but I had to come. She might need me." Hutt said seriously.

In the light from the fire Likea could see how earnest Hutt was. He nodded and placed his hand on Hutt's shoulder. Together, they silently sat watching Nadir.

Nadir eased the cramp in her lower part of her back. Taking a moment to rest she looked at the sleeping woman. She looked peaceful, without any trace of pain but her breathing was irregular. She picked up her knife and once more started to carefully cut around the arrowhead. The arrow had shattered on impact and pieces were embedded in several places. Finally, withdrawing the final shard piece and adding it to the small pile of bone shards beside her; in the irregular light from the blazing fire she carefully scrutinised the wound. She couldn't visibly see any more pieces except the largest shard still penetrating a bloody kidney and resting on a rib bone. Nadir's hand hovered over the shard and her hand trembled as she moved to cut. Her lips were moving in a constant prayer as she increased the tempo. Her hand steadied and with some confidence she boldly cut the flesh, soon the arrow came out. She quickly dropped the mass and rapidly tied off the blood flow. She gave a sigh of relief when the bleeding stopped and then gave thanks to the Light. She took another thread from her bag and began to sew the wound edges together. When she had tied off the last knot she sat back on her heels and watched the peace etched into the woman's face.

Slowly the greenish bubble disappeared, and the darkness of the night covered the women, now only the light from the fire flickered across them.

Nadir wiped her bloody hands on a cloth then wrapped the remnants of the arrow and the pieces of flesh together in parcel and tied the parcel tightly with cord. She leant over Veena, gently brushing her fingers over the serene face and with that action she woke her. Veena's eyes fluttered then opened, immediately a grimace of pain creased her face.

"I know it is painful but bear it for a moment," said Nadir. "I have done all I can. The arrow is removed but I have had to remove some of your flesh. With rest and care thee should live. My question to which I must have an answer is this. Will thee accept the life knowing a part of thee is no longer there or shall I give thee to the Light?"

"I accept. My children need me." Veena whispered.

"Then now thee will sleep and be pain free."

"Thank you, Guardian." Veena managed to say before she, once more, slept.

Nadir slowly rose to her feet, stumbling a little as the pins and needles in her feet ran riot. Waiting until the tingling started to disappear, she picked up the little parcel and walked over to Likea.

"Bring some of the cheetahs over. They must carry her, very carefully, to the hilltop. She won't wake but they must be careful, for I have sewn the wound together."

As Likea hurried away, her gaze turned to Hutt. Unafraid, he stared back at her.

Unsmiling, he reached out and took her hand and her fingers closed around his.

Nadir threw the parcel into the flames, watched for a moment then she let Hutt take her back to the sanctuary on the hill.

Chapter 16

THE ARMY OF SWAY

Jayca found the army early the following morning. He had barely begun his transform before Essura started firing questions at him.

"Enough!" shouted Jayca. "I have been aloft all night,"

Essura stared at him and then, in a quieter tone said "Jayca I apologise. What has happened?"

Jayca composed himself. "I need food." He said.

Essura gave him a dirty look. "You try me too far, Bird." He said but he called for food. Jayca laughed. "By the King's order – He has sent the falcons to find Aria, Hutt and maybe Likea. You are to release the cheetahs; they too go to the Lady's aid. They are somewhere in the Woodland. The message you sent was from the Guardian via a singing wolf. Tonka has marched around the Forest and has entered the Woodland. He has passed through the human colony and bypassed the Plains border. The King has marched and although he will get here this darkness or maybe the morrow. He will ride in relay, but he too must rest but you are to move at once."

Essura clapped his hands together.

"At last," he cried as he rushed from the shelter.

Jayca sighed. He sat down and pulled the bowl of food towards him.

With a belly now full, the food had nourished him enough for him to rise and go outside to watch Essura move his army. The first of the warriors were crossing the river. As they reached the far bank, they raised their spears in salute and urged the mounts to gallop.

The camp was in chaos. Both men and women were running in all directions each either carrying a message or a weapon. Cooks were hastily packing the wagon while others hitched teams. Essura climbed to the top of a barrel and shouted until his voice became hoarse. Jayca returned to the hut, sat and rested his head on the table. When Essura returned later he found Jayca fast asleep. Essura scribbled a note for him and left him to sleep. He too rode out of camp within the hour.

The King rode into camp late into the night. He brought with him his personal guard and five hundred more mounted soldiers. The camp was still reeling from the chaos of Essura's departure. Jayca went to greet the King and gripped the King's arm as he faltered dismounting. The King straightened and shook Jayca's hold free.

"I need food."

Jayca smiled warily. "And sleep, I think Sire."

The King gave a hollow laugh. "Maybe. Jayca now what news?"

Jayca didn't answer, instead he led the way into a shelter. He pulled out a chair and indicated that the King should sit. The King scowled but obediently sat. A woman brought in food and drink and set them before him.

"The minute you are out of my sight you take on this strange manner," complained the King but he gratefully accepted a cup of wine the woman had poured.

"Jaberill has sent back a messenger. He had taken the flight over the human colony. There is very little of it left, apparently. Massive fires have burnt out a lot of the Woodland and most of the buildings in the colony. He landed briefly and spoke with some of the survivors. The human survivors had some warning and they fled away from Tonka and hid. Jaberill didn't get to close to them in case they had been contaminated. He didn't think so though, for the misery in their faces and the tears from their eyes appeared genuine. Because of the fire they are short of food. From there he took flight and began a search in a pattern. As it was beginning to darken, they sought a refuge and begin the search at first light. That was when he sent the messenger."

The King cut another slice of bread and munched slowly. "Nothing else?"

Jayca shrugged. "Essura got away about mid-morning. He took the bulk of the army and the food wagons. The cheetahs went first they were long gone before the first mounted went. The singing wolf is still singing; we heard him at eventide."

"Has Preston returned?"

Jayca looked surprised. "Preston? No, did he go somewhere special?

"Mmmm. Never mind. "How much food is here?"

"Still plenty, the women had the children out all day gathering."

"Organise a wagon load to go to the human colony. Send two hundred soldiers with it. If all is well, they are to leave the food." He paused and looked at Jayca. "If not destroy the food and any that is contaminated." He yawned. "Now I will sleep. Organise food for morning light for me and my army."

Jayca rode with the King and his army. They crossed the forbidden river and rode in to the Woodland proper. They rested their horses around mid-morning, and it was then Jaberill's messenger found them. The falcon landed heavily, and the King ordered a healer to give aid. As soon as he recovered, he was brought before an impatient King although he showed no sign of his irritability to the messenger.

"Sire, I have a message from Jaberill." The King nodded and instructed him to continue.

Unable to contain it any longer, a big grin spread over the messenger's face. "Sire, we have found them. Jaberill is with them now. They were under attack, but we fought them off. The cheetahs are almost there." "Well done, messenger. Well done. Tell me more."

"Likea is with them, that is the Lady Aria, Hutt and another one. They are surrounded by Tonka but have a good position to defend. A rocky breakaway hill. They had repulsed an attack just before we landed. Tonka's main army is partially trapped in a quagmire. It must have rained very heavily for the plains are mud but the ones attacking the hill must have travelled in another way for they aren't bogged down."

"Is Likea and the Lady well?"

The messenger nodded eagerly. "The Lady is fine. Likea and Hutt have been hit with arrows, but the Healer had them in hand. They are well, Sire."

"Thank you, messenger. Your name?"

"Sire, I am one, Velon."

"Velon, I am in debt. Rest now and the morrow rejoin your flight."

"My Liege, I would like to return now."

The King laughed. "Velon. Rest awhile and leave later this day. You must rest for you are tired."

"Yes Sire," he said dejectedly. He saluted smartly and left them.

Jayca watched him leave." He is disappointed."

The King grunted. "Until he finds a willing audience."

Jayca looked at the King. "You sound disappointed. The news is good."

The King frowned. "As far as it goes. We are too far from them. They fought early this morning. Velon has only just arrived, how many more attacks have there been since he left?"

"He also said the cheetahs were almost there and Essura is hours ahead of us." Jayca reminded him.

"What if he is bogged down too?"

"Sire we have not had any rain and we are following Essura. Essura is probably following the Tonka's second army – the one that is attacking them now. Velon said they weren't bogged down."

The King stared at Jayca, then gave a sigh which then seemed to relax his serious facial expression. "Yes, you are right as usual, Advisor."

"My Liege, Is the one "other" that is with them, the Guardian?"

The King nodded. "I am glad she is. She has power and I pray that she stays with them until we reach them. I live to be grateful to her it seems." He sighed again and stood up. "Set the march, Advisor. We leave now."

They made good time with no incidents to hamper their travel but when darkness began to creep over the land, they halted to make night camp and rest the horses. The meal had been prepared and eaten when another messenger flew into camp. The bird requiring no time to recover insisted that he be taken immediately to the King. Jayca and the King were walking around the perimeter when Preston found them.

He bowed low and when he straightened, he delivered his message. "The message has been delivered and all is well, Sire." He said.

The King strode forward and clasped Preston's shoulders. "You found him?"

Preston smiled. "He was already on his way Sire and his own scouts had pointed the way. He is only one light time away."

"Preston you have gladden my heart. I won't forget you."

Preston blushed. "Sire it was my privilege." But he looked pleased and proud as he saluted and joined the soldiers sitting around the fire.

Jayca waited until they have moved on before he spoke.' You sent him to the Emir."

The King nodded. "It seemed the only solution, but that wily lion pre-empts me. He must have mustered his troops as soon as Tonka crossed his borders."

"So, where is he?"

"He should be on the other side of Tonka. When we move up, we should have Tonka surrounded. We will leave before first light, Jayca alert the officers. I am for some sleep."

Jayca watched him enter the crudely built shelter and for the first time in day his steps seemed to be lighter.

Nadir stumbled on the loose stones and almost fell to her knees, Hutt held her and tried to stop her from sliding. Like lightning, Likea was there and he firmly grabbed her to steady her feet.

"I have food for you and Jaberill has some wine. We have made you a shelter just beyond that rock, so you can sleep."

"The wine will be welcome," she said as she stepped over the remnants of the wall.

"Where have thee rested Veena?"

"In a shelter beside yours." Likea replied. Nadir nodded and walked on while Likea and Hutt went to fetch the food.

"Is she alright?" Likea asked.

"I think she is just tired; we didn't speak but her walk was awkward. Likea what is going to happen?" Hutt answered and asked curiously, worriedly.

"I think we will have to fight some more. Come light Tonka will move up more of his army. We will bring the cheetahs up here. Else they will be slaughtered and then we pray for the King."

"He will come." Hutt said confidently.

Likea hid a smile. "I'll take this food to the Guardian. You get something to eat and then you can help the warriors make some weapons."

"What are they making?"

"Spears, sharpened sticks. The points are hardened in the fire. An excellent weapon."

"I'll need one, where are the sticks?"

Likea pointed at a stack beside the warriors.

Likea found her kneeling beside Veena wiping her brow with a damp cloth.

"Guardian, I have your food."

Nadir looked at him and grimaced. "Later Likea; I need to see to all those wounded."

"No. Now Guardian. I saw you walk across this hilltop and your gait is unsteady. Whatever you did out there on the field has weakened you, so you need substance and rest."

"And what of the wounded? There is no other healer here." She replied tartly.

"No there isn't. And that is why you need rest. On the morrow we will face Tonka. Do you think he will ignore us because we are on a hill? Do you think he has forgotten that you and Aria escaped him? He has hundreds to sacrifice on this hill and we don't have that luxury. He will keep ordering them to kill us, some of us, if not all. We will either die or be injured. If injured, then you will be needed, if dead then we still need you to sing the lament."

She stared at him a moment longer then looked away. Slowly she rose to her feet then took the bowl he held.

"I believe thee promised wine." She said mildly.

Likea's lips twitched. "I'll fetch it now." He pointed to the next shelter. "That is where you can rest." He said.

When he returned, he found Nadir lying beside Veena, sound asleep.

Nadir slept for several hours. She lay awake for a few minutes listening to the sounds of the night. The cheetah guards were talking softly as the paced. There was sound out on the plains, mostly laughter and some shouting. Nadir sighed. There weren't any Forest sounds to be heard. Some light from the guards' fire cast a pale light into the shelter. She could make out a sleeping Hutt beside her also the meal, she hadn't eaten, and a small gourd of the promised wine. Without disturbing Hutt, she sat up and began eating the berries and bread and sipped gratefully at the sweet wine.

When she had finished eating, she carefully moved to the comatose Veena.

She ran her hands over the sleeping woman's face and felt the warmth emanating

from her body. Nadir dampened a cloth and draped it over Veena's brow. She pulled back the cloth somebody had lay across her midriff and by the dim light Nadir checked to see if the wound had bleed. The crude bandage was still in place and there was only a slight discolouration from seepage. Nadir nodded in satisfaction.

Nadir closed her eyes and began mouthing the Forest's prayer. The pale coloured aura shrouded both her and Veena.

After a few minutes Nadir rose and left the shelter. The bubble still encased the sleeping woman.

By the first light Nadir had visited all the injured and joined the soldiers at the fire.

Tonka's army had also awakened early for the noise off the plain grew louder and more raucous. Fires that had been smouldering burst into flame and the smell of cooking invaded the air.

Some of the cheetahs and falcons discreetly moved to the edge of the incline and could be heard retching. Likea grimaced. "What are they cooking?" he asked.

Nadir raised an eyebrow. "I don't think thee need to know that, Likea. Put it out of mind. It might help if thee stuffed some cloth in thy nose and breath through thy mouth. I'll see what I can do."

Nadir left him and returned to the shelters. Once there she began by praying a request to the Forest's benevolence. When she emerged minutes later the wind had changed directions and the smoke from the cooking fires was blowing back onto Tonka's camp.

Likea was helping the camp cook to prepare bread for cooking, he glanced up when Nadir returned and mouthed a thank you. She gave him a slight smile as she past and walked to where Hutt was practising with his spear.

"What are thee going to do with that?"

He grinned at her. "I made it. Jaberill said it is a fine weapon."

"It might be safer in Jaberill's hands. Have thee eaten?"

"No but I'm hungry. Aria is getting me some army food." He said as he took a swipe at a rock and yelled a robust "Ahhh!"

Aria dodged the next thrust. She looked at Nadir and rolled her eyes.

"Jaberill is encouraging him. Hutt put it down or I will give this food to Likea."

Aria said firmly.

They left him to his food and walked a few paces to the edge of the hilltop.

Both looked over the plain and as the light grew brighter the size of Tonka's army became evident.

Nadir shook her in despair. "So much destruction. So many lives lost. It will take so long to recover. Tonka will be remembered for all the wrong reasons."

Aria touched her hand. "Guardian, I give you my word that for the length of my life I will work tirelessly to eradicate Tonka's name. He will not be remembered for any reason."

"I think that it will take a lifetime and maybe more. He is ready." she said calmly. "Now he comes."

The watch men called the defenders to arms. The soldiers sitting down rose and reached for their weapons. Those eating hurriedly finished eating and took their places at the wall.

Tonka surrounded the outcrop; upon instruction of a single word his soldiers started to climb the hill. Three sides of the rocky hill were virtually unclimbable. Jaberill left only two warriors each on those three sides and drew the others back to defend the fourth. The first of the mutants were assailed by well thrown rocks. Those that fell, hindered those behind. Small landslides took down several of the enemy and with the weight of those pushing upwards many were crushed.

Jaberill had used his time well. When he rebuilt the wall, he left fist sized holes. Out of those holes poked the spears he had made and skewed any mutant who managed to get near the top. Again, and again those injured or those that tried to dodge the spear caused slippage and without anything to grab hold of they, slid to the bottom of the hill.

The defenders had taken no injuries which left Aria and Nadir with little to do. Aria filled a large bowl with water and carried it around the wall to give those soldiers a drink. While Nadir looked to making oaten cakes and seeing to those injured from the day before. Mid-morning came, and Tonka recalled his army.

Likea joined Jaberill at the wall. Out on the plain, they noticed movement, and both squinted to make out what was coming. As it drew nearer to the hill, they could easily make out what Tonka had done. Out of saplings he had cut and made a lightweight shield capable of covering at least twenty mutants. Jaberill frowned.

"I don't understand." He said. "If he had made several it would make more sense."

"He couldn't find the timber," said Nadir. Both Likea and Jaberill swung around to her. "What do you mean?" Jaberill demanded.

Likea frowned at his tone but Nadir caught his eye and waved him to silence.

"Tonka set fire to the woodland. He burnt the wood. Because of the wet earth he couldn't go too far so they built one. More will come they are just delayed."

Jaberill stared at her. "How many?" he croaked.

Nadir shrugged. "He won't need too many because he has changed tactics. Observe, he is arming his soldiers with arrows. The arrowmen will shelter behind the shield. They will climb and from behind the safety of the shield they will shoot their arrows. We have no shield and no arrows."

Likea rubbed a hand over his chin, his mind racing to find a solution. He visually scanned the area as far as he could see and saw nothing that they could use as cover; to move the soldiers back away from the wall would mean to leave the wall undefended.

"Have you got anything, Jaberill?" he asked.

The Falcon shook his head. "We have nothing here."

Likea ran into the crude shelters and lifted the few covers that they had used to cover the injured. He dragged them outside and went to the remnants of the heap of wood they had used for the cooking fire. He called three of the soldiers to help him and together they fitted a piece of timber to each corner and formed a rough and ready shelter.

"The arrows will pierce the cloth but shouldn't do much harm to the soldiers. The cloth will take most of the force." He told Jaberill. "That way we can still have some soldiers at the wall. We will have to move most of the warriors back."

Jaberill nodded in agreement. While Likea took the first turn under the cloth, Jaberill organised the next two covers to be made into makeshift shields.

They didn't have to wait long, the mutants sensing a shift in the fighting, climbed with vigour and the first volley of arrows flew over the wall. Barely had the defenders taken time to collect themselves when the second flight of arrows flew over the wall. This time Likea heard a muted grunt from the soldier holding a timber. Likea spared him a glanced and was about to order another soldier to take his place when he saw Nadir take the soldier and another cheetah take his place. Likea stabbed repeatedly through the spear holes in the wall and had the satisfaction of hearing a couple of cries of pain.

He chanced a quick look over the top of the wall and pulled a face. Even without the protection of the sapling shield, more haflings were climbing the hill.

He looked at Jaberill who was standing beside him.

"We have to defend the Lady, Likea we must man the walls." Jaberill stated.

"Bring half up, keep half back as relief. Tell them to throw stones again. Maybe we can start another landslide." Instructed Likea.

The crude shelters were working to a degree for only a few arrows hit the defenders. The rock throwing worked as another slide started and carried dozens of haflings to the bottom. The wooden spears were beginning to snap under the constant use. The arrows that missed the cloth cover were scattered all over the ground and a couple of the adventurous cheetahs picked some up and were thrusting them through the spear holes.

Likea stole a quick look over the wall again; in the distance he could see another of the sapling shields making for the breakway. He turned to the soldier beside him.

"Have you seen Jaberill?' he asked.

"He was hit. An arrow sliced open his shoulder. The white hair lady took him."

"Your name, soldier?"

"Falgara, sir."

"After the next flight of arrows, I want you to run to the far side and order half of the remaining soldiers forward. Find as many spears as you can and bring them back. Wait for the next flight to fall before you come back."

Falgara nodded and as the next flight fell, he set off at a run.

Likea continued to fight, sweat pouring down his face, stinging old wounds and biting into the new scraps on his hands.

The second shield joined the first, but it wasn't as successful as the first because it had to make its own path through the shale. The fight was continuous for it had become a war of attrition and Tonka was winning for slowly the defenders were injured by the barrage of arrows. The flimsy cloth shelters gave way to the weight of the arrows.

For the defenders now, their only relief was to hug the wall briefly and then fight again.

Likea glanced along the wall. Many soldiers bloodied, and many soldiers wearing crude bandages were now manning the wall. Likea looked up the sky and judged it to be mid-afternoon. The line of soldiers moved suddenly and Likea spotted Hutt. He was manning one of the spear holes with the spear he had made the night before.

As he Likea watched, he saw an arrow fly over the wall, strike a stone and it ricochet to hit Hutt. The arrow having lost most of its momentum, glanced off Hutt, it didn't penetrate but sliced.

Hutt looked surprised and dropped his spear. Likea jumped forward, grabbed at him and pulled him into the shadow of the wall.

In an instant, Nadir was there. Likea released the boy to her. She too clung to the wall to wait until it safe enough to move again. When it was Nadir took Hutt and ran to the shelter of the large rock where Nadir had been attending to the wounded.

Nadir returned to the wall not long after she had taken Hutt. This time she brought with her some cold bread and fruit and a large gourd of water. Likea gratefully took the gourd and drank deeply. Nadir gave him some bread. He nodded his thanks.

"Hutt?"

"He has a deep cut. I've stitched it together and I have put him to sleep. He does not need to see what happens next."

Likea searched her face. "What happens next, Guardian?"

"The shouting seems to have died down and the arrows are not so frequent. Didn't thee notice?"

Likea frowned. He risked a look over the wall.

"They are retreating. They are retreating?" He frowned.

The soldiers standing alongside suddenly cheered and laughed in relief.

Nadir gave Likea a smile.

"Look out onto the Plain." She said gently.

A broad grin creased his face. "Tis an army' but whose?"

"Thee eyes should be better than mine, but I think it might be Aria's father."

Falgara punched Likea on the arm and pointed excitedly. "It's the King and Essura. Our army is here as well."

Likea absently rubbed his arm "Tonka is wedged in. He is caught between two armies!"

He made to move over the fallen parts of the wall, but Nadir gripped his arm. "No Likea, this fight isn't yours. I need thee to gather herbs and food. We have many wounded and more will come."

For a moment he looked mutinous then the moment passed. "Surely Guardian. There will be no more fighting here."

Falgara once again came to him and Nadir. "We must leave you now and rejoin our army. Jaberill has ordered those slightly injured to assist you Lady. As has Booth the cheetah commander. Likea it has been my honour to serve with you." He gave them both a brief bow and led what was left of his squad down the pathway to the bottom of the hill.

Booth hobbled up and bowed low to Nadir. "Thank you, Guardian, for your aid. On my life I will see Veena will want for nothing should she recover. Her life is now my mission. We too will leave you now. The abominations that soiled this land must die. Likea, sometime, I would speak with you. You are a warrior without peer." He bowed to Nadir once more and joined his men making their way to the bottom. As they left, they put their weapons to any hafling still alive.

Likea averted his eyes. "I know they deserve to die, but Guardian they were not always thus."

"No and that is my shame, Likea." Nadir said sadly.

Likea heard the raw sadness in her voice and looked at her. He dared to touch her and placed his arm gently around her shoulders and hugged her briefly.

"Not your shame My Lady. Never yours. If a wrong has been righted, then it was you. If peace comes to us, then it is because of you. Those that you mend and live is because of you. Never your shame. Not ever." Likea said huskily, his voice breaking with emotion.

For a moment Nadir rested her head on his chest but soon she drew back and Likea dropped his arm. Nadir looked up at him and as their eyes met a wonderful warm spread throughout his body and his tiredness and pain slipped away and a great serenity swept over him and in her smile, he glimpsed utopia.

Her eyes filled with mischief and she tapped him on the arm with a pointed finger.

"We need food and herbs." She said.

The moment passed but Likea knew he had witnessed something beautiful and that the memory will ever remain.

Likea gathered some of those still mobile and they carefully made their way down the rocky path. He sent them out in pairs and in different directions to gather what they could while he collected some brush and wood. Only once did he glanced out over the plain to see the armies' manoeuvre into a position of choice; the fighting had not yet begun.

He worked steadily for a time until he had gathered a stack of wood. He sat on a log and began to make some brush into torches for the afternoon was gathering although it was still full light. He glanced up at a movement and seen some of the gatherers returning. He suddenly frowned and looked more closely for behind the gatherers was a mounted patrol and riding rapidly. Without moving his stare, Likea reached behind him and grasped his spear and brought it forward.

Suddenly he laughed out loud as the riders reached him. The King nodded his head in acknowledgement as he passed him. The mounted soldier behind the King raised the banner he carried higher. As the flag unfurled a great shout came across the plains. The King joined his army and now leads the charge.

Likea, unmindful of the dangerous slope raced up the pathway to the top of the hill. Nadia and Aria must have heard the shouting from the plain and both stood looking over the stone wall.

Likea grinned. "Tis the King," he cried.

He pointed at the racing patrol about to join with Essura.

"They have trapped Tonka between the two armies."

They watched in awe as the allied armies spread out in flanking manoeuvres, leaving Tonka surrounded.

Chapter 17

THE BATTLE

Essura saluted smartly as the King arrived. He looked amused.

"You made good time, My King."

"As did you," retorted the King as he dismounted. He looked out to the army of the haflings. "What is the situation?" he asked.

"I have been in contact with the Emir these last days past. He has the bulk of his army now situated behind the haflings cutting off their retreat. He has strengthened us with one thousand warriors. Those along with ours gives us gives us about three thousand. More if you include your guard."

The King nodded. "Include them. What of your strategy?"

"Basically, we charge them. But without the horses. The ground is too boggy for mounted warfare. We will only hurt the horses. Where the Emir has his warriors, the ground is firmer."

The King nodded again. "Do we have enough weapons?"

"Yes. At each rest time the soldiers were tasked to make two weapons before they slept." He pointed to the rear. "The wagons are coming in all the time. Tonka should have made his move hours ago. We had the men but not the weapons. I can't work out why he delayed long enough for us to encircle him."

The King turned slightly to look at the breakaway hill behind them. "I think that fortress pursued him to delay. My bird brigade informed me that those on that hill have held out night and day. The Guardian is there, and she is a prize Tonka wanted. I believe he felt that he could not leave her behind him."

Essura shrugged. "She is but one."

The King smiled at him. "Would you make her an enemy?"

Startled, Essura stared at him horrified. "No!" he protested.

The King laughed. "Nor would I." He sobered quickly. "Essura make ready for battle." He said formally.

Essura waved his officers forward.

The horses were gathered and taken to safely in the rear. One of the wagons was brought forward and was quickly unloaded. Each soldier was given a sword, a spear and a curved shield.

"What is that?" asked the King pointing to the shield.

"A shield. It is made from a hollowed-out tree trunk and cut into pieces. The soldier can protect his belly, but the main use is against the arrows. When we march forward the shields will be held over each mans' head. The front row is protected by the second row which has a longer shield. That way the first row has hands free to hold and use a weapon."

"How did you come by that idea?"

"When we came through the human colony. They use a similar object in some game they play. It seemed like a good idea and so we adapted it. We have been practicing and now we are ready to use it as a weapon."

The King took one and held it in the cord grip. "It is heavy." He said.

Essura nodded. "But it stops the arrows."

"I'll take this one," said the King, fitting it snugly over his fist.

Essura was horrified. "Sire, you can't mean to go into battle." He cried.

"I must. Tonka must die. That was my vow."

"Any soldier here can do that." Protested Essura.

"I am the King, Essura, and as such I must do my duty. He will die by my hand. Pass the word."

Essura shook his head but issued the order. When the King stepped into line, he found himself surrounded by twenty or more of his elite guard. Each one carried a shield. The King glared at his Captain who simply lifted one shoulder in a shrug and said. "My army to command. I have so ordered." His look at the King lasted a moment longer then raising his voice he shouted the command for advance.

Three thousand voices raised in a single shout stepped forward. With every third pace the single shout of Sway was cried out.

Tonka's army stood to meet the challenge; the bowman raced to the front and fired their arrows, but the distance was too great, and the shafts fell short. The noise from the hafling camp rose to such a pitch as though to drown the shout of Sway.

Tonka could be seen running up and down the ragged line of his warriors. The dishevelled line straightened, and the bowmen stood out front, once more with the bows loaded.

They released their arrows and as one, the second row of Sway warriors raised their shield and covered the first. The rattle of the arrows hitting the wood mingled with the battle cry and a muted cry of pain as an arrow found a mark. The soldiers stepped around their fallen comrade without missing a step and onwards they marched.

The bowmen fell back allowing the next row to come forward. The warriors of Sway passed the shields to the rear and moved alongside their comrades for now the fighting was hand to hand each soldier protected the man on his left. The fighting was so fierce that gaps began to appear in the lines and then the lines disappeared as well. The Kings guards were the only soldiers to be recognised for they still formed a solid block around the King.

Gradually Tonka's army fell back but were given no respite for the Sway soldiers pressed ever forward. The King's guard was very visible even amongst the many hundreds of warriors for a standard bearer had raised the King's banner high. At one-point Tonka rallied the haflings and they made a concerted effort to charge the King, knowing that should the King fall, the warriors of Sway would lose heart. Once Essura identified Tonka's plan he ordered two hundred of the black Bears into the fray. Even then the plan might have worked for the arrowmen seeing the Bears were without shields, reformed a ragged line and fired volley after volley of arrows. Seeing many of their comrades fall to the arrows, the enraged Bears charged the line of haflings. Witnessing the bears fall, several of the Sway warriors picked up discarded shields and without thought for their safety ran forward to cover the Bears. The hafling arrowmen faltered and the line broke, retreating only to fall victim to the hafling soldiers behind them as they to pressed forward. With nowhere to go the bears fell upon them. They were shown no mercy as the Sway soldiers crushed them with their mighty strength.

The battle raged for more than two hours and the armies were now several thousand paces from where the fighting had begun. Gradually the haflings were in full retreat, now running to the rear only to fall to the spears and swords of the Emir's warriors waiting patiently a few leagues beyond the battle.

The wagons carrying weapons, pulled by teams of oxen, were keeping pace with the fighting and the Sway soldiers were constantly rushing back to renew their weapons. As the fighting slackened off Essura ordered some of these men to put any surviving or wounded haflings to the sword. Behind these wagons came the lumbering flat board wagons and teams of civilians who gathered the wounded and the dead. The haflings lay where they fell while the wounded Sway soldiers were taken to the rear and to the healers who gave succour.

Nadir left the hill fortress and walked among the fallen and the wounded, with her she carried her bag, now filled with the herbs and plants that Likea had earlier gathered.

Without cloth to wrap the wounds she instead used a broad leaf to hold the herbs to the flesh and wrapped it with a piece of vine.

Likea walked beside her and helped to lift where necessary. Twice he sent inquisitive healers about their own business when they came to question Nadir, who studiously ignored them and continued her chosen task. When they came upon fatally wounded soldiers, Nadir roused them from stupor and spoke with them. Wherever she could, Nadir helped them to begin their metamorphous, those incoherent or beyond conscious thought, Nadir gave them to the Light. Both Likea and Nadir spent their final daylight hours until just before darkness engulfed the land in this manner. Nadir soon stopped and walked towards the last stage of the battle. With Likea in the lead, pushing through the ranks of soldiers, to make a path for Nadir until they came to an opened area and stood side by side. They watched as the King's guard withdraw and the only combatants were the King and Tonka.

The King walked forward and stood before the hafling lord.

"Tonka, I have vowed to destroy you. You will die by my hand." The King's voice rang loud and clear.

Tonka lifted his head. "I have waited for this moment all my life. My sole purpose has been to fight you. You had everything, and I had nothing. You! My brother! I am what you made me, Sethe. It was you who condemned me, ordered me away from the Sway to live with the other mongrels." He spat. "I know what I am, a mongrel. A hafling, neither one thing nor another. What fault was mine?" He shouted.

"The initial fault lay elsewhere. Sway knew that, but you broke the law, Tonka, from where there was no going back. I could not save you, but it didn't have to end like this."

Tonka sneered. "It has to end like this. I will kill you and you have no heir and my legacy will live on, but your legacy ends now."

The King sadly shook his head. "I will have an heir Tonka. My son took a bride and she carries the Heir."

"Noooo!" Tonka roared. "I killed Vidal. I saw him mortally wounded."

"But you didn't kill his bride. The Lady Aria carries his seed. She is safe with the Guardian".

"The Guardian," Tonka whispered. He lifted his head higher and peered into the deepening gloom. Suddenly he saw her, calmly standing beside Likea.

Tonka roared his anger as he pointed at Nadir. "I will destroy you! I will not fail this time!"

"Thee have already failed, Tonka. Thee army is no more. Your only success is the misery thee have caused but even that, in time, will pass." Nadir said softly but clearly. She turned away to walk back through the crowd.

Her obvious distain enraged Tonka and he made to run at her. The King raised his sword. Glinting in the twilight, it flashed once as it struck Tonka in the throat. Tonka fell at the King's feet the blood pooled in the churned earth and slowly seeped away.

The King stood still looking down at his dying brother. He allowed his sword to fall from his hand and slowly fell to his knees. He lifted Tonka's head from the wet earth his hands cupping his brothers face. Tonka tried to smile, instead the action only produced a ghastly grimace. 'I almost won". "He said. "I hated you Sethe with my very being. I hated you. You have not beaten me, only taken my life. My legacy will live on and on." He rasped as blood oozed from his mouth.

Slowly the light faded from his eyes and the King gently lay the monstrous head down. He stood up and took the cloth offered from a soldier and wiped the blood from his hands Essura came to stand beside his King. He nudged Tonka with his boot.

"And now, My Lord?" he asked.

"Now we must bury or burn them, so nothing can feast on them." The King replied bleakly. "He was my brother, Essura. He was so young, so happy and yet he grew to hate me." The King stared down at the body then again, he slowly knelt in the mud beside his brother. He brushed the long mane of hair away from Tonka's face. Gone was the hate filled lines and the sneer from his mouth. In death Tonka looked peaceful.

The King pulled his arms free of his jacket and gently lay it over Tonka's chest, bringing the cloth higher to cover the wound on his neck. Slowly he rose to his feet and never taking his eyes from his brother asked for digging implements.

Essura gently touched his arm. "Lord there is no need for you to do this deed."

"Yes, there is. He once was of the Royal House and it is all I can do for him. Leave me now. You have your own work to do."

Nadir and Likea slowly climbed the breakaway. Midway, Nadir stopped and looked over the plain. Thousands of pinpricks of light dotted the battlefield. What little sound that came their way was muted. Gone was the roar and shouting of the battle, the crash of weapons. Occasionally came the sound of a cry of pain, but even that was subdued.

Nadir sighed and started to climb again, she stumbled on a loose rock but Likea gripped her arm.

"Guardian why have they lit so many fires?"

"They will bury the haflings. They are using the fires to see by. On the morrow I will ask the Forest to change the wind, so the smoke and odour will blow away from the army then they will be able to burn some. It will be quicker."

She sighed again. "This plain will no longer support life. It will become a desert. The trees and grass will die for the life-giving rain will cease. This land will be forever more barren because the poison from the haflings will leach and poison the soil. The Proto Forest will not sanction the living of any creature or plant coming from this place."

She gripped his arm. "Come, soldier help me up the last few steps. I need food and so do thee, then we sleep for the King will come in the light time."

Nadir was awake and attending to the wounded long before daybreak. When Likea found her, she was standing over Hutt, watching him sleep. She glanced up as Likea approached and smiled.

"He is healing well."

"Will you wake him?"

She shook her head. "No not yet. The burning has commenced, and he doesn't need to see it. While he sleeps, he is calm. If he were awake, he would be all over the place."

"What now, Guardian?"

"The King is approaching. It would be a kindness to his age if we went to meet him," she laughed. "Better rouse Aria for I think her father comes as well."

Four horsemen broke away from a patrol and rode closer to the breakaway. Nadir and Likea walked towards them as the King dismounted. He gave the reins to a guard and faced Nadir. He bowed low to her.

"Ask," he said. "It will be granted."

"There is nothing – I have all I need." Nadir responded.

She stood aside to allow Aria to pass. Aria in turn bowed to the King who took her hand and helped her to rise. He smiled then beckoned the Emir forward and smiled tolerantly as they embraced. Then it was Likea's turn. He made to bow but the King grasped him by the shoulders.

"Nay – not this day. Likea I am indebted. Ask what you will, and it will be yours."

"The debt was mine, Sire. I gave my word to Helment and now I have been able to fulfil my bond."

"We will talk later, Likea" said the King and looked about him.

His eyes clouded. "Where is the boy? Is he slain?" The King asked worriedly.

Aria looked around and it was she who answered.

"No Sire. He sleeps – he was wounded, and the Guardian wished him to rest."

The King breathed a long sigh of relief. "The Queen will be glad." He said.

The Emir grinned at him. "You too I think, Sire." He laughed.

The King chuckled. "I have missed him," he confessed.

He looked at Nadir who was standing apart from the happy group.

"I would speak to you, Guardian." The King requested.

The others tactfully withdrew to allow them some privacy.

Likea bowed to the Emir but it was to Essura that he spoke.

"How did you get here so fast and with so many? I surely thought the Light was ours." He asked.

"A war was brewing because the King would not name the Heir, so we already had the army marshalled. I was in the Woodland border because we had word that Tonka had circled the Forest. When the singing wolf passed on the message about the Lady, the King sent messengers throughout the Kingdom and beyond.

Once he had named the Heir – the rightful Heir - the factions on our borders had no claim to the Kingdom. The Kingdom was safe from attack and most of those other armies joined us. When Jayca arrived with the message and orders we marched across the river. The King had almost caught us this morning, but we have been in contact for many days and knew of the situation. He sent the falcons ahead." He nodded sagely. "A wise King. It was he who slay Tonka as he had vowed although I think it cut him deeply to do so, but he showed no remorse."

Likea frowned at Essura's words – he looked puzzled but turned to the Plains King and spoke to him.

"But you Sire, your army was abreast with the Kings. You had so far to come – how did you do it?" he asked.

The Emir chuckled. "We had word of Tonka's movements many days past. When he passed on our boundary, we had already massed in pursuit, but My Liege King had sent his swiftest, by name of Preston, to us. On his word of my daughter and her child my army knew no tiredness and we forced marched. In all, a good days work." He said in some satisfaction.

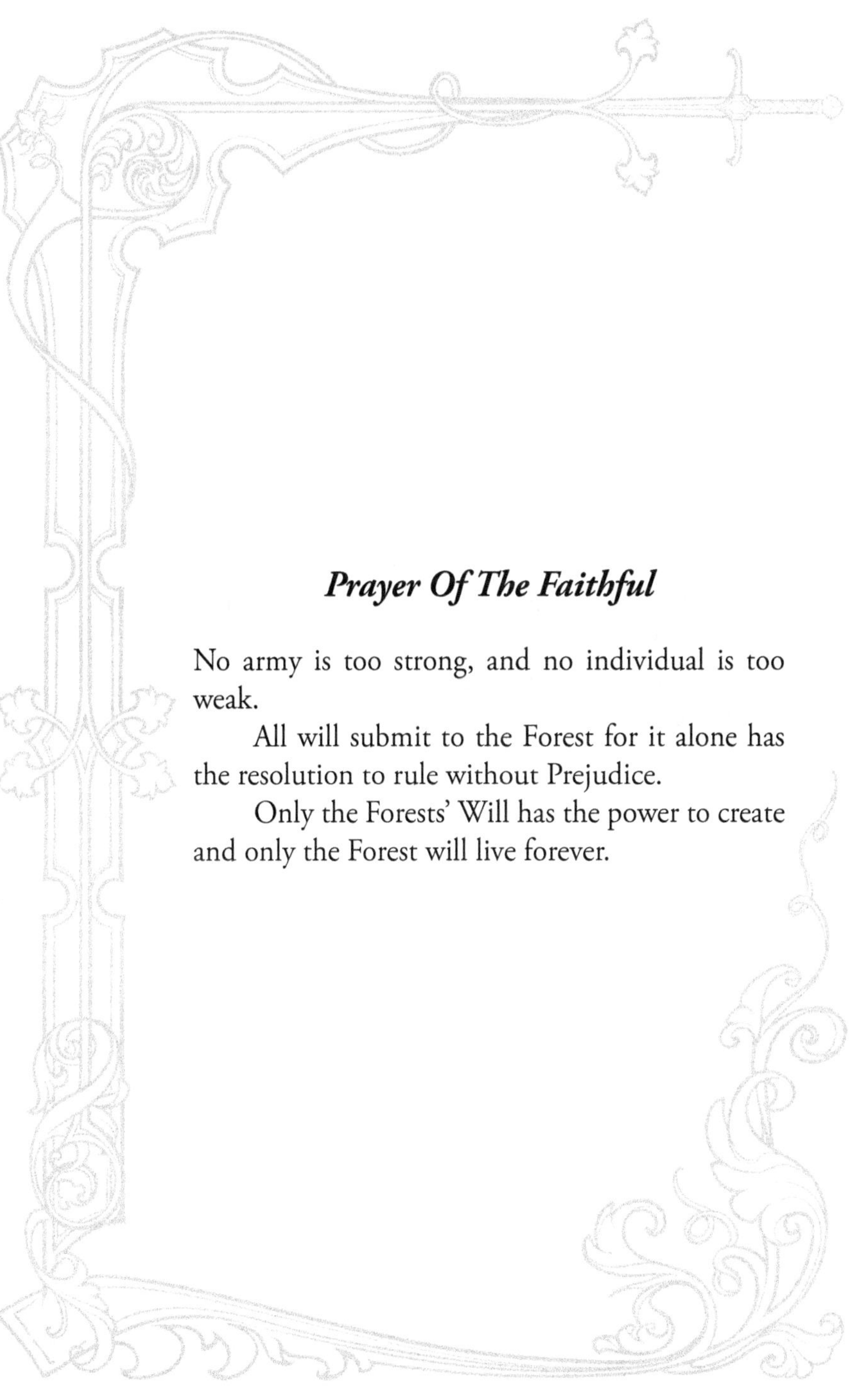

Prayer Of The Faithful

No army is too strong, and no individual is too weak.

All will submit to the Forest for it alone has the resolution to rule without Prejudice.

Only the Forests' Will has the power to create and only the Forest will live forever.

Chapter 18

THE GUARDIAN

"**I** cannot thank you, Nadir. I have nothing fitting to offer you." Expressed the King gratefully.

"My needs are few and those the Proto Forest provides." She replied.

"I would give Hutt. He is the first of the sleepers that you have known. You do have a fondness for him, I think."

Nadir shook her head. "He is human and needs to be with his own kind. Likea would care for him better than I."

"No-one would care more than thee, Guardian." The King said softly but Nadir denied his words.

"Nay. I am beyond the human life for I have entered my third regeneration. The Light is now a part of me for I fly within it. I cannot provide the human side that he craves, and he cannot join me in flight. It would be an unbalanced act – far kinder to settle him with his own."

"Then I will grant you entry into the Kingdom." He offered.

Nadir shook her head in refusal. "Even after so many, many seasons Ambrose's name is still feared. Unrest, suspicion and fear would follow me."

"It would change in time, Nadir. They would know you and love you as the Forest does now."

"The Kingdom holds nothing for me. I want for nothing – need nothing, Sire." She said firmly.

Nadir looked directly at the King and half smiled. "The Forest needs a Guardian and the Kingdom needs its King. We both have a great deal to do to repair the damage that Tonka inflicted. Some of the abominations will escape and they will grow strong again. Better that thee remain aloof from me."

"You are far stronger than I. You could have sided with Tonka – you knew that he could not harm the Forest. You knew that the Forest would never allow him to contaminate the sanctuary. Why give me back Aria? You had cause to destroy me and a powerful ally to help you."

Nadir smiled tenderly, turned slightly to look where the Forest lay. "The cause I had to hate thee faded and died many seasons ago. Even before I was given the first regeneration. It was not thee that condemned me to the Forest, and I understood that you were only my gaoler and not my judge. The Hiatus was the judge and it gave me mercy. So, thee see I had no cause. I truly found the Light and my belief has never faltered."

The King nodded his understanding. He offered her his hands and she grasped them.

"Then we will not meet again." The King said, sombrely.

"No. My legend will grow in mystery and fear and thine will grow with love and affection. That is how it should be and that way we will both keep our Kingdoms safe and pure."

Nadir stepped away. "I will send Hutt to thee," she said.

"Thank you. I will order him to accompany you to your home. Likea will go with him and bring him back to the Kingdom."

He raised his hand to her forehead and lightly touched her he then turned on his heel and left without a backward glance.

Aria waited until the King had left before she approached Nadir.

"I have to leave but there is much that I would like to say," she confessed, and tears began to stream down her gentle face.

Nadir smiled at her. "The Covenant prophecy is fulfilled. What else is there? Only I ask thee one thing. Watch over Hutt. Likea will have much of his teaching, the King will give him love, but see that he is taught the Covenant properly."

Aria touched her forehead to Nadir's for a long moment. Tears continued to fill and fall from her eyes. "I promise," she whispered emotionally. With one final look, Aria then hurried to her fathers' side.

Nadir and Likea were alone on the hilltop watching the soldiers file past as they began their journey home. The burial details were still in the field - as were the parties of the King and Emir who had gathered to share a meal and bid each other farewell. Aria was to travel with the King to Sway.

"They will give me the honours that should be yours. You deserve them." Likea said.

"What good are they to me?" Nadir retorted. She turned and continued to pack her bag with food, barely glancing up as some of the passing soldiers hailed her.

"It should be known that it was you that saved the Heir." He argued.

Nadir snorted. "I am not even human let alone the true life of my totem. What good are accolades to me? However," she paused for a moment then continued. "Likea of thee I ask one thing. I have entrusted Hutt to thee. Care for him for he is one of mine and not one of the Kingdoms."

"That is my pleasure and not a chore."

"Then I am satisfied. Now I must wake him and send him to the King. While you wait for him thee can collect more food and some horses for us. I will meet thee back here, for now I must go and find my singing wolf."

Hutt was still drowsy when Likea carried him to the King. The King seated Hutt beside him and Aria plied him with food. The Emir was speaking with Essura and from their conversation Hutt learned of the battle from the previous day. Hutt dropped his mouth open in shock – his food forgotten as he listened to them talk. Aria gently lowered his spoon back to his plate. The action galvanised Hutt and he turned to the King.

The King looked amused at the fury etched onto Hutt's face, but he spoke kindly to the boy and with Aria's help he calmed him and let Essura speak of the battle.

The King kept Hutt with him for some time until Hutt finally re-joined Likea. When the Royals were mounted and about to leave, the King nodded as he passed Likea and Essura sketched a salute. Aria, riding beside her father, smiled and waved to him.

Hutt was raging with disappointment that he had missed the battle. His anger so strong that Likea was hard pressed not to laugh. Likea collected the horses and lifted Hutt onto a sturdy pony and led the way back to Nadir. They returned to the breakaway and spotted Nadir walking towards them and beside her was the wolf, Velma.

Goaded by the sight of Nadir, Hutt launched into another tirade.

"I can't believe that you let me sleep through the biggest battle ever waged." He cried.

Nadir shrugged. "I forgot about thee."

Her obvious disinterest inflamed him further and he started ranting again.

Nadir mounted, then looked at Likea.

"I was sorry that I gave the wolf a voice for now he sings constantly, but I would gladly listen to him rather than the wailing of Hutt."

Likea laughed. "Then let us leave both Hutt and Velma to sing a duet."

The Forest loomed comfortingly closer. On the edge of the trees sat a lone, grey wolf. He was looking out towards the Plains and he seemed to be waiting for something or someone.

End